T5-ADA-556

```
LP              3952322
FIC             20.95
Dwy             May94
Dwyer-Joyce
The storm of wrath
```

DATE DUE			
AUG 16 1995			
SEP 28 1995			

GREAT RIVER REGIONAL LIBRARY
St. Cloud, Minnesota 56301

GAYLORD MG

SPECIAL MESSAGE TO READERS

This book is published by
THE ULVERSCROFT FOUNDATION
a registered charity in the U.K., No. 264873

The Foundation was established in 1974 to provide funds to help towards research, diagnosis and treatment of eye diseases. Below are a few examples of contributions made by THE ULVERSCROFT FOUNDATION:

A new Children's Assessment Unit at Moorfield's Hospital, London.

•

Twin operating theatres at the Western Ophthalmic Hospital, London.

•

The Frederick Thorpe Ulverscroft Chair of Ophthalmology at the University of Leicester.

•

Eye Laser equipment to various eye hospitals.

If you would like to help further the work of the Foundation by making a donation or leaving a legacy, every contribution, no matter how small, is received with gratitude. Please write for details to:

**THE ULVERSCROFT FOUNDATION,
The Green, Bradgate Road, Anstey,
Leicester LE7 7FU. England
Telephone: (0533)364325**

Love is
a time of enchantment:
in it all days are fair and all fields
green. Youth is blest by it,
old age made benign:
the eyes of love see
roses blooming in December,
and sunshine through rain. Verily
is the time of true-love
a time of enchantment — and
Oh! how eager is woman
to be bewitched!

THE STORM OF WRATH

From all over the world the treasures had come — the necklace, the bone-handled knife, the minute keg, fastened with a gold buckle, and the tiny paint box. They led Constance-Tenacity Fitzgerald to her birthright. There was mystery all about her, and a nightmare that came true, of a midnight journey to a country cemetery. She was heiress to Lissarinka House, destined to marry Phil and be mistress of Puck's Castle one day. Then came the great storm — and with it disaster.

*Books by Alice Dwyer-Joyce
in the Ulverscroft Large Print Series:*

THE MOONLIT WAY
THE DIAMOND CAGE
THE GINGERBREAD HOUSE
THE BANSHEE TIDE
FOR I HAVE LIVED TODAY
THE STROLLING PLAYERS
PRESCRIPTION FOR MELISSA
DANNY BOY
THE GLITTER-DUST
DOCTOR ROSS OF HARTON

ALICE DWYER-JOYCE

THE STORM OF WRATH

Complete and Unabridged

ULVERSCROFT
Leicester

First published in Great Britain in 1977 by
Robert Hale Limited
London

First Large Print Edition
published January 1994
by arrangement with
Robert Hale Limited
London

Copyright © 1977 by Alice Dwyer-Joyce
All rights reserved

British Library CIP Data

Dwyer-Joyce, Alice
 The storm of wrath.—Large print ed.—
 Ulverscroft large print series: romance
 I. Title
 823.914 [F]

ISBN 0–7089–3015–8

Published by
F. A. Thorpe (Publishing) Ltd.
Anstey, Leicestershire

Set by Words & Graphics Ltd.
Anstey, Leicestershire
Printed and bound in Great Britain by
T. J. Press (Padstow) Ltd., Padstow, Cornwall

This book is printed on acid-free paper

In this Silver Jubilee Year
of 1977
I dedicate this to
THEM

Prologue

I HAVE it still, the heirloom. Of course, I have it still. I hope that I shall never be parted from it till the day I die. If I could take it with me into the next world, I would do it, but that is beyond the bounds of possibility. Yet maybe it might be a thing you could smuggle past St. Peter. He would know the story behind it. Just for now, I have only to open the small cardboard box, lined with cotton wool, link my fingers into the chain of a necklace and lift it out. It does not tarnish with the years, changes not in the slightest, as far as I can see. I drape it round my neck and it reaches well down my front, this necklace of extraordinary fashion. It is still marked MADE IN JAPAN on a small ticket, that is fastened by greying white cotton to one of the black metal links. The beads are wood, honey-coloured wood, and each alternate bead is the same. There are eight beads all told and there are two varieties, separated by four inches of black chain. First comes an egg-shaped bead and then a cube and each bead is embellished by a cup of gilt metal at either end. You could go counting round the necklace, as you might a rosary, if you had a mind to, but there are only eight beads, as I said, so it might be a prayer you were making to a foreign god.

It winds five times round my wrist as a bracelet, and it has a value out of all proportion to what you might think, if you saw it. It was never of any importance perhaps, only to me, yet it has a beauty that is all its own. I put it back in its box, wondering why the black of the links never lost their beetle sheen, nor the gilt its richness. It is not too light, nor is it too heavy, a pleasant thing, just right for fingers to fidget. The beads make a rattling sound like the brittle branches of a frosted tree, but they are warm from my neck. The box is lined with cotton wool. The top layer covers it and the black and the gold and the honey are all hidden and the lid is on. I put it back carefully in my jewel box and look at the other strange things, that live there, extraordinary objects to rub shoulders with diamond clips and rings and ear bobs and baubles and bangles.

"Gold and frankincense and myrrh," somebody said. Gifts from all over the civilised world, but that was not the way of it, or perhaps it was. There were so many little things, and they are all here under my eyes. Of course, the most important was the small gold keg, banded with leather, swinging from its lizard strap and with the neatest gold buckle. That was the real heirloom. It made me believe that it was possible to love somebody, to lose him in death and still to love him . . . and for his love to last out all eternity too. Maybe, just maybe, there was a chance of it, so the gold keg is the most precious jewel I have, locked safe with my treasures.

1

Lissarinka

I HAVE only to sit in my special armchair today and lean back against the printed velvet of the upholstery. Deep crimson it is and printed velvet it must be, because Siamese cats have an aversion to this particular fabric. They are great on claw-sharpening and no carpet is safe against them. Seo has the moss green carpet, where my feet rest, so tufty with her activities, that it might be as well to run a midget lawn-mower over it, if there was such a thing. She has unpicked stitches wholesale out of the red Turkey stair carpet. Now and again, I make a pilgrimage up the flight on hands and knees with a needle of wool and do my best to disguise the bald patches, before the man from the shop visits the house again. 'Hotel quality' the Wiltons were and 'guaranteed to last out a lifetime', if one did not insist on possessing a familiar called 'Seo'. Worse than that we had had generations of Siamese cats and each one of them called by the same name. They seemed to change from one cat to the next by powerful magic and they threw the torch of this craze for claw-sharpening from grandmother to mother to daughter.

So now, a cat called Seo sits on my lap and I rest my head against the high back of the Windsor chair, close my eyes and listen to the familiar boiling-kettle-purring of a sleepy Siamese. Her paws are gentle reminders of the past as they knead dough against my knee. Maybe she does possess the power of witchcraft, for in my mind's eye I am a child again, a mile out along the bog road to Carrick. I have a range of choice in the corridors of the past. I have only to walk down the passages of my brain and I have a basket and the season is Autumn and I am gathering nuts. Perhaps I have a milk can on my bicycle handle-bars and a crooked stick to reach after blackberries to make bramble jelly in the kitchen of the big house. There are such a variety of exciting things to do. I am convinced that the children nowadays never have such adventures ... and I have so many friends. Across the valley is Puck's Castle with four boys, like the steps of stairs. Their lands run alongside ours of Lissarinka. We have horses grazing the fields and we used to play Cowboys and Indians. Sometimes, we buried treasure and that is when we turned pirate, but the trove we hid had no resemblance to what was pillaged on the Carribean. We also stored up items of interest for posterity and the furtherance of science and knowledge generally. We plotted charts, but we never made much a hand of finding anything we buried. This is a strange part of country and it is Ireland, where 'the Little People' are recognised as legal inhabitants. They would be quite capable of spiriting away any object we chose to bury and we chose our subjects with care.

There must be coin of the realm of course, but that never exceeded the value of the angled threepenny piece. Even that we counted as generous. There were lead soldiers in variety, but they were ones that had had heads grafted with a match stick. The uninjured mercenaries were far too precious to inter in the earth, for they had to live to fight another day. The others had the glory of being found by posterity, so that the world might rediscover knowledge of the military of long ago, or the 'Cowboys and Indians', come to that. We always were prudent enough to inter something expendable. There was a day when we buried a copy of the *Leinster Tribune*. It was a weekly paper, that came out every Wednesday, published by Fergus's father in the nearby town of Ballyboy. We wrapped it in cellophane and then in corn silk and finally put it two feet down in a grassy hill, in order to preserve a sample of newspapers of the world for the people of the future. We were very conscious of the atom bomb and what it might do to civilisation in the blink of an eyelid, between one moment and the next and perhaps we were not far wrong about that.

We buried a china robin, I recall, but only because it had got its head knocked off and stuck on again with Araldite. It was important that future christians, if any, might see a replica of the bird that had pressed its breast against the thorny crown of Christ crucified.

We roamed the country in a gang. There was always an intense activity that whirled around us, as an approaching hurricane might move. Closest were Philip, Connor, Dermot and Tomas McCracken from Puck's Castle. There was an understanding that Philip and I would marry one day and unite the two estates, that ran side by side. I was not in the least aware of what love was or what marriage might be and neither was Phil. It was a wild part of Ireland, well off the path of civilisation and there was still innocence and good church and chapel attendance and a strong belief in the 'Little People'. There was rife superstition and no doubt whatever that Puck's Castle was haunted. There was a stain, the colour of wine, on the hall flags there, a stain not to be rubbed out, like the blood on Lady Macbeth's hand. I had seen it a thousand times. There was 'a Green Man', who appeared in the kitchen there on Hallow E'en Night and frightened the maids out of their wits.

Times have changed now and maids are few and far between. Mostly they have crossed the seas to England to seek their fortune, where the streets are lined in gold . . . where an Irish policeman can hold up the traffic with 'one wave of his hand' as the old song says, such power did he possess. It is a tangle of old memories and I am wandering through a lovely land. There is a sandy dustiness to the bog road and a red sealing wax colour to the rowan berries and white bog cotton and dark peat stacks and small pools, of an impossibly deep brown clarity. The road is the same today as I always remember it. It runs straight along, till it reaches Lissarinka back gates. They are painted white and have a strange latch for the convenience of anybody riding a horse. You do not need to dismount, just lean down and unclip an upright bar and the gate moves open. Safely through to the avenue and the gate swings closed and the latch clicks shut. Then comes the curve of the drive, sweetly upwards through the trees, for here is a green cool tunnel. Round the curve, the country road disappears from sight and the house is waiting, set about a hundred yards from the top of the hill in a sheltered hollow, with trees all around and above and below.

Lissarinka means 'the fort of the dancing', if you translate the name from the Gaelic. Maybe it was an unlucky thing to build a house on a fairy hill, but it is a place of rare beauty. There are foxgloves and nut groves and nooks where the primroses and the bluebells and the cowslips come early every spring. There are mossy banks and violets. Here is no cruel fortress like Puck's Castle with its blood stain on the hall of the tower, the ghosts, that walk the battlements. No wonder the boys preferred to spend their time in Lissarinka, but as I think this now, I know they are all grown up and boys no longer. I am back in the kingdom between my temples, so I decide to visit the front drive of the house and turn to the past again. The front gate is black-painted and the name of the house is picked out very grandly in gold paint and it is no different today to what it was, when I was a child. The avenue is clean of weeds now too and it runs straight along for half a mile, before it rises a little to the wooded hill and the house itself comes into sight above your head. There it is, well up the hill, with a flight of four shallow grey stone steps to the front door, a pillar at each side and the door itself white, and with a lion's head brass knocker, polished to rival the sun.

There is a view over the country from the top step, that is worth a pause today as it always was. The Bog of Allen is flat, they say, but there are wooded valleys and always the hollow hills, so loved by the fairy people. There are stone walls and fields, with fine stock . . . cattle and horses and sheep. Always there is a donkey, walking 'the long meadow' or maybe stretched out in the middle of the road, as a declaration of independence against civilisation. The cottages are scattered along the sides of the sandy narrow road and not one of them without a clucking of hens, a clamp of turf, a stack of hay, a woman at the half door. You have only to turn your head and there are the battlements of the castle pushing out through the tallest trees in the district, reaching for heaven. Across three miles, in this clear island air, you could see Phil McCracken, if he were to come out on the leads, but he will not do that now. The years have run past and plans have gone awry. A life that was mapped out to glide smooth from start to finish took a skew and a swirl and ran agley. Yet still I think it was not the building of the grey stones of Lissarinka that angered the fairy folk. Today with my eyes closed, I look over at the battlements of the castle and in my mind's eye, there is a mist that comes down and it might not be possible to see a person, that had climbed up to walk the perilous height. Legend says the mist comes because two young lovers leapt to their death in the tower and still the crimson stain is on the flagstone below, but Tim-Pat always says that Mrs. McCracken did that herself once a week with chickens' blood and I thank God that I have Tim-Pat still. I remember Tim-Pat for ever . . . from the day when I walked the stable yard the first time and felt the cobble stones harsh against my small soft shoes. He picked me and carried me and his whip-cord quality was a match for any stone. There was a wonderful comfort about the leather and tobacco and warm-stable-essence of him. He is a shortish wide-shouldered man with a screwed-up smile — a gnome man. He has always struck me as being the man who looks after the whole place. My father might be a more superior being, but Tim-Pat has the know-how, the sheer hard work, the wisdom about smaller issues. I never remember a time when he did not see to the horses, milk the cows, foot the turf and cart it home, save the hay. His wife, Bessie was as different as a full-blown rose might be to a wood carving of a leprechaun, such as they make these days to sell to the tourists. Bessie had a round laughing face and skin like a peach. She was all softness and her waist took a bit of encircling. Her soft breast was a haven to bring troubles to. I remember telling her one day that she had hair like an empress because it was all gold and done up in a crown on her head.

I re-kindle the boil of Seo's purring with a stroke of my hand and look through the window in front of me, look down the slope of the avenue towards the road and ask myself how it can be possible that Bessie's hair is snow-white now and Tim-Pat is iron-grey and monk tonsured. He is even bent down a little with the years. It was only yesterday that they walked one on each side of my Sheltie, down the avenue yonder and along the Carrick road for a mile, so that I could buy a sugar-stick called 'Peggy's Leg', that was the colour of honey and had an unforgettably delicious taste. The past is stored with memories, of sounds and tastes and smells and sights, with all the things that happened and each part fitted in to each other part, to make a picture in the end of it. As I sit in the old armchair with closed eyes, my thoughts go helter-skelter down the slide of one day after another, of one month after another, of one year after the next. Yet there must be some first point to come to. There were birthdays and picnics and one school and the next, and college. There were events that will never let go of memory, nor lose their pain. Yet it was all so happy growing up, being called Miss Fitzgerald instead of 'Constance-Tenacity' and there was a strange name for any girl! There was that small shock of surprise that one might be thought grown up, even though the 'Constance-Tenacity' had come out of nowhere. Tim-Pat could make me no wiser about my name and he told me that my parents must have just chosen it.

"Don't go asking about it either. I can tell you your GrandMaw's name and your Greatgrandmaw's on both sides and there was never a Constance-Tenacity but your own self, that I heard tell of."

There was a worried look about him and I thought it might be in case I asked my mother about my name and she might think I did not like it, but then nobody likes the name their parents choose for them. At any rate, it seemed that Constance-Tenacity had come 'from out of Nowhere'.

"I wish I had dozens of brothers and sisters," I sighed, to Tim-Pat but I was young at the time and had no sense to speak of.

It was well before the golden day, when somebody had addressed me as

'Miss Fitzgerald'.

Tim-Pat was quick in anger about my wish for a big family and anger was unusual between him and me.

"Anyway why should you be wishing that?" he asked in a hard voice. "Haven't you got the whole world in your hand and nobody to be stealing the glory off of you? You'll be the queen of Lissarinka when the time comes and no son and heir in the house to put your nose out of joint for you."

Indeed it was a long time ago, this passage of arms, away down the years and me with a very little wisdom indeed.

"They're over-protective," I said confidentially, meaning my parents, and then I thought that Tim-Pat might not be acquainted with the phrase. I had only just learnt what it meant myself, so I filled him in on it.

"I can't do anything, but I'm caught. If I had three or four sisters and a couple of brothers, I'd be able to have a smoke in the hay loft without the whole household going mad at me about it."

He shut one eye and screwed his face up to a lob-sided acid drop and looked at me out of the other eye.

"There's times when I give up all hope of putting anything into your skull, Constance-Tenacity. For one thing, a hay-loft's a daft place to strike a match, let alone go 'haling cigarettes. It's worse still, if you're not turned nine yet. You're only rotting the lungs out of your chest. For another, them fags has been hid up in the bricks of the harness-room for enough weeks for the mice to be crawling all over them and desecrating them."

There was a twinkle in his open eye and then the serious look again, creeping like a cloud over the brightness of his face.

"Don't go hinting to your mammy nor yet your pappy that you're lonely for more childer in the house. They worship the ground you tread and you ought to be down on your bended knees to them for the way they treat you. The thought that you miss brothers and sisters would only bring down tears to drench their eyes."

He took out a pipe with a short stem that was as much a part of him as his right arm, cut the plug tobacco, rubbed it between nut-meg palms, stuffed the bowl with it, as if he was carrying out a precise surgical operation.

"As to brothers and sisters, haven't you enough friends? The place is crawling with them . . . the young McCrackens and the doctor's son, not to mention the son of the *Leinster Tribune*?"

This last had a noble Roman sound about it, but it was only Fergus Kennedy of Ballyboy, whose father edited the local paper, the one, which came out every Wednesday.

"They'd be my own flesh and blood," I explained. "That's different from friends. Besides Fergus Kennedy's grown up, and he's always up in Trinity College at his studies."

He took out his aggravation by striking a match on the seat of his breeches, lighting it up first time in a way that I never failed to admire, but could never imitate.

"You've got riches and happiness and grandeur. Don't go reaching for more or you'll maybe find yourself with empty hands. I'd be afeard to talk the way you do, for 'tis flying in the face of God. You did it yesterday too, flew into the face of God. Don't think I didn't see you, riding your pappy's horse bareback in the seven acre field and only a halter for bridle, a horse that has the devil in his soul. Och! You'll come to a bad end."

Then he laughed and took me off with him to help drive in the cows and not a harsh word between us.

The memories vanish like turf smoke that is blown in the wind, but perhaps there is a way to catch them, set them out in order, index them into a sequence that will start off in the long ago and circle about, to end up with me neatly back sitting in the chair where I am now a grown up woman with Seo in my lap. I think of all the cats, that have sat thus, so alike one to the other, each one as destructive to the carpets and the upholstery, each one with claws vanquished by printed velvet. I wonder if Seo is a Witch Cat as Bessie says they all are. I wonder if there might be the danger that I could step back in time and find myself lost to this gracious room forever. Seo's fur is soft against my lips, as I bend my head to kiss the point exactly between her two seal brown ears. My mouth leaves a smidgeon of lipstick on the blonde plush on the top of her head.

"Have you the power to turn back the years, Witch Cat? If I were Alice in Wonderland, I might step through the looking glass, but that was another story."

Seo opened her mouth in a silent protest, for well she knew, that I had only to summon up the past in my head.

"I wish I could get back to the beginning of it all," I mused and that would have been the night of the first storm.

There was a sudden wind that shrilled over the wood, whined in the sashes, moaned in every nook and cranny of the house, groaned in the boards of the floors and along the landings, creaked the stairs, where no foot trod. Something scratched at the window and Bessie always held that that sound meant that one of the animals, whom we had loved and lost in death, was outside, and begging to come back for a while. Automatically, I got to my feet and opened the lower sash a twelve inches, thought that that might not admit one of the bigger dogs and raised it a good two feet and laughed at my own superstition. There was a storm on the way. The expanse of the sky was blown to emptiness, except for a few wispy fleeting clouds. The leaves of the hillside were dancing and shining and twinkling. I sat down on the chair and Seo approved of the open window. She stood, shaping for a leap to my lap and in the backdrop of the fall of Lissarinka hill, there was a pinkness in the dying light and a sullen angry look, that I had not noticed before, when I looked directly out. I picked her up and settled her on my lap again and was surprised that there was no lipstick on the fur between her ears, where it had surely been half a minute before. An extraordinary idea came into my head and I dismissed it at once. Bessie would have really believed that this was not the modern Seo, but one of the cats from years ago, that had leapt, light as a feather, through the open window. That was how big magic would be done, but I knew it as the trick of my fanciful mind. Seo's purring had intensified all the same, as if she had not seen me for a long time. She reached up for my shoulder and rubbed her velvet nose against my cheek and her whole body vibrated in a lithe ecstacy. Then came another breath of the coming storm and the curtains billowed into the room like the sails of a ship. I got to my feet quickly and closed the sash again, else the next billows might have sent the flowers flying to the floor in their tall vase. I had taken Seo under my arm and I looked out at the whitening of the leaves of the weeping willow on the lawn. Surely it seems to be smaller than it had been? Weeping willows had a habit of growing too big and Tim-Pat had said a few days ago that this one had outstayed its welcome, but seen from the angle where I now stood, it was small and dainty. Perhaps Seo had done mighty magic? Maybe she had jumped out into the garden and sent back a substitute kit from the past, hoped that I would not notice the lack of the lipstick, pink on her head. I smiled to myself at the thought and sat down in the chair again and leaned my head against one of the flaps of the Windsor back, smiled down at Seo in my lap again and asked her if she was one of the old, non-forgotten seal-pointed queen cats who had walked Lissarinka in her day, and watched for mice in the stables, slept in the basket under the hot-water towel rail in my nursery bedroom. I have no way of proving if I slept, or if I just closed my eyes and remembered. The weeping willow could have been a trick of the light. Whatever came about between one minute and the next, I shall never know. I was not downstairs any more, but up in the nursery playroom, with the cat under my arm and Bessie was there, the tray between her hands.

"Time for bed soon, Constance-Tenacity."

This was a part of Lissarinka given over to children, a suite of playroom and bedrooms and school-room, bathroom ... all self contained and it had catered for generations. I was the only one left of all the young people that had gone before, but there had been many along the years. They had left evidence of changing times in the desks and the blackboard, the well-worn rocking horse, the Noah's Ark with Mrs. Noah and all the animals in the world, shelves packed with familiar books . . . Robinson Crusoe, Enid Blyton, Little Women, Arthur Ransome, Mrs. Tiggy Winkle, Dickens, Dickens, Dickens, the big volumes with the green binding. They were there, all the old remembered friends, school books too with Latin primers and sum books and more sophisticated Greek prose.

The desk had a fine taste in notepaper with a flowered motive that matched the violets on Bessie's special nursery tea cup, which was made of bone china and which was so valuable, that it had been repaired with strips of metal. A few years ago when I had friends in to play and we had wanted lemonade instead of tea, Bessie always made her own private tea by putting leaves in a perforated spoon and standing it in the cup, warmed of course, and then infusing it with boiling water.

I caught a warmth from the big fire place and turned to look at it. There was turf piled up alongside in an old oak cradle and a skip of logs, that had been sawn from the dead apple tree. It was tea-time by the cuckoo clock, but I had thought the cuckoo had stopped years ago. He came out as I thought this and went through his usual performance and I knew I was dreaming.

Yet it was a most realistic dream. The leather seat of the club fire guard was as more vivid a red than ever and the brass front of it was as highly polished as Bessie could make it. Even the fire was jealous of its brightness and sulked a little and the peat turf sent up greyness along the curve of the throat of the fire place. Across the room, the dresser was stretching to reach the ceiling. The blue and white saucers and plates were ranged like soldiers on parade, and the cups hung from little hooks. If I opened the drawers, I knew every knife and fork and spoon, all a little the worse for wear and inherited from the downstairs dining-room and kitchen.

My dream thoughts drifted on and on, turning this way and that and then I saw my reflection in the mirror over the fire, saw myself fifteen years of age, but knew well that I was no such person. I was a grown-up lady with a Siamese cat in my arms, yet there was no pink tinge to the fur between her pricked ears and there should have been. Therefore I was dreaming and the dream was drawing back and the years were spinning out like a fishing line, reeling away, away, away, away. Or maybe it was just memory and a vivid imagination. If it was a dream, I must not forget its nature, but it was no dream, for I could remember it . . . knew what must happen next, as clear as crystal. It had all happened before. I tried to hold on to this knowledge and it turned into wisped gauze that broke away from my mind and vanished inexorably. My senses recorded Bessie and her face smiling and hair, gold as an empress's crown, not snow white as now.

"There's a storm coming up, Honey. I've closed all the windows and put the wedges in the sashes. There'll be thunder and lightning later on, for there's a threat in the sky. I'll stretch a cloth over the mirrors in the rooms yonder. I don't want you to be struck by a bolt of lightning and you safe in your bed."

"I've told you that that's all nonsense," I said primly.

Was I not fifteen turned and knowledgeable about old-fashioned superstitions? What possible power against lightning could cloth over a mirror have? Besides, Lissarinka had a splendid lightning conductor and it would earth any shafts that fate directed against us.

"It's better to be safe than sorry."

We were to have high tea . . . rashers and eggs and homemade soda bread, with good farm butter from our own cows. There was blackberry jelly and Sally Lunn and a Victoria sandwich.

It was not often that we ate alone in the nursery. Almost always, there would be some of the McCracken boys or John Morton, the doctor's son, or one or two of the others. It just happened that this was term time and I had been sent home from boarding school, because I had been ill . . .

Yet somewhere through it all, I knew that this was not reality. I was a woman grown and I had been caught up in a spell. I had stepped back through the years and what was about to happen had happened before. This time, I must remember it, but it was hard to recall the dream past the awakening.

Tea was over now and I had gone down to say goodnight to Mimsy and Father. I was in my bed and the start of the whole story had come round again. There was something that I tried to remember, but it had vanished. I looked at the glass of milk on the bedside table just as it always was, covered over with a gauze netting, weighed down with blue glass beads. Mimsy had come to tuck me warm in the blankets and Father with her, shutting the wooden shutters across the windows.

"We'd best have the shutters across. It's blowing a half gale outside and Tim-Pat says it's going to be a holy terror."

I assured him that I loved a good storm and that when I was full grown, there would be nothing I would prefer to putting on a long cloak to walk out through the thunder and lightning.

"Maybe you'll change your mind when you're full grown," he smiled at me and kissed my cheek and my mother kissed me again and I felt sleepy and happy and safe and loved, and the wine-red velvet of her dress brushed against my face and the sweet scent of her wrapped me round.

There was Bessie turning down the light and following them through the door and the door was not closed, but left ajar, so that there was a streak of light down the side of it, to keep me a part of the house and not shut away alone. The stair carpet muffled the sound of their feet, but I knew they would be safe downstairs. Outside the wind was making a sound as one might hear on a ship at sea, a continued roaring and swashbuckling. Now and again, there was the dash of rain against the windows, but the shutters made nothing of that. Seo was supposed to be asleep in her basket under the hot towel rail but she had waited till they had gone downstairs. I felt her light on the clothes, as she jumped up on the bed and snuggled herself into a round ball against my side. Her nose touched my cheek, as if she too kissed me goodnight and after a while, she began to snore very softly.

There was no memory of anything out of the ordinary. We had had storms at Lissarinka before. Tomorrow, the Castle hobbledehoys would be over to see what damage had been done for their school broke up today and they would be home. With luck there might be a tree down across the avenue and we could help to saw it up. The house shuddered now and then and some soot fell into the fireplace. I was glad of the streak of light from the slightly open door, glad of the warmth of Seo against my side and the way her little snore turned into a purr, when I stroked her. Her eyes reflected red in the darkness when she blinked them at the doorway, but she was very sleepy and so was I. I would play the pretend game. I chose a ship at sea in the Caribbean and soon there might be ship wreck, but no great sorrow to it, for the whole crew must be cast ashore on a coral island. Phil would be in command as usual. It was a island of paradise, with fresh water, with fruit growing, so that one had only to reach out a hand for it. There was a log cabin to build and furniture to make and the shells of turtles to use for kitchen utensils ... and goats for milk and bread fruit for bread and a great many things stolen from Robinson Crusoe, but I was as sleepy as Seo. The brightness of the tropical sun dimmed down to the nursery bedroom with its shutters pulled across. The streak of light from the door switched off as my eyes closed. A slate fell from the roof above my head, slithered across the other slates and crashed on the terrace below, but it was all remote and unreal as a dream. There was nothing but darkness and the ship sound of the wind and the thunder grumbling now and then, but far away and farther ... then nothing, nothing, except the soft foot on the floor and the breathing beside my bed, as Bessie crept in to see that I had not been frightened by the elements. I had only a dreamy knowledge of her and took her presence for granted, one of the grace and favour gifts that were my heritage. I was Constance-Tenacity Fitzgerald, only daughter of Lissarinka, only child, and heiress to the whole estate. I was destined to happiness and there seemed no possibility of my ever being anything but happy. I was safely asleep in my bed and time was running forward, or running in circles perhaps, circles that went round and round for all a person might know, but if the course of the running of time were to be altered, who is there to say, what might happen? The Little People lived in the hollow hills. There were few in Ireland, who would deny their existence or their jealousy about privilege. No man would plough across a fairy ring, far less walk across it. No woman gathered blossoms of the May — the Hawthorn, nor took it into the house. Yet, long ago, somebody had thought to curve out a hollow and set his house near the wooded top of a fairy fort. He had called it Lissarinka and set its name proudly in gold paint on the front gates and it was a happy house. As far as I knew, it had always been a happy house . . . and tomorrow, the storm would be over and Phil would come with the rest of them and there would be exciting things to explore . . . and so to the dark emptiness of deep sleep.

The slam of the door woke me to darkness and it seemed that I had been asleep for a long time. The streak of light had gone and the drawn shutters shut out any trace of the night outside the windows. The wind hurled itself against the house in a tempest, but muted, as it had been when I went asleep. Yet my door should not have been shut. It was always left open. A draught must have blown it on its hinges till the lock clicked and held. I got out of bed and felt with my feet for my slippers, could not find them for a while, because sleep still muddled my senses. After a while, I found one and then the other, wondered why I had not thought to turn the switch of the bedside lamp, but it was not worth the effort of waking up enough to grope for it in the pitch dark. I knew the way to the door with my eyes shut and had my hand on one of its panels, when I heard the voices, Bessie's first and then Mimsy's.

"Come back to bed, Ma'am. I'm telling you, you had one of your bad dreams. That's all it is. There's nobody outside the house. How could there be in a tempest like that? The screeching of the wind woke you up and you thought you heard something."

Mimsy's voice was softer and hard to hear, compared with Bessie's. I had to strain my ears. Then my hand found the handle and I turned it softly and opened back the door an inch. Through the crevice, I could see sideways along the stretch of the Turkey carpet with the banisters of the top landing straight in front of me. The light had been turned low, but my mother was standing over by one of the windows, trying to snick back the catch of the shutters.

"Come away from there, Ma'am. It was that blast of wind that blew through the whole house. Sure, can't you see the way it's nearly shut the nursery door to? I thought a minute or two ago, that same door slammed shut, but I see 'tis open a pieceen. I'll have to let more light in or we'll have Constance-Tenacity out to see what's happened and then I'll have two of you on my hands, instead of the one."

The door was pushed open six inches and I almost took the swing of it on an eyebrow.

"It's no wonder it got you out of your warm bed and filled your head with fancies, Ma'am."

"I heard the children crying, Bessie. It wasn't a fancy. I've never heard them so clear. You always say that animals come back from the dead and scratch the windows and the door to get in. We all know it's silly and superstitious, but you've made us all as bad as yourself. We get up and open the door or the window and they come in, Bessie. You know they do. Why can't you believe me that they're outside there this minute, the children . . . all the little children? They were so small and weak. They'll not survive the cold and the wet. Let me get the shutters open quick. They sounded happy at first. They were singing, then they didn't like the lightning and they wanted to come in to us, to the warm of the house. Open the window just a few inches, please, Bessie. You'd do it if I said I heard a dog howl . . . "

I knew that my mother sometimes walked in her sleep, but it was a thing nobody talked about. She was the sort of person one would expect to be given to sleep-walking. I watched her now, as she fumbled at the catch with Bessie pulling at the wine velvet drape of her sleeve. The wine red and the Turkey carpet and the dimmish light turned the whole picture into a rich strange oil painting. I had named her well when I chose to call her 'Mimsy' as her pet name. It had been my term of love because she was so gentle and kind and charming and pretty. She was not practical and downright like Bessie, for all Bessie's superstitions. Bessie had taken over the running of of the house and it was just as well, for my mother could never have done it. Yes, 'Mimsy' was just right for the way Mother moved like a grasshopper through every conversation, the way she fluttered in from the garden with her arms full of flowers and forgot them in the hall, the way she could never remember. We had been reading 'Alice' one day and had come to ''Twas brillig and the slithy toves . . . all mimsy were the baragroves', and all the rest of it.

I had asked Bessie what it meant and she told me it meant 'anything you want it to mean, Honey'.

"Then 'Mimsy' is magic-talk for Mother and I hereby christen Mother 'Mimsy'," and we laughed and 'Mimsy' she became and remained 'Mimsy'.

She was quite delighted and said she felt flattered. The name went with pretty flowing dresses and with fun and laughter and sometimes with strange fancies.

"It sounds like Ophelia, doesn't it, Constance-Tenacity?" "There's Rosemary. That's for remembrance" and "You must wear your rue with a difference. There's pansies. That's for thoughts. There's a daisy. I would give you some violets, but they withered all when my children died . . . "

It was a misquotation for Ophelia's children had not died, but her father, yet there had been a small unease in my mind, that 'Ophelia' might have suited Mother better than 'Mimsy' . . . Ophelia with her hands full of long purples . . . and somewhere in the dark part of my mind, I knew that Ophelia was mad and wondered, but when I brought the subject up with Bessie, she turned me off it. 'Mimsy' was what you might call 'fey' and she was the mistress of Lissarinka and one day I would be mistress of it myself and she hoped that I was half as clever as my mother was with all the poetry and learning she had in her head . . . and not to worry about Mimsy seeing children, that weren't there. It was all in her brain, poor thing.

Now I was looking at Bessie's arm about Mimsy's shoulders and the coaxing voice.

"Come back to your bed, Ma'am. You'll catch your death of cold."

Mimsy had turned away from the window and was walking along the carpet and I saw the tears that over-spilled her eyes and rolled down her cheeks.

"They were so small . . . so small and so perfect . . . just the same as fairy children might be, but they were all taken . . . one after the other and I was left with nothing . . . not even hope. They were so beautiful and tonight they were crying to come back to Lissarinka . . . to come back to me. Why can't I let them in?"

I heard Father's exclamation, before I saw him come out of their bedroom door and Bessie was glad he had come.

"Has she had one of these damn sleep walkings? It's been months. Oh God! I'd hoped that they were done for good, but the sound of the storm would make anybody have nightmares."

He had taken her into his arms and she seemed to cower against him for comfort . . . for protection . . . for reassurance.

"Come back to bed, Moll. It was only your bad dream and it's done with."

"Were there no children?" she asked him, lifting her face to his and the tears dripping down her cheeks still, and Bessie was whispering to him that Herself had thought there were children "Beyond in the front drive."

He put up his head towards the ceiling and sent back the shadows with his deep laugh.

"You've forgotten. It's cats and dogs that come back from Hades on visits. I'm worn out getting up from my comfortable arm chair to let them in and it's all Bessie's fault for starting it in the first place."

"But the children all died," she persisted. "I'm no good to you, Richard, for your house is empty."

He took her by the shoulders and shook her and I was ashamed of being an eavesdropper to such a scene. Bessie was stealing away in her chequered carpet-slipper-boots and her grey flannel wrapper and I noticed the gold hair up in rollers and the gauzy scarf round it. She went down the back stairs and presently she would be up again, to see if I had been disturbed. In the meantime, I closed the crack of the door a little and stayed listening to what was no business of mine.

"Am I not children and house and fortune enough for you, Moll? That child named you aptly when she put 'Mimsy' on you, for your head is full of nonsense."

"You're children and house and fortune enough for me," he went on after a bit. "I'd count the whole world well lost, if I still had you."

"But you would have liked Lissarinka running over with sons and daughters, Richard. It's made to be full of graceful and beautiful children."

Again, he laughed and swung her round, bent his head to kiss her, asked her if she had forgotten Constance-Tenacity.

Her voice was a wraith of sound that

crept up from the red carpet to the Adam-green-walls and echoed down the well of the staircase.

"Tenacity? Constance Tenacity? But she's different. Can she fill the gap made by sons . . . sent from Nowhere, like a miracle? Sent from Nowhere, manna from heaven, rain in the desert, the olive leaf in the dove's beak . . . a rope cast to a drowning person?"

"Sent from Nowhere," he echoed and there was a sadness about him and I could understand nothing of what was going on between them. "I suppose you could put it like that."

"They're crying again," she mumbled against his neck. "I can hear them, I tell you. You can't be deaf to them . . . not you. Let them in, Richard. At least open the window and if they want to come in, they may do it."

He turned on her and across the landing, I could see the lines etched by the years on his face.

"They're dead, Moll. Face up to it. They're dead and they'll not be standing outside with the dogs and cats, who have known our fireside. They're gone to God, to eternal happiness. Nothing you can do can ever bring them back again . . . nothing you and I can do can ever replace them now, and in the meantime, and for the rest of our lives, please God, we have Constance-Tenacity, sent to us from Nowhere . . . with the whole world held between her two little fists, and the courage that's in her heart. You've settled for her and I've settled for her. Constance-Tenacity and your own self . . . I've torn the world in two . . . split it up the middle. She had one half and you have the other. If you go to Puck's Castle and then take a world tour from there and back again . . . pause to look at Mrs. McCracken's bloodstain on the flagstones of the hall as a tourist attraction and go to the Barbadoes and Nicaragua and Nombre de Dios Bay and home again, you'll not find a happier man than myself. This I swear to you . . . Moll, my darling. Turn your back on the past and look to the years to come. Watch our daughter go up across the skies and ride the comets. Let what is past, sleep in peace, until we're past ourselves and then what's it all matter?"

He lifted her in his arms and took her back to bed and presently Bessie came up the backstairs and crept into my room, quiet as a mouse, to see if I had been disturbed, maybe if I had overheard anything. She could have no idea of how disturbed I had been, but I was in bed and my slippers were side by side on the mat, my eyes lightly shut, my breathing regular. She could not see the invisible rats that raced round and round in my head, as if my head were a wire trap from which there was no escape. I recognised the scene I had just witnessed as high drama, but I could understand none of it.

There had always been a mystery about me ... recognisable in the stable conversation, in the kitchen gossip, in the commands that I must not torment my parents with requests for brothers and sisters and no firm reason given. I had half thought that Mimsy had been through some dreadful experience. I knew that she was not normal mentally, yet she seemed happy as mistress of Lissarinka, but 'I had come out of Nowhere'. That statement was a bomb underneath my existence. Could a person come from Nowhere? I fell asleep wandering in the maze the problem set me, but in the morning the storm had gone and the shutters were open. The sun streamed in and it was a different world from the night of the landing and the whispered conversation.

After a while I ceased to worry about the prospect of coming from Nowhere. I was home from school, but soon term would start again. In the meantime, Lissarinka was mine to enjoy with all its freedom. Then there was just one more year at school and after that the finishing school in France, but that would be fun. Then life stretched out before me and not a care in any part of it down the whole vista. I pushed back the thought of the scene on the landing and got ready to meet the day. There was storm damage to view and Tim-Pat might let me use the chain saw. Mimsy was happy. Father adored her and it did not matter if she had strange fancies. We all loved her and Bessie ran the house like clockwork. Soon, I would be home to help, with all the knowledge I had amassed from my

French finishing school. "God was in his heaven," or so I believed and "all was right with the world."

I was hungry for breakfast . . . porage and bacon and egg. I must hurry downstairs with Seo, the cat, at my heels, with no trace of lipstick between her chocolate ears. Yet I was full of dream and sleep and I was in my printed velvet chair . . . full of dreams, that had gone past and were over for aye. Seo was on my lap, fast asleep still and there was no doubt that the smidgeon of lipstick was still on honey-brown. Then Bessie came into the room, her hair snow-white, only a memory of the gold that had lived there in years long gone.

"Him-self will soon be home, Ma'am. I don't know what he'll think if he finds you fast asleep and the flower vase blown down and the roses strealing all across the carpet . . . "

I looked out at the weeping willow and knew that indeed it had grown too big, but Tim-Pat would see to it one day . . .

2

The Door To The Vault

THREE years later, came the big storm, the tempest that nobody forgot. Mrs. McCracken had it that Puck left his castle and walked up the side of Lissarinka Hill and perhaps he did.

For myself, great changes had come about, for my schooling was finished and Bessie was of the opinion that I had acquired 'a grand polish'. I spoke French like a near-native. I cooked like a near-chef. I knew most of the rudiments of running a house, but the French order of nuns would never have chosen Lissarinka as a model for their teaching. Still, they had guided my faltering efforts and they had done the best they could with the bad material I seemed to be. I was able to indoctrinate Bessie into the art of cooking 'coq au vin', which was, to her mind, 'the ruination of a good roasting fowl'. She was far more pleased that at last I was taking an interest in my own appearance. I had a wardrobe that filled her with delight. I had outgrown my look of a young filly foal, 'all eyes and staggery long legs'. Bessie thanked God that I used make-up with discretion. In her own words, I did not look 'like a painted-up kept woman', as most of my generation did, when they came home from being finished.

I had gained an enormous knowledge of the facts of life, by convent standards, but the nuns had only built on a sound foundation of farmyard observations, which I had picked up for myself at no expense whatever. Bessie was proud of me and that was something. The boys showed a changed interest in me, too. They themselves had altered out of recognition. Phil, who was destined to be Master of Puck's Castle, had attended an agricultural college and was all jodpurs and high-necked sweaters and master-complex-six-feet-tall. Still, his hair was sunshine around his head. He was back in Puck's Castle, with a deal of power in his hands and he knew how to use it. The tenants might say he would never be the 'decent man his father was before him', but he knew the power he possessed and he used it . . . used it, as he used his whip at the Point-to-point races, to bring him home the winner.

Connor had chosen the Navy for his career, and he was in Dartmouth, or through it. He appeared at rare intervals, still completely in Phil's shadow, still with no word to say for himself, very handsome in a photograph taken in uniform.

The two young brothers, Dermot and Tomas, were seniors in boarding schools and they had no idea in the world what they wanted to do with their lives. They were twins and they were identical . . . looked alike, thought alike, one soul in two bodies. Bessie had it that they were Puck's own progeny, for the devil that was in them, but their own father thought they were a pair of 'omadauns'. If they did not soon take their fingers out, they might both end up as young age pensioners. Still, there was no hurry. The Castle could support them all. They were grasshoppers. They idled their time away and they had a tremendous adoration for my new image.

Fergus Kennedy, the son of the *Leinster Tribune*, seemed to have disappeared. He had got his Trinity degree in something or other and he had been working in Fleet Street, picking up the facts of Press life. It was a rough, tough existence and he had lived in a bachelor flat and had done some sort of managerial course. He ran his own life, 'drank, or learned how to drink level with the best of them', or so his father summed Fleet Street up. Bessie told me confidentially that Mister Fergus had not been too happy beyond in England. She had it that he had left his heart in Ballyboy and that he could not wait to get back to the things that mattered to him. Presumably that meant the *Leinster Tribune*, his father's newspaper, which he was destined to inherit.

So we were all very young and unsophisticated, very unwise too perhaps, the night of the second storm. We would never have agreed that night, that we possessed any such qualities as unsophistication or inexperience.

We were all so sure of ourselves and we knew it all, every last one of us.

Then the big storm came and Puck left his castle and walked up the hill to Lissarinka House.

It was Bessie that came to tell me about it, for I never even woke up. The devil had walked in the night and had ripped a path through the trees ... a path that ran straight from Puck's Castle to Lissarinka House and all the lovely elm trees blown down like 'as if you was to fling down a box of matches'.

I stood at the bedroom window, which she had unshuttered for my benefit and there was a new track through the woods on Lissarinka Hill. There was a clear way mapped as if a bulldozer had gouged it out. The row of ancient elms, notoriously prone to elm disease, had suffered. It had been a lovely avenue, double flanked by old trees, running from Lissarinka down the side of the hill towards the church and up the next hill to Puck's Castle. It had always been the short cut to the Castle and now a whirling dervish of a tornado had spun the elm trees higgledy-piggledy. The way to Puck's Castle lay wide open now. You could see the battlements and the side of the hill on which the Castle was built. You could see the little grey stone church on the tiny hill that stood between Lissarinka and the Castle. Beside the church you could see the graveyard ... the tombstones, the marble angels. When I stared long enough, I could make out our family vault. We lay, the folk from Lissarinka, in privilege, in rich privacy, in a railed-off plot, surmounted by a marble plaque and statues brought all the way from Italy. There was a below ground room with shelves where Lissarinka coffins were stored in dead grandeur. I got an uneasy feeling as I stood at my bedroom window, as if Puck, Nick, the Devil himself had opened up the way from my window to the place my people lay buried, all the ones that had 'gone before' from Lissarinka. I had come from Nowhere, they had said that night and I remembered it now, and Seo was impatient in my arms, the Seo we had then, and put up a paw to my face to remind me that it was time she went outside.

I emptied her out of my arms and

had a bath, chose a safari suit, a most glamorous garment, yet suitable for an expedition to the tattered jungle that the elm trees had become. I must go and see what damage the storm had done, but I did not know that something might have been done, which could never in this life be undone. I had even lost my desire to be allowed to use the chain saw, for I was child no longer.

My safari suit was Paris, a cream jacket, finger-tip length, with pleated pockets, with shoulder epaulettes, and slacks to match it, of superb cut. I tied a bright embroidered band, Indian-like, round my brow to bind my straight dark hair down as if I imagined myself to be Pocahontas.

At last, I stood on the front step to survey the scene. The front garden seemed to have stood up to the storm remarkably well. From the top of the four steps, I could make out very little of important damage. The weeping willow was as graceful as usual, but it would have stooped against the ferocity of the storm and when peace had come, it could rise again. The sun dial was on its side and the brass face had rolled ten yards away, but that was a matter that would be put to rights very simply. There was a tree down across the avenue to the back gate, but it was an ash and would make good burning, when the winter came. Of course, there were leaves everywhere and bits of twigs and small tree branches and the ornamental urns on the terrace were blown over and all the geraniums and alyssum and lobelias shot out in a muddle on the gravel of the drive and across the lower step. From the front of the house at this level, the track of the storm through the woods, that I had seen so well from my window, did not seem much. The other trees of Lissarinka woods might have moved together to shut out the view of Puck's Castle. Yet I knew there was a space that had been shorn through the trees and that probably one might walk along it and come out at the church, at the cemetery itself, at the family tomb. There were 'Bessie thoughts' in my head. We had a family banshee according to Bessie and if we were to die, one of our family, it was the banshee's duty to comb her hair and keen out her lamentations up the side of Lissarinka Hill, on the eve of the death.

The arrival of my friends from Puck's Castle distracted my attention from family legend and their greetings made Seo jump out of my arms, to which she had returned. They had arrived in a clapped-out Daimler and they shouted news at me from a hundred yards range. They arrived as the Strolling Players might have done in Olivier's unrivalled production of Hamlet and they set all thoughts of banshees and witches and warlocks to flight, even if they lived in a Castle, believed by half the population of the district to be haunted by the devil himself, whether he happened to be called Old Nick or Puck.

They cried out to me in competition one against the other, till the open sports Daimler stopped at the foot of the steps with a bang from the exhaust that sent the rooks flying from the trees . . . and Phil yelled at his brothers to shut up. The Daimler betrayed the broken down fortunes of Puck's Castle for it was what my father called 'vintage plus, yet not quite plus enough'. Phil and Con sat in front and the twins perched on the hood at the back and I looked at Phil, trying to see him for the first time again, trying to make up my mind if he was really the one for me. I saw the halo of sun round his fair hair, turning it to pure gold and then subtracted the tight line of his lips and the hardness of his jaw.

"Christ! That was a hell of a storm, Constance-T," he shouted. "We've called to see if Bessie could give us breakfast. Our place is in chaos. Even the chicken's blood is washed out with the floods and Ma's in hysterics. We thought we ought to do a recce, came to collect you."

Of course, Bessie could give us all breakfast. She never failed. Con, dressed in neat navy slacks and a roll topped white sweater was far more mannerly.

"We didn't manage to achieve breakfast," he murmured "It's like old times."

Dermot and Tomas had jumped from their seat on the back, as if they were a trained circus act and the words tumbled out of their mouths. There was awful havoc from the storm — trees down all over the place and half the lead off the castle roof. The water had come in, gallons of it. Did I know there had been a big whirlwind? Ma knew all about it. Puck had taken a scythe, like Father Time, the old bloke they had at Lord's.

He had left the Castle and cut a swathe down to the church and up through the graveyard to Lissarinka, to make a path up the hill. It was all some kind of a curse or spell or what have you. When I met Ma, I was not to contradict her, but of course elms were a hazard even without the Devil.

"You're first in the running to be the next mistress of Puck's Castle, when she'd gone. She says Bessie's brought you up to be a true believer in the supernatural."

"For God's sake, shut up," Phil said.

Then we were all in the kitchen, eating plates of porage with brown sugar and cream and some of us were sitting at the table and some standing. Phil took the seat at the head, as if it were his right. I resented that a bit and wondered if he ought not to have invited me to sit there in my own house as his hostess, but he was talking about the sun dial, that had been blown over and Con, as sea-man in embryo, was telling us how to set it up again with a compass, but nobody paid him much attention.

Bessie's voice reached us above the din, from where she stood over by the black-leaded stove.

"Now, who's for rashers and eggs? I want to know this minute and no more prating till I do . . . and don't let your eyes be bigger than your stomachs. The way ye always treat this place like a hotel, I don't know how I ever put up with it."

Maybe the storm, that whirled round Lissarinka kitchen, was as powerful as the storm of the night before. It whisked plates here and there and emptied cups of tea, made nothing of rounds of golden soda-bread, sent home-made marmalade flying down the pots, sliced the slab of creamy butter to its death. Only when they were all full and myself too, did a silence come down and Bessie said there must be an angel passing.

Then he came in across the silence, Fergus Kennedy, and I had not seen him for years. He had been educated at Trinity College in Dublin, had been in Fleet Street in some executive job, learning to be the Editor of his father's 'Tribune'. Here was the 'Son of the Tribune' then, a few years on, with the sophistication of London on him, his hair as dark as ever it had been, his face serious, his voice pleasant, his smile kind, a little deprecating shyness about him, as he searched round the room for me. He might have been a different species of being to us, assembled in the kitchen. He had a cream silk shirt and a Trinity cravat, a jersey with a V-neck with his college colours, brown brogue shoes, like chestnuts, well cut slacks.

"I did knock but nobody heard. I thought you'd not mind if I came in."

His eyes found me and there was surprise for half a second.

"You're Constance-Tenacity, aren't you? We haven't met for years."

God help me! I had been leaning with half my bottom on the big kitchen table, where I had no right to be, when I was hostess to company, even if it were only the boy-men from the castle, whose second home this was. If I had known Fergus was going to arrive, I should have seated myself more decorously, I thought, and then wondered why it mattered. I stood up and mumbled a welcome, held out a hand to him and saw that he was boy no longer, but man — sophisticated, desirable man at that, with hair as dark as my own and the same gentle shy well-mannered way to him, for he pulled out a chair for me to sit down and I was used to such attention in Paris by this, but not in Lissarinka.

I managed to ask him if he would like a cup of tea and he accepted one, but declined anything to eat and this to my mind, put him a step above the locusts from Puck's Castle. He told me there was a reason for his visit. He took no more notice of the others except a brief nod, just looked down at me, told me he was home at last. Then he went on with it.

"A man came into Ballyboy this morning early, stopped at the Press office. He was on his way somewhere with a turf lorry and he knew that we're keen on news. Maybe you don't know yet, but St. Brendan's Oak is down in the storm. You know the one I mean, by Killeen Church, the old tree in chains?"

We did not know it was down, but of course we knew the tree very well indeed. Everybody in the parish knew it. We had listened to tales about it, since the first day we had started to listen to tales of the supernatural from Bessie or Mrs. McCracken, or indeed, from any of the inhabitants of the surrounding countryside.

Lissarinka stood on its hill and Puck's Castle was maybe three miles off on another and lesser hill, but between the two houses, there was a valley and here stood a grey church. There was a gentle climb from the church up a little slope to maybe two acres of mossy grass, that was the graveyard, a place of peace, if ever there was one. It was not a formal cemetery with yews and cedars, just a piece of an Irish hill, where cowslips flourished and where primroses sheltered in against the graves, where often one might find a hare sitting safe in her form. There were blackbirds with their rich song. Sometimes, the willy wagtails flew up from the stream below by the church.

If Mrs. McCracken were to be believed and a great many other people too, St. Brendan had come walking past Killeen Church one day a great many years before. Bessie put it at two thousand, but she cannot have been right about that. However, we did not argue about it, for it was an interesting part of local lore. St. Brendan had broken off a stout oak branch higher up Lissarinka Hill, used it as a shepherd's crook, for was he not one of the greatest shepherds of all time? At the church in the valley he had come on a running brook, had stooped to drink of the water and had pronounced it 'as good as the water in the springs at Biorra' and that was high praise indeed. In thanksgiving, he had driven the oaken crook into the bank of the rivulet, had proclaimed that it would stand till the day of judgement and that pilgrims would call it a Holy place. It was the sort of thing you meet in every part of Ireland and we had all taken it for granted. As long as we could recall, people had come to the staff, now grown into a tree. It looked enormously old and it was quite extraordinary, for there was a custom that a supplicant must tie a rag or a ribbon on one of the branches or twigs, rather in the nature of lighting a holy candle. Below the reach of a tall man's arm, the tree had the look of the 'Wren bush' on St. Stephen's day. There were stories of prayers that were answered and miracles that were wrought, but although Mrs. McCracken was a great believer in the powers of the tree, her sons were not so sure. Phil always proclaimed that his 'Ma' was well off target.

"Ma's cracked," he observed one day. "It's the law of averages. Some prayers are answered and some ain't. You can't win 'em all."

Still we had an affection for the oak. It was a thing, that we had known all our lives and we were sorry to hear it had been a victim of the tempest. We got to our feet, intent on going down to have a look at it. It was, or had been a great shamrock of a tree, in three parts, three great trunks, held together by chains, that might have held a ship's anchor. It had split apart years and years before and people, who loved it, had bound it together again. As a small child, I used to rub my hand against its bark and hope that the chains did not hurt it. I used to grieve a little in case it had wanted to get free and had been chained down. I am given to wandering from subjects and it is a bad habit, that links me to Mimsy's grasshopper mind. I forgot to mention the clear cool stream that gushed out of the oak's side and the way people brought bottles and filled them at it, for the water could work miracles. I have forgotten the smooth slabs of stone, which time had worn hollow on the banks of the stream, under the shade of the tree, where prayers might be said in this silent holy place, where the only sound was the trickle of the water and the song of the blackbirds. It was such a place, where the great God Pan might have been involved even before Christianity.

Now, Fergus Kennedy had come across the kitchen to claim my attention and there was an urgency about him. Bessie was beside me and he wanted her to listen to what he had to say.

His voice was low.

"This concerns your father, Constance-Tenacity. I haven't seen the tree myself, but the Press van's trying to get through. The roads are blocked, but they'll soon be cleared. My father thought I'd best come on here and warn your father, or failing that, tell Tim-Pat."

We waited and there was silence in the kitchen, broken only by the ticking of the clock. Fergus was looking at me, wondering if I could be substituted as a receiver of confidential news. He decided that I was, especially with Bessie to back me up.

"The man on the turf lorry said that the heaviest branch has come down on your burial vault in the graveyard, done quite a bit of damage. It might be best to get it seen to before — "

Bessie's face had a pinched look about it that I could not understand and she cut in on him.

"We won't tell the Mistress a thing about it . . . just the Master and Tim-Pat."

She was thinking quickly what was the best thing to do. I could sense the cogs of her brain skidding in puzzlement. I knew that there was something I could not understand between Fergus and her. She gathered the rest of us into a bunch with her eye and was at her most authoritative.

"And if the rest of ye are going to have a look at it, take the swathe, that's been cut down the elm avenue. The Master will want to know what damage is done there and ye can take your time about it. I'll send ye down a nice picnic lunch later on."

Bessie was snatching information from Fergus like any herring gull on a fish quay. Tim-Pat was fetched and he huddled by a window with Bessie and Fergus and there was talk and more talk, with the rest of us shut out. Then they turned round and warned us that Mimsy must know nothing about the damage to the family vault. Bessie said she would keep Mimsy in bed on some pretext or another, till the whole mess was cleared up. Tim-Pat drove off in the Land Rover with Father. Then a message came to say we were to walk down along the fallen elms as Bessie had said, till we reached the church. Father wanted an assessment of the damage and we were on the spot. We went out to the front steps and Fergus put his hand under my elbow. He knew by my face that I was a little put out that he had been taken into the silent confidences between Bessie and Tim-Pat and my father and I had been lumped with the McCrackens, shut out in a strange kind of way. Of course, Fergus's father and my father were very old friends, but after all, I was the daughter of the house.

"I wish Puck had kept himself in full employment maintaining the stain on the stone steps of the hall at the Castle," he whispered. "This is a whimsical part of the world, with its superstitutions and its Little People and its God-awful legends. I think we must be all half daft."

His lips tickled my ear and he opened one of the secrets for me.

"It doesn't matter a damn about the elms. It's just a slowing up procedure on our friends here ... and there are others arriving. The oak tree has broken the vault door and your father doesn't want anybody down on the scene, till he sees the full extent of the damage ... especially not your mother."

I remembered suddenly how Mimsy brought flowers to the graveyard every Sunday when we went to church, how she walked down the steps to the Gothic door of the vault and set them eight feet below the level of the ground. I had never thought it strange that she should be so devoted to her people-in-law.

She had no children but myself and I had seen her do this all the years I recalled and everybody took it for granted ... "Mrs. Fitzgerald and her flowers for the tomb."

We reached the dry stone wall that bounded the woods from the grass in front of the house. Across the wall was a place of incomparable beauty in spring with its lakes of bluebells, its clumps of primroses, its trailing ivies. There the wild orchids hid and the tiny sweet strawberries in summer.

Fergus helped me over the wall, as if I were a fragile creature, not capable of clearing it with ease in five seconds, but perhaps he was paying homage to my French-built safari suit, which was unsuitable for any safari, when you really thought about it. Phil was jealous. At least I had succeeded in that. He snorted his derision, as he caught up with us and finished the apple that he had picked up from the copper bowl in the hall on his way out. The juice was trickling down his chin, as he squared himself to face the swathe of prone elms, yet they were not prone, but tossed with their trunks this way and that, no order about them in the world, flung down as if they had been devil-thrown. He made sure my eye was upon him and he showed off like a small boy, flinging the apple core, with a fine pride in his physical prowess.

"Bet you can't beat that," he challenged and he was speaking to Fergus, who ignored him.

There was a small round stone at my feet and I picked it up, not thinking it might be a foolish move to make. My mind was too tangled up with the Gothic door being broken and why it was important that Mimsy should not know, about the flowers at the vault every Sunday, about the memory of Mimsy and Bessie on the landing outside my door on that other night three years ago and all the talk about children crying outside the windows, ghost children surely.

There was no fairness in aiming a stone against an apple core and well I knew it. Yet, I flung it far and far and far and it passed the path of the core by ten yards. It was not as if I did not know that it never paid to beat Phil at any game. We all knew it. For all his adult status, he acted like any small boy.

He bent down to the stone wall and chose two equal pebbles, pitched one across to me. It might have been wise of me to fumble the catch, but I even caught it in my left hand, thinking only of Mimsy on the landing and of Bessie's whisper.

"Come back to your bed, Ma'am. You'll catch your death of cold."

My shot went impossibly far, for the distraction in my thoughts, and Phil's fell short of it. He was angry and more jealous than ever. He took to ignoring me and went off along the elm avenue, now sadly in ruin, with no backward look at me.

He set his brothers to the task of jungle

warfare and they were like a small troop of Tarzans, scaling half prone trees and swinging from the branches. Only Con kept aloof of them and stayed near Fergus and myself, and Fergus and he were like two huntsmen with very good manners for they found all the easy ways for me to traverse the avenue and I wondered if they were concerned with my smart clothes and not with me.

I recall every item of the gear I wore that day. It was one of those outfits, one never forgets for the rest of one's life. It was a creamy buttermilk shade and it had been made in the Rue de la Paix and that shows how I had graduated from Lissarinka. The patch pockets had buttoned-over flaps at breast and sides. It had a leather belt, polished like a Sam Browne. I had a dark green shirt that matched my canvas rope-soled shoes. I think even now, I might have passed in the fashion spots of France, but maybe memory is the glory. My hair was shoulder length and was brushed till it shone. I still hoped that I looked like an Indian princess, as I watched Phil, who was pretending not to watch me. At one stage, he reached a high branch and gave out a prehistoric cry like Tarzan, as if he challenged any man to speak to his chosen mate, but I took no notice of him. I was surprised that I did not care very much if he were angry with me. Fergus and I had come down as far as the bubbling spring, that turned into the stream, which joined up with the one at Killeen Church.

We walked side by side past the place where crocus beds would bloom again in the Spring. On down the slope, we went with Con discreetly behind us ten yards, along small paths, through ivied patches, where the rooks always made May a noisy month. Down we dropped under the still-standing trees, to the wild crab, which provided fruit for our crab-apple jelly every year. Then Puck's Castle was in view again, first the battlements, then the sheer stone cliffs, which were its walls then the steps to the front door. At last we could see down into the courtyard and from here, it was as small and perfect, as a child's toy fort.

The church was in the hollow at our feet soon, but the great oak that should have sheltered it from our vision, had turned into a dozen oaks that lay scattered about the ground. I stopped short in pity at the sight of it. It hid a section of the cemetery, covered our family burial plot with a tangle of its branches and twigs and leaves. The Land Rover was parked down by the church and my father and Tim-Pat were over by the vault. I could see the Press Van from the Tribune parked near the Rover. The light was so clear that I could see the lettering on the side of it clearly, a quarter of a mile away with a young chap standing beside it, as carelessly as if it was nothing for such an important tree to be struck by lightning.

Fergus was making sympathetic conversation at my side and Con had drawn level with us, but I took no heed of them, just hurried my pace a little.

Then I found myself standing near the vault, running my finger along the broken railings. The plot that held the underground room was sizable enough, but the oak tree had invested every part of it. There were branches that lay covering the grass. There should have been a flight of steps that led down to the Gothic door, but a great limb of the tree had come straight down into the well of the steps. There were limbs of tree lying on every side among the other graves. It seemed a dozen oaks had grown up to take the place of one, yet they lay askew and must soon die. I stood on tip toe and tried to see down through the leaves, to see if I could catch a glimpse even of the door and there it was, just the tip and there was no doubt that it had been burst open. It was ajar. If a person could squeeze past the branches and shift the trunk over . . . if I could somehow get down there, I had only to push open the door and go inside into the darkness and I would be where the coffins ranked on their shelves. The small hairs on the back of my neck stood on end and I shivered a little, but Fergus gripped my elbow and I looked round and saw my father and Tim-Pat were with us. I could feel the love that bound me round in Lissarinka almost a physical thing. An old countryman stepped forward and took his cap off, stood facing me, his mouth pulled down in sorrow, his cheeks like an old apple.

"Don't mind it, Miss Constance. We'll have the grave mended again and your mother isn't to be breaking her heart over it."

He shook his head sorrowfully.

"St. Brendan will be breaking his heart over it and no shame to him! Hasn't it carried his blessings since the dawn of time rose up the skies?"

I asked him if there were no saving any part of it and he said that maybe there was and maybe there wasn't.

"And aren't you the fine lady grown?" he said and his face had lost its sorrow. "Isn't the grand mistress you'll be making for Lissarinka House and the sun shining on your black hair, till it's better than a raven's wing for the glory, that's in it?"

"If there's any part of the oak left growing, we'll set it again," I said and I had collected quite an audience by that time, for the McCracken clan had arrived and the boy from the Press Van and same straggle of farmers and their wives.

I felt moved with some strange power that I had never experienced before, but I think that it was Fergus's arm on my elbow that gave me the power of speech, like the spirit that sat on the heads of the disciples. I felt almost like a young prophetess, full of faith in what I was saying.

"After all, it only takes a twig, stuck into the earth to grow into a tree . . . given time. It only takes one acorn, laid in the mould beside the stream. St. Brendan would never see it die. We want faith, every one of us and maybe a bit of courage. 'If we screw our courage to the sticking point, then we'll not fail . . . '"

That was Shakespeare and I wondered whom I was trying to impress. It could only lie between Fergus and Phil, and Phil turned barbed spears against me.

"Courage, the girl said," he sneered and there was no liking for me in him, not one little bit and we practically engaged to be married. "It's as well to talk about courage and replacing a tree, that's lasted almost two thousand years replant it with a careless twist of the wrist and the sun shining and the birds singing. I'll have you know that there are times, when Puck himself comes down here to

76

walk this hollow."

I do not know what got into me. I could feel spiritual strength such as I had never felt before, as if the dead people in the cemetery had lent me the power, that had quitted their bodies.

"I will replant the oak," I said. "It won't be anything but a young tree, till I lie in the vault myself, but when we're all forgotten, it will have found its majesty again. Surely St. Brendan would never take away his blessing from it?"

I tore off a sapling from one of the fallen branches of the oak and found a clear space by the brink of the stream. I smoothed the earthy leaf mould with my hands and so I made its bed. Then I borrowed a stick from a farmer who had come to watch what I was doing. With great care I made a deep hole through the soft richness and set the sapling upright, sprinkled down a handful of mould, all firm with my feet and smoothed off the soil again with my hands.

I had plenty of watchers by the time I had finished. They found ash plants and made a palisade of protection for my tree.

"May the Lord bless the growth in it," said an old man. "And may St. Brendan himself leave his grace with it, as he did with the other."

There was a murmur of 'Amen' from all about me, and suddenly I wondered what had got into me. I had taken it into my head to play the oracle, taken it into my head that I should be the one picked out to plant a new oak tree, if such a thing ought ever to be done. Yet the people were glad I had done it and I was surrounded by heady praise, that I had in no way earned.

Only Phil was angry with me.

"So it only takes a twig, stuck in the earth to grow into a tree, given time. I hope you crossed your fingers against the devil. I'd like to hear you repeat it, when the sun's gone in and the moon's come out. Come down here then and ask St. Brendan to forgive you for the pride you have in yourself, and what you can do and what you can't do, and what you shouldn't even attempt to do."

They were all against him and on my side.

"Och! Mr. Phil, you should think

shame for speaking to your young lady like that."

They were careful about my set sapling all the morning and trod carefully past it during the operation that followed. There was not a man, nor a woman nor a child who risked disturbing my effort at tree planting and I think they believed I had done a good thing.

Then Fergus broke up the planting incident, took me off down the hill to the Press van and introduced me to his photographer. The tension and the drama and the anger seemed to be over. Even the exhaltation had left my heart. Whatever strange power had invested me had gone as swiftly as it had come.

It was a lonely part of the country but more people came, drawn by curiosity as the news spread that St. Brendan's Oak was down. There was plenty of time for conversation and many discussions as what must be done and there seemed no hurry whatever to do it. At one stage, two nuns arrived in an estate car, which belong to the Ballyboy Convent and they knelt on the row of stones, the praying stones, and said a rosary and the people knelt too, for it seemed a correct thing to do, to thank St. Brendan for the loan of the giant oak tree for all those years. Even the McCrackens knelt down in the background and I joined them at peace again, although we were of what the nuns would have called 'a different persuasion'. Then we all got to our feet again and began the business of clearing up. It was a slow leisurely job and it was such a change from the quiet of ordinary life that there was a holiday atmosphere about, for all the prayers. Only my father and Tim-Pat were not enjoying it. They were preoccupied and serious and I wondered why. Usually at an affair of this sort, Tim-Pat was the most mercurial man in the gathering. Still, I did not give it much attention. Presumably it must be a sad thing to have a family burial place disturbed, though I did not seem able to care much about it myself. I was far more interested in realising the importance of the old tree I had taken for granted all my life. The nuns were determined to bring some branches home in the estate car and there were plenty of willing hands to saw off suitable pieces. There had been miracles wrought by the hundred, one of the nuns exclaimed, and all by St. Brendan's tree. They would divide up the branches and any person, that asked, would be given a small piece of the wood. Who could tell what power there might be in the smallest bit of it? Put like that, it sounded that the oak might not be mere firewood. One farmer brought a cart, another tractor, a third a lorry. Soon there were saws at work trimming off the green twigs and even the twigs might have 'prayer power'. I believed it myself out there in the sunshine and with the birds singing. Did I now know for myself that Tim-Pat's withered lung had been healed, just because Bessie had prayed on the stones beneath the tree? Hadn't the doctors given him up and wanted to send him to Dublin for some big operation that might have killed him? Then Bessie had 'worn out her knees praying' and Tim-Pat had been his old nutmeg self again and no surgeon's knife to drain his life away from him. It was the same with us all. We were simple folk and maybe we believed in the old gods more than we did in science. So the tree was trimmed of its leaves and cut into movable holy segments and presently there was order returning to what had been a patch of land inhabited by a ruined oak. There were heaps of leaves and piles of logs and the tractor was going to try to pull up the big limb of the oak that lay stretched down the stone stair to our vault. It was the high spot of the whole day. The hours had slipped away and a farmer had brought a crate of beer in his car. Another had fetched sandwiches and buttermilk and a fruit cake. There were men with bottles of John Jameson whiskey and John Power. Bessie had sent down a perfect packed lunch, with chicken carved on cardboard plates and crisp salad, even two bottles of Vin Rosé and glasses. It was like a day at the races with 'the master's flask' sent down in the basket and brandy in it and a bottle of cider for the McCracken twins.

Of course, it was as good as a day at the races. My friends and I were here, there and everywhere. Somebody had produced a chain saw and he was the star performer with the speed which he severed branches and no effort to him.

But the time had come for the tractor to pull the limb of the tree up from the steps of the vault and it was going to be a tricky business. No wonder that my father and Tim-Pat were tight in the lips about it. If anything went wrong, the whole structure of the family tomb might be broken and it had been there for hundreds of years. It must be a very sacred thing in our family and I was beginning to worry a little. The chains that bound the limb were the same cruel links that had held the oak in one piece. Somebody had taken a length of the cable and connected it to a tractor bar, that provided tremendous strength. Then the tractor moved on with a roar of its engine and the limb moved and moved an inch at a time. It groaned once or twice, as if it did not want to be hauled to the level of the earth and cut into logs to be taken away, to be made into holy relics. It was old and tired. I was sorry for it to be left at the end of its life, lying there with all the faces staring down at it. Maybe it was comforted that the nuns held their hands clasped in reverence. It was old and dead and finished and I did not believe it was interested any more in the imaginations of man and what he can think up about the powers of magic or religion or witchcraft, call it what you will. It yielded, an inch at a time, and came slowly up the steps and now we could see the door with the Gothic arch, and it was open a little. As soon as there was space, Tim-Pat was there, testing it, almost guarding it, not leaving it, even if the oak trunk were to fall back upon him. At last it was out on the grass and slowly the men were stripping it of its leaves and branches and it was a huge strong limb, that a carpenter might make good use of, but it was for holy purposes only and the chapel wanted pews and the church wanted a reredos. Even the chapel in Ballyboy was after the wood. The local carpenter had decided that it would be to his glory to carve a lectern of some of it — to cut out a great spread-winged eagle of it to fly in the Ballyboy Catholic chapel for hundreds of years. There was great going and coming among the religious folk and it was all peaceful and happy, for there was no war of religions in the parishes, only amity and that was how it should be, so between them they divided out the wood and the place grew tidy and more tidy and there was a man, who collected up all the leaves and the churchyard was almost its old self again by tea-time. Tim-Pat never went far from the Gothic door. Perhaps there was a freedom of helping oneself to parts of the tree. Maybe, he feared invasion of the tomb. I confessed to myself that I was far more intrigued with making an impression on Fergus than I was on anything else and this was a completely new emotion to me. Glad I was of the Indian headband and the fact that my hair was as black as a raven's feather — that my gear was becoming and that I was young and active and brimming over with life. Fergus watched me all the day and I was conscious of this, I who had never been particularly struck with him before. It gave me pleasure to give Phil pain, for Phil was jealous and that added to my stature in some new strange way.

Then at last, everything was cleared away and the churchyard was stripped of all the oaken pieces that had come from the division of one. There was no root left, for it had pulled itself out like a tooth and it had been hauled up on a farm cart with a rope and a pulley. The hole had been filled in and the ground raked over and the wood was gone and the twigs and the leaves. The cemetery wall was breached, but soon men's hand would pile stone upon stone and it would be itself again. All that remained was the Gothic door, shut but not hanging straight, the broken railings, the stone steps. One could push the vault door open and go in, but Tim-Pat stood there, like the angel at the gate of the garden of Eden. I wondered what the vault was like inside and there were plenty more people with the same curiosity, from their whispering, but my father had no intention of making it a show for curious eyes.

It was all nearly over and people were beginning to go home in twos and threes. The tractor had gone and the horses and the carts, the nuns' estate car with its relics in the back, the van with the Press camera and Fergus too. It was no good without Fergus. I got a strange feeling that the sun had gone in and indeed it had, but it was Fergus's going, that had turned the church flat gray and made the flowers lose their colour and the whole little hollow its magic. The McCrackens were there still, as full of energy as ever, but they were not for me. For the first time in my life, I was bored with them. I was glad when Father said it was time we were getting back to Lissarinka.

He picked up an old chisel and levered a staple from a farm gate and he took the Rector aside and borrowed the padlock and the key of the graveyard from him. I watched as Tim-Pat made the Gothic door of the vault secure, hammering in the staple and fastening it with a piece of chain, turning the key in the lock, that rightly belonged to the cemetery gate.

"That's hold it till tomorrow, sir. Byrne, the carpenter, will make a job of the door tomorrow and get it set on its hinges. Don't be bothering your head over it."

They were standing at the foot of the

steps and I leaned down and smiled at the seriousness of them, but Father took no notice of me, only came up the steps and got in the car and drove off. Tim-Pat pushed at the door with his hand and stared at the studs in its surface for a moment. Then he came up the steps more slowly and I laughed at him, for I thought it a joke that they must think it necessary to lock up the dead. There would not be one person in the whole parish with the courage to go into that place of dead bodies in the night. Well I knew it. It was quite easy to cut up a fallen oak, but if it came to going in to look at the dead in a mausoleum underground once the sun went down, there would be no great rush.

"Why are you locking it up so carefully, Tim-Pat? Is there a skeleton in the family vault?"

We were alone at the head of the steps, but he looked round quickly to make sure nobody had heard me and then he turned a glare upon me, so angry that I could hardly recognise him. His face was screwed up as if somebody had given him a sponge of vinegar and gall to suck, when he had thought it soaked in clear cool water.

"Don't ever say that, Constance-Tenacity — not to me, nor yet to your father, nor your mother. Their people are lying down there in their last rest, their father and their mother and so on and back for a hundred years and more, ones they love and have reverence for. 'Tis mortal sin to make fun of the dead and they at peace for ever in such a quiet place — all tears past and all sorrow done for them . . . and no foolish girl's chatter out of an empty head. Go on home with you now and try to learn to behave yourself, for you've done nothing all day but flaunt your tail feathers like a peacock at Mr. Fergus. You're grown up now and it's fine game to play one man again the other, but don't go mocking the dead. If I catch you talking to your mother about any part of this day, I'll have the hide off of you and it's no good running to Bessie with tales either, for she's of the same mind as myself."

He went off for six steps and then he turned back to me and I daresay I stood there with my mouth open with surprise, for I could not see how I had given him such offence.

"I've got to go in to Ballyboy for the messages. Take care of the key of the lock for me. Give it to Himself when you get to the house. But I tell you now, there's those in that vault, that will deal with you, if you don't keep a still tongue in your mouth."

He thrust the key at me and I put it in my pocket and forgot all about it. Then I joined up with the McCracken boys and we went to take a last look at the sapling oak, safe behind its palisade. Phil had lost his anger, but he was inclined to be short with me and that meant he was sulking. As usual, when he sulked with me, I got a feeling that the whole world was against me. Father might have given us a lift home. Tim-Pat could easily have dropped us off at the gate to Lissarinka. Any of the farmers might have done the same. Instead, we found ourselves trudging back up the hill, through the fallen elms. Quite suddenly we were tired, but Bessie had supper waiting for us in the kitchen. She listened to our account of the day with a great interest and was delighted that I had taken it into my head to set the young sapling.

"If you hadn't done it the way you did, sure what would the people have to hope for in the days to come? You mark my words, that tree will come shooting up like a Jack-in-the-Beanstalk. There's nobody like yourself for the green finger when it comes to setting a plant or a bush or a tree. Even Tim-Pat can't touch you for it."

We took ourselves off to the old playroom on the next floor. It was a pity that the twins gave such publicity to the fact that Fergus Kennedy had been 'taken with me'. It annoyed Phil, bellowsed his anger against me again . . . made him mean.

The conversation took on a lunatic turn and he harked back to my planting of the tree, and what I had said about planting an acorn. It was a foolish conversation, that went from bad to worse. I should try planting a few acorns sometimes, for all I would get would be a thorn forest and then I could play at being the Sleeping Beauty, but see if he'd tear his armour getting in after me in a hundred years ... me, with my miracles caught in the branches of an oak tree and all my fancy talk.

I might think I was great, because my family had a vault and a banshee, but that sort of thing did not make me better than the next man ...

"Courage," you said. "Why didn't you go into the vault, when the door was open? Your father went in, but not you. You were afraid because there were dead bodies in it. Even old Tim-Pat hadn't the nerve to go in properly, just stood there like a gawk, guarding the door."

The talk went on with the usual virulence of youthful discussions and there were things said, that would have been better left silent.

"I wasn't afraid to go in. Dead bodies never harmed anybody."

"Why did you hang back then and cling to Kennedy's arm?"

"I didn't."

"Oh, yes you did ... "

So it went on and the twins sided with Phil. Only Con said nothing.

Phil was at his most arrogant. His face

was the face of a war lord.

"Go into the vault tonight then. You still have the key."

It went on for a long time and I wished they would take themselves back to Puck's Castle, for we were all losing our tempers and we were old enough to have more sense. It was no good now for me to open the door and go in. Phil dared me . . . dared me . . . dared me. I must steal out of the house by myself at midnight and go down to the churchyard. I had the key. They all knew I had it. If I wanted to prove I wasn't a coward, it was easy enough. I sighed and thought of the hard thing it was to be in the early years of adulthood. It showed that grace and beauty of teenage was a myth. Youth was hot hell and frustration.

Of course, it was a dare and a dare had always been as honourable a challenge as a gauntlet thrown down by a knight. Yet we were children no more, Phil and I.

"You daren't."

"Of course, I dare, if I wanted to traipse all the way down there again. I've had enough for one day."

"You'll not get out of it like that."

"On my word of honour, I'm not trying to get out of it. I'll not go tonight. I'll do it tomorrow night."

"And the door will be fast shut by then and you'll not have the key. Your pa won't miss it tonight. It's tonight or never."

I decided at that moment, that I would never marry Phil, never again think it might be a good plan to unite the lands, that ran side by side. He was the most objectionable man I had ever met and there was an infantile side to him. He was childish for all his years, yet now he held me in a trap. I sighed with weariness, with sorrow too, that love had run like sand through my fingers and turned to nothing.

There was no escape but to pick up the gauntlet.

"Very well then, I'll go down to the vault at midnight. I'll bring the key and I'll open the door and go in . . . right in. I'll touch the far wall, if there is a far wall. What's more, I hope that the devil you're supposed to have as a paying guest at the Castle will roast you all and serve you with apples in your mouths. Bessie's quite right, when she says you're a herd of wild pigs."

They went off at that, restored to laughter and maybe to their senses.

"Don't be silly, Constance-Tenacity. We were only assing about," Con said and Phil backed him up for once.

"Can't you take a joke? It was only a joke. Challenge withdrawn and you may keep your honour . . . and we all love you and we'll love you forever."

They were wild ones. The playroom door shut with a slam, that almost turned it inside out and they went down the stairs like enough to the herd of pigs, which was one of Bessie's similies for them. They did not seem to have improved since their childhood days. There was an excuse for the two younger ones, but Phil was strange. There was something not quite right about Phil . . .

I went to sit in the rocking chair and stared at the panels of the door. My heart was beating fast and thoughts were rocketing round my head.

It had been such a strange day and night, so happy-sad mixed up. I had not found favour with Phil. I had fallen out of love with him and I doubted if I had ever been in love with him. Fergus had attracted me like a lodestone. I wondered if I made some excuse to go into Ballyboy the next day, if I might meet him in the street. I had never thought much about him, just liked him, liked the quiet calm way he had, and his kindness.

Then there was this question of the dare. I was glad they had withdrawn the challenge. It was all a tease. It was so childish for me to get involved with tom-foolery at my time of life. I was so tired, I was almost out on my feet. I began to undress and found the key in my pocket and my first reaction was that it had not shed rust on the safari suit. Now that I had time, I took a good look at it and was surprised that it was so ordinary. There was nothing sinister about a key that opened up a gate to let funerals pass through, yet it was the key to the cemetery gate padlock. It should recall the screech of the gate's hinges and the smell of flowers, too sweet a smell of funeral flowers . . . and the low bier-like cart that would be waiting a little way up the path. The coffin would be laid on the cart and pushed along the gravel path, if the new grave was very far along what they called God's acre. It was a pleasant bit of land, a quiet resting place, but I had never seen it at night. The moon was full and I pictured the shadows, that would be thrown by the tombstones. I imagined the way the statues of white angels might take on a false movement, if one turned away for a moment.

Phil had stipulated midnight and then he had called the whole thing off, but my mind fretted still. I admitted that I was afraid to go down the hill to a place where the dead lay. There was no doubt that Phil would set up some stage ghost to terrify the wits out of me, even if he was now a grown man. There was a cruelty about him, that his brothers did not possess. Yet even without the possibility of an organised haunting, I was afraid of the place. I was a coward. I pushed the thought of my cowardice from my mind, yet it jumped out of its banishment like a Jack-in-the-Box to torment me.

I had a long leisurely bath and went to bed. Presently Bessie would bring my Horlick's upstairs and Father would come with Mimsy to say goodnight. Seo would appear from some secret place, when they were all gone and wait for her share of the Horlick's in the saucer. She would lap at it with her small pink tongue and tuck herself in against my side. Then sleep would come to her and she would make the little snoring sound that turned so easily to a purr, if I stroked her . . .

Phil had taken back the challenge. Thank God he had taken back the challenge! Fergus Kennedy would never have treated me with such harshness, Fergus, with gravity in his eyes and a slant to his brows that made my heart quicken . . . Fergus . . . Fergus . . .

3

A Sprig Of Everlasting Flowers

"THOSE friends of yours are improving with age," Bessie said, as she came into the bedroom with the Horlick's on a tray. "It must be the gentility of the Castle rubbing itself off on them at last. They went and saw your mother and thanked her for the lovely picnic lunch and she not knowing what they were talking about. Then they came into the kitchen and behaved very well-brought up, but I suppose they're young gentlemen now. Mr. Philip said that I'd have to go over there, when you and he are wed, for they haven't a decent cook in the Castle. Still, I think Mr. Con is the pick of the bunch, but then he'd always be off at sea and that's no life for a bride."

I had no intention of marrying Phil. I opened my mouth to break the news to her and then Mimsy came drifting into the room, round the edge of the door, very graceful in her flowing flowery dress. She wandered to the window and looked down on the evening garden and the moon was visible in the sky, from where I sat, propped up in my bed.

"It's lonely out there, Bessie. It's always been lonely at this time, when the day had gone and the night hasn't quite come."

Bessie took her arm and brought her over to kiss me good-night, solid, three-dimensional and real in a way that Mimsy never was.

"Constance-Tenacity is half dead with sleep, Ma'am. She's had a hard day."

"And what was so hard about the day?"

Her lips were butterflies against my cheek and Bessie had frowned a warning at me, that I did not understand in the slightest. Why must Mimsy not be told about the fallen oak and the vault? Good heavens! She would see what had happened on Sunday when we went to church.

"Herself was helping clear trees the whole day and there are dozens and dozens of them. If Tim-Pat had let her, she'd have had a go with the chain saw, but then she had on her lovely Paris suit and it wouldn't have done at all, at all. Mr. Fergus Kennedy was with the McCracken boys and they had a fine time of it . . . the son of the *Leinster Tribune*, you know who I mean, Ma'am. I think he has hearts for her and no wonder, for she's grown up a lovely young lady. Tim-Pat said today that she looked as if she was crowned by a rainbow."

Mimsy was lost at that and I jumped out of bed and put my arms about her, felt terror because she was so frail. She might have been a child in my arms and I wondered if my birth had drained all the strength from her body into mine . . . maybe her strength of mind too.

"You mustn't think of getting married and leaving me," Mimsy said and I assured her that I had no such plan.

"They all left me," she whispered. "The ones that play out there."

She nodded at the window and I knew it had been one of her bad days and that was why Bessie had not come down to the Churchyard to see the fallen oak.

"They sing sometimes. Don't you hear them singing?"

She got up and walked up and down the room and I thought that she was Ophelia and Lady Macbeth indeed and I loved her with my whole heart and there was a great fear upon me that she might die. Yet there were worse things than death . . .

She stopped and looked down at me, her face smiling. "I'll tell you what they sing. They sing nursery rhymes. They're only small of course. 'Boys and girls come out to play, the moon doth shine as bright as day.' Poor little things!"

Bessie was determined to break it up and she did it with practised ease. Her arm was linked in Mother's and she was so very normal and natural that there could be nothing strange going on. Father would be getting impatient with the 'coffee downstairs going cold on him'.

"Look at the poor young lady and her eyelids sticking to her eyes with the weariness and you putting dreams into her head so's she won't sleep. Come on away with Bessie now, like the loving darling you are and there's the dinner to be planning for tomorrow and the bills to be paid. I have the cash books from the shops and you know it's your job to help me with them. I can't do the figures without you . . . "

That was a kind untruth too, for Bessie ran the whole place with my help now, but we drew Mother into a net of protection and involvement and with such tenderness.

"What will ye have for pudding tomorrow, Ma'am? The hens are laying well and you love Queen of Puddings. I could make up the bottom part now and have it all ready and set, but you'd put me right, as you always do and not let me make the meringue top like flannel. It's all in the cool oven, but you keep me right about that and I don't go mad with fright, for there's nothing the Master hates like a Queen of Pudding, and it falling down on him the moment I bring it to the table . . . "

"Thank God you remembered the monthly accounts are due, Ma'am. If it weren't for yourself, the tradespeople would never set eyes on their coin."

"You're not to fret about anything, Ma'am. Sure, haven't you the whole house between your hands and you run it like the Queen runs Buckingham Palace? I don't know what I'd do, if I hadn't you at my elbow, when a thing goes back on me. But it's not too bad with Constance-Tenacity to help and all the French cooking. You don't know the comfort it is to have somebody to run to, for Tim-Pat may be a good man in the yard, but he's not worth a ha'porth, if you wanted him to turn his hand to rice pudding . . . "

It was all the other way about in an Alice-through-the-Looking Glass sequence, but Mimsy never understood the kind subterfuge, that was perpetrated on her and in a way we all entered into it, never laughed at her fancies, nor pointed out her illogicalities — only loved her more. Now she went off to pretend to help Bessie with the grocer's book and the butcher's bill and the ordering of menu for the next day. Indeed my eyes were heavy with sleep and the darkness had come down. The light from the staircase through the open crack of the door was growing brighter, as the night darkened outside the window and I was half way between sleeping and waking and surprised that Fergus had come to my dream island to walk with me and to talk with me and perhaps to play out fantasy with me. Always, it had been a faceless person, but tonight, it was no knight in white armour, no Hamlet, no hero of stage or screen. It was the son of the *Leinster Tribune* and we were acting out an iced spun-sugar romance, Phil McCracken was a piece that never fitted into the jigsaw of a day-dream. Tonight the story in the dream had a beauty that was not to be found in real life and I walked in a world of marble halls and maybe pink champagne and I drifted into sleep maybe. I built something as beautiful and as delicate as a spider's web in the frost of a sunny winter's day, a web that spanned the long darkness of the yew walk tunnel, yet glittered with the diamonds of the dawn light. It was quite dark outside, when they woke me up, or I thought they woke me up. It was as strange a sound as the harp of a spider's web might have made and it was allied to it and fitted into the dream quality. The voices must surely have come from another world. They were high and light and full of youth and laughter and happiness, with fun running over at the brim, yet eerie too, as if fairies had come out of Lissarinka and were descanting against the growling sound of the wind in the chimney.

"Boys and girls come out to play.
The moon doth shine as bright as day.
Leave your supper and leave your sleep
And join your playfellows in the street . . . "

Over and over it went, like a disc caught in a groove. I woke up or thought I woke up. I shall never know, if I got out of bed and went to the window. It was late, for the darkness was silvered by the moon and the moon was far up the sky and full and the clock in the hall struck eleven. I could see the front drive clearly and the trees were swaying as if they wept for their fallen comrades, yet they could not put the light into mourning. There was nobody out there, no sound whatever, only a great silence and a feeling, strong in my breast that there had been people there just now, maybe children who had joined hands and danced in a ring under my window. There had been a play I had seen once, where children had come to fetch another child away and they had been dressed in old-fashioned clothes. Bessie had said I had no right to look at it, but it had been on some Television programme and I had seen it, getting past her censorship for once. The children had sung and the little girl had got out of bed and looked through her window and the children had danced away down the road, far and farther away and they had lured her to follow and now it might be myself caught up in the action of the play. I could remember it very well and they had worn Dickens-clothing and maybe the boys had on Mad-Hatter's top hats and the girls Kate Greenaway Dresses, or maybe I was dreaming and it was time to get back to my bed, yet arrived there and safe, I could hear it in the distance, getting fainter and fainter.

> "Boys and girls come out to play,
> The moon doth shine as bright as day
> Leave your supper and leave your sleep
> And join your playfellows in the street . . . "

Then there was nothing but blackness and a sleep as deep as death, yet in the morning, when the sun woke me by shining in my eyes through the window, I felt tired and for a little while, I remembered strange nightmares, that had pursued me. Of course, it was a heritage from the day before and the graves and the vault and St. Brendan's Oak and the fact that I had been over-tired. The wisps of a handful of dreams trailed through by mind, the sight of the door — the Gothic door — to the vault and the shrill scratching sound it made against the ground and how hard it had been to open the padlock that held a chain. It was all dream how the chain had resisted giving up its grip on the padlock. Then there was a long room and shelves and coffins and one small coffin, tucked away at the back. I had come upon it and been terrified and had woken up with sweat on my brow and running down between my young-girl breasts . . . then darkness again . . .

In the last moments before I was wide awake, I remembered the singing of the children, that I had thought I heard below my window the night before and I clung to the last fragments of the dream . . . padlock, chain, coffins ranked along the shelves and a small white coffin. Wearily I swung my legs out of bed to go along for a cool bath. There was no reason that I should be weary — no reason for the dark shadows that had come under my eyes. The surprise of finding muddy green shoes under the bed edge startled me back to my full senses. Beside them, kicked out of sight obviously, was an old pair of denims, a black sweater, a dark anorak. I noticed in the bath that my hands were grubby, yet well I knew they had been clean, when I had sat up in bed drinking Horlick's.

It worried me for there was no possible explanation why I should have thrown down the clothes so carelessly. I threw them carelessly into the bottom of the wardrobe now, for I did not want to face Bessie's questions. I put on the safari suit again and went down the stairs to find Father at breakfast. As I kissed his cheek, he smiled up at me and said I had done too much to it yesterday and then Bessie came in with my scrambled eggs and asked if I was feeling all right.

"You'll have to rest today, Honey. It doesn't suit you to be trying to build a two thousand year oak tree in one day."

Out in the yard, I found the car I had had as a present for my birthday, left out in the stable yard and the tyres muddy, with the mud not dry. There was a dent in the bumper, that had not been there before. There was grass caught up behind the bumper, between it and the mudguard, as if somebody had backed into a tall grass verge. Then Tim-Pat came into the yard with one of the men from the farm and I sidled round the car and hid from them, yet did not know why.

"They say 'tis haunted," the man was saying. "Of course, 'tis haunted and you can say old Shamus was three sheets in the wind. He always has drink taken at that time of night. God knows what hours Mrs. Keogh closes and he'd be the last man out of the pub."

"So he saw somebody coming out of the tomb?" said Tim-Pat in a sarcastic voice. "And all in black she was."

He took out his pipe and clamped it between his jaws with his nose almost touching his chin.

"It wasn't long gone twelve," the man went on. "A slight woman came out of the door, stopped to shut it after her and make the door fast. There was a sound that a child might make, a sort of a sob. Then she was gone and after a while, the noise of a car starting up and away."

I crept into the harness room and climbed to the hay loft and hid, did not even come out when the McCrackens came from Puck's Castle, looking for me. When they had taken themselves off, I put my head in my hands and remembered with a great clarity, the muddied shoes and the dark clothes I had found in my bedroom. I remembered the car wheels and the grass in the bumper. I thought of Mimsy and the way she walked in her sleep. I remembered that I was her daughter and the seeds of madness ... Oh God! Bring it out into the open and admit. Maybe Mimsy was a little mad. Maybe I had madness inherited within myself. Perhaps I had got up in my sleep. If I had heard the children singing in my demented brain, then it was not impossible that I was capable of getting out of bed and putting on camouflage clothes and silent shoes, of taking the car and driving down to the vault in the cemetery. The dream was no dream but reality, the shelves with the coffins, the Gothic door. I crept down from the loft and went to my bedroom stealthily like any thief, took out the clothes and looked at them again. Something fell from the pocket of the anorak to the carpet at my feet and I picked it up — a sprig of what they call everlasting flowers. It was not three inches long, but it had no place in my pocket. Surely I had not found it in the vault and brought it home with me?

The blood drained from my cheeks and my heart bumped against my ribs and then I heard somebody coming and ran across the room and into the bathroom, where Bessie found me.

"Ah, there you are, Honey! We all thought you were lost. I'm killed with the work I have to do below stairs and I don't want your mother near the church for a bit. Would you ever take the flowers down there and do the altar for Sunday? You do it better than any of us, the way the flowers sit so lovely for you."

She had the roses all ready for me in the hall.

"Take a tin of Brasso and a rag. Give the vases a shine, while you're at it. I'll make a special chocolate cake for your tea with walnuts on top of it, as a reward for your holiness."

I had taken my car and driven to the church. The roses lay along the seat at my side and I had thrust the Brasso and the duster into one of the side pockets of the dash. Suddenly I wanted to get to the church, as if I had been lost in a desert and had come to cool clear water. It would be dim there and quiet.

113

Bessie could never understand how the thoughts in my mind were whirling, as stars in the sky might whirl in the head of a drunken man.

I remember nothing of the short drive, remember nothing of parking the car and taking the roses in my arm. I only recall that I knelt in the front pew, where we always sat, my face in my hands. I knelt not on the hassock but on the bare flags, with some idea that prayers might be more readily answered if I did that. The cold chill of the stone was a penance to my knees, as I prayed that Mimsy was not mad. Then came the quick guilt of voicing such thoughts to God, but He knew them anyhow.

"She's not mad, only a little strange. It's for myself I pray and you know that. Please don't let me lose my mind . . ."

My whisper echoed from the ceiling and came back into my ears.

"Lose my mind . . . lose my mind . . . lose my mind."

It was best to get to my feet and fetch the flower vases, go to stand before the altar after a long time, when I had done all the small tasks. I had polished the brass of the vases for so long that it winked sunshine at me. Then the scent of the roses came stealing down like a blessing. I put my hand into my pocket to find my handkerchief to rub the grey of the Brasso off and my fingers found something.

Before I lifted it out and identified it, I knew what it was already — the key, that opened the padlock, that held the chain, that closed the door to the vault, that held the coffins ... It was like the House that Jack Built. I said it again in my mind. This is the key that opens the padlock, that holds the chain, that closes the door, that shuts the vault, that holds the coffins. Into my brain came the whisper from last night and in some strange way, it matched up with the nursery rhyme of today.

> "Boys and girl come out to play
> The moon doth shine as bright as day
> Leave your supper and leave your sleep
> And join your playfellows in the street ... "

This is the key that opens the lock ... that holds the chain, that closes the door, that shuts the vault ...

An icicle was drawn down from the top of my spine, down along the vertebral column, that kept my body erect. In a small flash, I pictured all the skeletons, that must lie within a stone's throw, each of them bones, a bunch of hair, a rag, a few teeth, maybe a ring or two, a faded ribbon, God knows what! I had only to open the door and go in. More and more, I was beginning to feel certainty that in the night, I had been stepping the paces I now trod. No, I would not have gone into the church, just driven my car straight to the graveyard, wanting to get it all over and done with, and muddied the tyres. I would have put on the dark pants and anorak, a camouflage against the night, and I would have parked the car near the bank by the vault. I had forgotten to give Father this key last night. Again, I had forgotten this morning and I was sorry for it now. If I had not found the key in my pocket, there would have been no challenge issued to me by myself, that I was a coward. The McCracken family mattered not at all. I put the challenge to myself, threw the gauntlet down at my own feet and picked it up. The key was nothing spectacular nor yet dramatic. I felt that it should be like the key to an old-fashioned dungeon with great words upon it, but it was a small tin key and had probably been bought in Woolworth's. It was curved and tinny, worth only a few pence, not the sort of thing for one to risk one's reason for. I wondered if I might be doing just that, for I was very frightened. I could not understand why, except that the dreams of the night had come back in force to haunt me. My legs were stiff as I walked along the centre aisle of the small church and the echoes of my steps seemed to say "Don't go. Don't go. Don't go. Nobody knows. Nobody knows." Even the door of the church groaned as I turned the iron ring handle and warned me that I might be setting out on a path, that I might regret. I looked down at it severely and told it aloud that one of these days, I would bring down an oil can and put paid to its noise.

"Disturbs the church services ... "

I said. "It's time somebody took the trouble to oil you."

My sentiments did nothing to dispel the eerie feeling. I walked the path from the church gate, on down the small incline to the stream at the foot, where the giant oak had stood all the years till yesterday. It was remarkably quiet and empty in the hollow and there was a feeling as if somebody had been there and had just gone. It was neat enough, only for a straggling of twigs and leaves and the churning marks, where a tractor had cut up the grass. Presently, the carpenter would come to fix the door of the vault. What did it matter if he had no key? He had only to take a screw driver or a chisel and lift the staple out like a loose tooth. In one hour or perhaps two, the door would be as firm on its hinges as it had ever been. I had only to wait and he would come along. I would produce the key as an excuse for my presence. We might go in together, and there was a coward's thought!

I climbed the gravel path that led towards the tomb, yet I did not seem to exist in any sense of reality, only in a nightmare again. Here it was, after too short a time and the scrape marks of a grass bank, where somebody might have driven a white car against the turf in the dark of the night, yet the moon had been shining and how could I know that? The railings were broken. There was no barrier to prevent me from walking down the flight of steps, one by one, slowly and more slowly. At last my hand stretched to touch the Gothic door, to move a finger from one stud to the next and know that all my excuses had run out.

There was no proof that I had walked in the night and that I had driven my car against the bank that was now high above the level of my head. The key was in the lock and the lock was shaking and not my hands and that was a lie, if ever there was one. I was in the dream world, though the sun was shining and a blackbird had perched somewhere nearby and was filling the emptiness with his song. If the key would not open the lock, there was nothing I could do, but there was an increasing suspicion in my head that I had opened it maybe at twelve midnight and not known such unease as

I felt now. Then the key spun and the padlock was in my hand and the chain slipped and fell at my feet. I had only to push the door and it opened and stuck and opened again and surely I remembered the scruntching scratch of the bottom edge of it against the floor? I must open it to the full for there would be no light. With wisdom, I might have gone back to the church and brought the box of matches from the vestry, but I had no wisdom, nothing about me that was real, yet in front of my eyes on a small ledge just inside the studded door lay a sophisticated red leather torch, initialled in gold, with my initials. It was proof enough that I had been here before in the night, that I had parked my car too close to the grass bank, that I had not dreamed the nightmares in the darkness. I had lived them. I had walked in my sleep, as Mimsy walked in her sleep.

There was a whisper about the vault, a smell that met me at the door, of damp and decay and mouldering and dead flowers and surely of the rheumatism that inhabited the limbs of aged men and women, of rotting cloth and yet a dry as dust smell too. I picked up the torch and switched on its confident beam and looked down a narrow corridor of a cell that seemed to have no end, but to run along till it met in nothing at last. There were shelves at each side and I tried not to be frightened that they held coffins, fine coffins too with splendid brass fittings, though the years had not done much for the brass. There was a plaque on the shelf below where each coffin stood and a name on it. I went slowly along the passage between the two sides of the room and saw that the shelves were broad. There were other coffins farther back, but I had had enough of the place. Surely my courage had been proved, if only to myself? I decided to see how far back the place ran and I walked on a step or two, and the light picked up the end very soon, with a shelf that ran across. There was something white on the shelf on the right, that held the white light of the torch like a magnet, and drew me like a lodestone.

It can only have been a step or two more, when I was beside it and the spot light in my hand showed it in every detail. It was a small white coffin, beautifully fashioned, created by loving hands, laid there with reverence and surely a great sorrow? There was an aura of sadness, like a physical thing, that wrapped it around about and I felt tears thickening in my throat. There was a child here, a small child. It could never have walked, talked, laughed. On top lay a bunch of flowers in pastel colours, pink and mauve and light yellow and blue and lavender. Somebody had disturbed it and there a sprig from them on the floor at my feet. I picked it up and recognised it as the same as the flowers, the artificial flowers, that had fallen from my anorak pocket not so long ago. It was a posy in memory, of course, deemed suitable for a dead love, a posy to last along the years that would never be. I picked it up. There was a metal plate screwed into the white lid. It was not brass, but some black enamel metal with words etched out on it and they were dusty from the flowers. I had to wipe the plate clean and stand on tip toe, lean over and point the torch down from the level of the top of my head.

CONSTANCE-TENACITY FITZGERALD, THE ONLY SURVIVING INFANT OF RICHARD AND MOLL, DEARLY BELOVED AND LOST TO ALL BUT GOD.

It did not register. It meant nothing to me. Then one by one, the knowledge sentences came flowing into my brain. It was my name. These were my parents' names. The coffin was not old, not years and years old.

Then I went on with my scrutiny of the plaque and my heart stopped for three seconds and went on again with a great throb that seemed to burst my chest apart.

The infant's birthdate was there and it was my own birth date. I looked at it for a long time, but there was no doubt. The child's birthday and mine were the same, day, month, year. The date of death was there too, not three months after. I stood on tip-toe to read it the clearer, wondered if I had walked in my sleep again into a dream from hell. I wanted to get away. I had never wanted to get away from anywhere, as I wanted to get away from that vault, but I pushed the sprig of the posy into my pocket, walked backwards out along the path to the door. I should not have been surprised if it had slammed shut, if I had been locked in there for all eternity, but it opened at my touch, sticking a little as it had done before, grating against the ground.

The air outside was sweeter than any air, I had ever breathed. I filled my lungs with great gulps of it. Presently I remembered that I must shut the door and replace the padlock. There was a C-shaped handle and the staple, that Tim-Pat had driven in. I had to find the chain and thread it through handle and staple, exactly as it had been. Then I was free to go. I crept up the steps and there was nobody about. The blackbird was still filling the sky with his full-throated song. The brook murmured from the bottom of the rise. I took to my heels and ran, ran down the small hill and past the parked car, on up the incline and through the church door. I had a right to be in the church, if anybody came. Had I not been arranging the flowers for the altar for Sunday in another age, centuries ago, or in some eon, yet to come, on another planet far out in space, maybe not even created now? I wondered if this was how a person felt before they went mad. I was swinging like a roundabout chair plane half way between sky and earth, with no reality whatever in any part of me. Yet the church door creaked in the old way, when I turned the iron handle, groaned on its hinges, as if it complained of the damp in its bones and I remembered that I had threatened, promised, to oil it.

"I don't disturb the services," it said now or I thought I heard it say. "I've made the same noise for a long time and nobody has ever been rude enough to make a remark like that about me . . . "

I crept along this aisle in the Alice-Looking-Glass-World, and my legs were a diver's legs clad in lead weighted boots. I might have turned into some clumsy mechanical man with the effort it took to lift first one foot and then the other, but at last I reached the pew. I knelt down on the flag stones and put my head on my arm on the front ledge. Automatically I said the Lord's Prayer, but I thought no more about the meaning of the words of it than I ever did. I went back over it again and tried to pray.

"Our Father, which art in heaven ... hallowed be Thy name ... " and thought Constance-Tenacity ... Constance-Tenacity, but she was in a white coffin and she was dead. It was no good trying to pray. I had lost all connection with God in His heaven. I sat back on the seat of the pew and lifted my prayer book and still I was a marionette, with no power to direct my actions. My hands were shaking and it took me a long time, before I got the front cover to open and there was the familiarity of the fly leaf and my child's writing on it from thirteen years before ...

> Constance-Tenacity Fitzgerald, aged 5 years,
> Lissarinka,
> Ireland, Europe, The World, Space.

The faded wavering letters were undulating like the waves of the sea and there was a sickness in my stomach.

> "If this book should chance to roam
> Box its ears and send it home."

Then down near the bottom of the page was more adult writing and though the writing was older, the ink was younger.

> THIS BOOK WAS STOLEN FROM CONSTANCE-TENACITY FITZGERALD INFORM THE CIVIC GUARDS AT ONCE.

It had been a way to pass the time during a dull sermon and there was still an echo of laughter in it. It was childishness like "Boys and girls, come out to play."

The sun shone through a stained glass window, sending a shaft of silver through a saint's breast-plate, that struck my chest like a spear and with it came a thought that stopped the breath in my mouth. Constance-Tenacity, the child in the coffin could never have come out to play. She had died before the time for playing. Yet did she come out to play in the moonlight? Here was a waking nightmare, if ever I knew one. Had she come out to play last night with others like her? Had she come like the children I had seen in the play? Was it beyond the bounds of possibility that she had stood in the drive of Lissarinka House under the window last night and willed me to come to her, not a small baby any more, but a grown-up girl in a Kate Greenaway dress with boys in Lewis-Carroll-top-hats. Had she joined hands with them and played Ring a' ring o' Roses, and Oranges and Lemons, and finally danced away down the avenue, looking back over her shoulder to see if I had heard her . . . if I might follow.

If I could imagine the door spoke to me just now, then I must be going insane. My hand felt in my pocket and touched the bristling artificiality of the sprig I had picked from the floor of the vault. I had not imagined that there was a small white coffin there. I admitted freely that the speaking church door was imagination, but not the coffin, not the name plate, not the date of Constance-Tenacity's birth and her death.

Now I was afraid to get up and leave the church, for the door might speak to me again, when I knew it had no power of speech . . . and Mother of God, if Constance-Tenacity Fitzgerald was dead and entombed in her white coffin, what was I? Somewhere floating in the back of my brain, somebody said I had come from 'Nowhere'. Had it been Mimsy? I could not remember ... could not reason or remember or get rid of the paralysis, that bound me, body and brain. I had written the words I had just read in the prayer book ... 'If this book should chance to roam ... ' It was my baby writing first and then my better writing and my more adult humour. 'This book has been stolen'. Well I remembered doing it. I even remembered the text of the sermon, that had been so boring. 'Consider the lilies of the field, they toil not neither do they spin. Yet Solomon in all his glory was not arrayed like one of these ... ' something like that. Yet I was dead and buried. I had just seen my coffin and my mother was mentally unbalanced ... I must be completely insane. There was no other explanation. It was no dream. I pinched my arm to see if I could wake up and find myself back in bed, but still I sat in the pew, waiting for the courage to face the way to go back to Lissarinka House, afraid to put my hand on the lock of the church door, in case it might speak to me again.

"I don't disturb the services," it had said, but it could never have spoken, except in a crazy brain. Then it groaned again and I had not moved from my seat, only sat there like a half dead woman, frightened out of any wits I might possess. The door lock groaned and it did not speak this time, just complained in its familiar way and that must mean that somebody had come or was coming into the church. There were steps on the aisle and they were a man's steps, approaching me, pausing at my side and a man's voice, with nothing supernatural about it, full of life and laughter.

"White roses for Sunday from the hand of Constance-Tenacity and as perfect as always. Are you sure your name isn't Constance Spry, or is she not jet-set enough for you, these days?"

I sat as still as any marble statue, totally unable to think of any remark to make. It was Fergus Kennedy and probably he was the last person I wished to see me, as I was. It was strange how he spoke about names, when my whole brain was involved in the importance of being Constance-Tenacity. It was like 'the Importance of being Earnest', I thought, with no sense in the world.

"White rose of Lancaster or is it York?" he went on. "I never can remember, but think of the importance it had at the time, and now, it doesn't matter. Then men died for it. It makes you wonder."

I turned my head to look at him.

"Lancaster-red, York-white." I said in the voice of a stranger, in the voice of a dying creature, in the voice of a ghost and maybe I was a ghost at that.

He was startled by the look of me. He grabbed me by the shoulder and asked if I were ill. He shook me gently and presently he took me into his arms. I have no idea what he thought was wrong with me, but he was filled with concern. There were tears that had started to trickle slowly one after the other down my face.

"Has Phil been mean to you? Is that it? Take no notice of him. It's just his way. He adores the ground you walk on. It's just a lover's quarrel and soon patched up."

"Who am I?" I asked him and my voice was a whisper, as mad as myself, that crept up among the rafters of the old church and echoed back to the creaking lock of the door and forwards to the white roses of York.

He was startled more than ever at that, but I pursued him with the tenacity I was alleged to possess.

"Who am I?"

Mutely I held out the prayer book with its child's inscriptions.

"I wrote that, didn't I? You must know the silly things you do in church to pass dull sermons and that day it was about the lilies of the field. I remember writing it. Just tell me who I am. Please, Fergus."

He humoured me, for he thought I was ill and perhaps I was. He pretended to make fun of me, but he was worried and maybe he remembered Mimsy.

"You're Constance-Tenacity Fitzgerald, of Lissarinka House . . . "

Then he thought to cheer me up a bit and added some light flattery.

"You're the most lovely lady in the whole of the country and if you weren't more or less fixed up to marry Phil McCracken, I might let myself fall in love with you."

Again came the laugh from the sane land.

"Are you set on marrying Phil, for it's a fact that he's not fit to clean your shoes? Maybe I could get you to change your mind?"

I was still in the crook of his arm and I could feel his heart beating against my shoulder and I clung to him and felt great comfort in the clinging. I was glad now that it was he who had come and not Bessie nor Tim-Pat. He was so down to earth and solid and not given to dreams, nor fairy lore nor ghosts nor yet demons, and yet I was demon-ridden.

"Constance-Tenacity Fitzgerald is dead, Fergus," I whispered against the side of his face. "I think I'm a ghost."

He held me back and looked into my eyes for a bit. Then he cradled my body against his and held me tightly and asked me why I thought such an extraordinary thing.

"In God's name, tell me what's happened?"

I muttered it against his ear, the whole story and very disjointed it was. I do not know how he made out much of it, but his only emotion was sympathy for me and a great understanding and he listened to me in silence as I went on with it, sentence after sentence . . . all about the children, who sang under the windows of Lissarinka and about Mimsy and my fears of going mad, about my sleepwalking and the artificial flowers, which lasted down the years that were never to be . . . about the white coffin, and the child, that had been born and had died . . . had been born on my birthday, "the only surviving child of Richard and Moll."

It went on for a long time in fits and starts and he had great patience with me and never interrupted me, except once, when I told him the lock on the church door spoke to me.

"That damn' lock is never done speaking to somebody. I'll oil it myself one of these days. The sexton is bone lazy."

It was such a normal thing to say, it recalled me to reality. In a way it recalled me to life, for I had given myself over to the land of the insane. I went on and on and he heard all the whole story of Constance-Tenacity. Then he held me in his arms for a long time, as if he loved me and was loth to let me go, but let me go he did, though he still held my shoulders between his hands.

"My father and your father are great friends . . . probably the best friends that ever were . . . very close indeed," he said and nothing more after that.

Then after a long time, he went on.

"You're well cognisant of my father, 'the Tribune' . . . " Here again the laugh of sanity, that frightened off the vultures, that sat all about me, waiting to feed on my brain.

"Your father entrusted a great part of your education to 'the Tribune' . . . French and Latin and Greek, you had from my father, on Tuesdays and Fridays after school hours and much talk of my father's philosophy. It was to supplement your education . . . early education at the Ballyboy School . . . and it did you both a great deal of good. Your father always said your horizon was stretched beyond the Wicklow Hills and it all due to 'the Tribune', even before you were accepted into that fine finishing school of yours. All the same, they put a fine polish on an uncut diamond. I hardly recognised you the other day."

There was another pause here, as he took out a handkerchief and caught a late tear that was trickling down my cheek.

"My father and your father had very few secrets between them and I was a horrible little boy, though it's a long time ago. I'm years older than you are, but I had long ears and I listened, when maybe I wasn't supposed to be listening. Then 'the Tribune' took me into his confidence, when I grew up. I know more about you, than you do yourself ... in some ways, but nothing like the whole of it."

I was looking up into his face with alarm and he kissed me on the corner of the mouth and put his arm about me again, told me that it was better to have an arm about you when news broken, that might cause shock and surprise and perhaps sorrow.

"It's not that it will make any

difference. You're not some mad creature out of Jane Eyre. You're a beautiful girl and what went on before you were born is none of your doing . . . or afterwards. It's all so simple. It's strange you never guessed it for your mother sometimes comes out with strange things. You're an adopted child. That's all it is, legally adopted and heiress to everything any daughter of Lissarinka might expect . . . a thousand times more attractive than she could ever have been, I have no doubt, full of grace and charm and beauty, with the whole parish at your feet and the heir to Puck's Castle to be your husband, unless you have the sense to show him the door."

I had told him about the finding of the coffin. I had told him of the name on it. I had told him everything and this was the answer, but there was more to it.

"There's one person who could give us the full story and that's Bessie. Presently, we'll find her and we'll let her know what's happened. She'll tell you the full story of what went on. Maybe she'll let me sit in on it and hear the bits I did not overhear, as a long-eared boy . . . and later, when I thought one day, I might be falling in love with you my father told me . . . but that's no matter now."

It was a strange thing the way his last words affected me like a current of electricity. Here was I, more or less engaged to marry Phil McCracken, although we both seemed not to be all that interested in the fact. Phil and I were brother and sister and he bullied me as he might bully his sister, if he possessed one. His kisses gave me no pleasure, nor the fact that he partnered me at tennis matches and at any dances we might attend. Our lands ran together and it was the economical thing that we should marry and unite the two families, but I was no Fitzgerald. I wondered if the McCrackens knew this . . . this fact of my adoption. I was astonished that I did not care, if Phil took it into his head to jilt me, because my blood might not be up to his in nobility, even if my potential possessions were.

Then, unforgivably, Fergus took me more closely into his arms and he kissed me as he had no right to do. He kissed me for a long minute and I walked in the fields of heaven and thought myself a wicked woman, to move from one affection to another with such carelessness. In his arms, I even stopped caring much if I were only an adopted child. I forgot the child ghosts, who might have come from their graves at midnight to dance under my window. I forgot everything except that I was Fergus and Fergus was I, whoever I might be.

Then we went slowly down the aisle and out through the church door.

"Leave your car here and come in mine. I'll walk down and collect yours later."

Phil would never have had such consideration, but still I was being very untrue to him.

Fergus helped me into the passenger seat and then clicked his tongue and went off to the boot of his car. I could hear him rummaging about in it and then he went to have a look in my white Aston Martin. He found it after a while, an oil can, and he went back to the church door and oiled the hinge, grinned at me and told me he had put paid to the voice of the church door and now he would try to put paid to any other worry I might have.

"Your father is in Ballyboy today and Tim-Pat's with him. They won't be home for hours yet. We'll go up to Lissarinka and find Bessie. She'll tell us what she knows. She's always held that it shouldn't have been kept quiet. It would have been no shock to you years ago, as it must be now, but it doesn't matter and it doesn't change a single thing. You're still the same person you were and are and will be and nothing is changed, nothing . . ."

He leaned over and kissed me again.

"Now do you think you're a ghost?" he said.

4

The Switch

ON the swift drive to Lissarinka, the scenes from yesterday, flashed across my mind like pictures thrown on a projector. There had been a secrecy between my father and Tim-Pat, a guarding of the door to the vault. There had been the moment when Tim-Pat came up the steps and I asked him if there were a skeleton in the family tomb, for the way he made the door fast. There he stood now, on the slide of my memory, his face full of fury.

"Don't ever say that, Miss, not to your father nor yet to your mother. Their people are lying down there in their last rest."

'Their' people he had said, not 'mine', and "If I catch you talking to your mother about any part of this day . . . "

I had rarely seen him so put out. There seemed to be a determination that

Mimsy must know nothing about what had happened. The whole household had thrown itself about her in a barrier of protection against some awful fact. Was it the white coffin and the child that lay inside it? Had Mimsy's brain closed against it and against other children, dead too? I had forgotten all about 'only surviving child', but I remembered it now. Bessie might tell me soon. She called me Constance-Tenacity. They all did. They celebrated my birthday on the coffin-plate birth date, but I must have been living out a lie . . . and here was Lissarinka and Fergus helping me out of the car and into the house the side way, where we were unlikely to meet anybody. We went into the old library at the back, settled me into a chair and put my feet up on a stool. Then he went off but returned in no time with a tumbler, half full of sherry and a tartan rug. He put the glass in my hand and tucked the rug round me, told me to drink the sherry up at once.

"I've got to find Bessie. Then we'll have to get Mimsy settled somewhere. Just get that sherry down you. You've had a shock. Then close your eyes and don't worry if I'm not back for a little while ... quick as I can."

I drank the sherry and soon, I was floating in a half dream. For some reason the thought of the children that sang under the window came to my mind, almost took possession of it, the children that I imagined might have climbed the hill and joined their cold hands to dance in a circle.

> "Boys and girls come out to play
> The moon doth shine as bright as day
> Leave your supper and leave your sleep
> And join your playfellows in the street."

Had Constance-Tenacity had brothers and sisters ... all dead now? Had I really heard children sing and were they child-ghosts from the vault? I thought of the blood stain on the hall of Puck's Castle and knew that it must be a supernatural thing. Phil's mother could never do anything so ridiculous as getting chickens' blood and keeping the stain fresh on the flags. She was just a superstitious lady, who liked ghost stories and family traditions. I was a favourite of hers and she approved the idea that I would be her daughter-in-law, but she could not know I was an adopted child. Did Bessie know who I actually was? They were a long time coming back, Bessie and Fergus. Perhaps she would not let Fergus tell me what she must tell me. I took the sprig of artificial flowers out of my pocket and looked at it for five minutes, put it away again and the sherry closed my eyes in sleep. Bessie was on her knees by my side when I woke up and her face was white and unhappy. Fergus was standing over by the mantlepiece watching us in the mirror.

"You never went down to the tomb last night?" Bessie said to me. "It was a bad dream you had."

I took out the sprig of flowers again and gave it to her and her eyes were filled with tears suddenly, for it must have brought back memories of an old grief.

"Fergus told you," I said. "I went

again today and I found the torch I'd left there last night. Fergus won't have told you anything that's not true. I know she was born the same day as me. I know she's dead. I'd have come to you for help, Bessie, but Fergus found me in the church."

She gathered me into her arms, as she used to do, when my child self cut a knee and ran to her to get it kissed better, but my wound was deeper today.

"He said you knew what went on, that you'd tell me who I am."

My face was against her breast and her voice rumbled out to me.

"You're Constance-Tenacity and you always will be . . . legal and proper. I always said they should ha' told you from the start but they wouldn't have it and now it's a nice state of affairs. The day you were old enough to understand, that was the right day, but we'll have to make the best of a bad job."

She set me back against the chair and walked the floor for a while, muttering that Mimsy had been put to lie down for a bit, so we had the place to herself and myself and to Fergus.

"And he deserves to hear what I know. It's his right, for God only knows what you'd have done, if he hadn't found you today and you thinking the church door was talking to you ... "

Fergus was a great believer in strong drink. He went to a cabinet and produced more sherry for me. He poured out a stiff Glen Livet whisky for Bessie and one for himself, did not even offer to insult it with water. Bessie took hers with one gulp and it caught her breath, as if she drunk fire.

"I don't know how there are folks that like the taste of that," she said and it was a sensible house all at once and there was laughter and Fergus was there and nothing could be too bad. It was as if somebody had banished the demons and goblins and turned on the day, turned on the pursuit of happiness.

Bessie put down the glass on a small table and sat herself in a chair, which she pulled up to mine so that we were face to face.

"It all happened a long time ago," she began and I remembered all the old bedroom stories.

Fergus had come to sit on the arm of my chair and I was glad of his hand on my shoulder. It did not seem to matter to him, if I were only an adopted daughter.

"Your father and mother were married a long time ago and there couldn't have been two happier people in God's world," Bessie said. "They had everything life had to offer them . . ."

"But Mimsy?" I whispered and she hushed me, told me that Mimsy was not the same in those days and then said no more about it, except muttered that perhaps a wicked fairy god-mother came to the wedding, or "that is what old lady McCracken would say, if she hadn't more sense."

"I wasn't house-keeper then," she went on after a pause. "There was a Scots woman, called Morag Cameron. I came because Morag had to go home to Scotland. Her mother was ailing and she had to look after her. When the mother died, she stayed on over there and she and I never lost touch with each other, as you know from all my prating about her and the letters we get — and write."

Father and Mother loved children. Father had wanted sons to come after him on the land.

"When we heard that your mother was expecting a child, we went off our heads with joy. There was such a welcome waiting for that first son, that you wouldn't believe it. The Mistress wasn't like she is today. You understand that, Honey. Och! The clothes we had and the toys, as if a new-born infant wants toys. Herself and I were like two wee girls waiting for a birthday dolly, with the sewing and the knitting — and the Master with a Sheltie pony ready and nothing good enough but a toy train set for a son."

Her face had lit with remembered joy but now the shadows chased each other across it as she remembered that it had not ended happy ever after.

"Twenty-three years ago it happened almost to this day. One night, she wasn't well. She hadn't eaten her supper and she thought she had got a cold in her tummy. I put her to bed, but she had pain, that ran from her back to her stomach and down her legs. There was . . . oh! Honey,

I don't have to break your heart, like mine was broken. She had a son . . . a pretty little man, but they said he wasn't 'viable'. They meant he had to die but he was dead, before he was born . . . no time even to put the sign of the cross on him, no time to fetch the doctor, only myself to look down at him and think how like he was to a perfect weeshy doll, but no breath in him and no cry. She hadn't felt him move for a day or two, but she'd told nobody, hadn't known she should have been terrified."

My attention was riveted on every word she said and well I understood it. There was not much that girls of eighteen did not understand, things that their elders and betters never dreamt they knew and the McCrackens and I were modern generation.

"The doctor said it was just bad luck. There was plenty of time to come and they could fill Lissarinka with sons, for they were young and healthy. 'Perfect baby making machine,' he said, but he was a man of science. She put it all behind her, or we thought she did, but what mother can forget a dead boy?"

Most of the time now, Bessie forgot her present audience. She had been so much part of the family that she had suffered with them and now she re-lived every dashed hope. Sometimes, she paused for a long time, while she got her voice steadied.

"The next year, she was expecting again and this time with the doctor watching every move she made, no riding horses and she didn't like that. She was the life and soul of the whole parish and she entertained and ran the house and there was nothing blind to her. Gaiety and wit, she *was* gaiety and wit, and a husband adoring at her feet and half the men in the parish too. You'd not recognise her . . . "

She pulled herself up short and demanded of herself why she should make a short story into a long agony.

"Long agony it was, with every year a century and every hour a year . . . "

She looked at me and remembered me and kept back some of the pain and the waiting and the yearning.

"She was expecting again and there was more joy than the first time. We were all half crazy and the clothes all brought out for the baby, the cot and the pram and the sheltie, as if a baby be wanting a pony straight off!"

She turned a glance at me over the top of her glasses and remembered that I was a farm-bred lassie, thought to toughen up the history.

"You're born and bred with farmyard animals. You know there are cows that can't hold their calves? You'll know that too, Mr. Fergus?"

He nodded his head and thought to save her the pain of memory.

"How many times, Bessie?"

"Four times . . . all sons, all perfect and every trick in the doctor's book to stop the tragedy. She went up to Dublin and over to London and she had tests and injections and God only knows what . . . all sons, and children that might have come out of the side of Lissarinka Hill for the lovely wee creatures they were — and only living breath denied to them."

"Where . . . are . . . they?" I asked in a whisper and she looked at me grimly.

"They're in that vault you visited today, but they have no right to be, for they had no time to be baptised. They were stillborn. It's tom-foolery, if God would send a baby into the world dead and not have it back again into his blessed acre, to lie till judgement day."

"I didn't see them, see the coffins."

"They were there just the same, but it was the kindness of the clergyman, who had allowed them to be put there in secret and out of sight, till the last day, when they'll rise up to the throne of God."

There was a long silence, and I waited but she said nothing, till Fergus prompted her.

"And Constance-Tenacity, she lived three months?"

Her voice was breaking so much that he had difficulty to understand her.

"She was a different one . . . strong. She was born alive, held on to life, where a male child might not have been able to. That's why they called her the strange name. 'Tenacity'. Your father used to joke about it and say she'd live to be ninety. She was perfect in every way and we were so thankful. She'd everything we saved up for four sons, more besides. There was such a celebration for her birth that you'll never know ... a bonfire on the top of Lissarinka Hill, that could be seen for ten miles, a great christening party with folk invited from all round ... "

She stopped up short and the joy went out of her and the woe crept in. The sides of her mouth went down and her face was the mask of tragedy.

"And the wicked stepmother wasn't asked and she put spell on the baby," I whispered and she looked at me and nodded her head.

"It's no good going over sorrow, for it never gets less, only more, so that a person can't bear the pain. I'll tell you the rest. Then you'll know what happened, see how you come into it. Don't think that we love you any the less for it — love you more for you saved Moll Fitzgerald's life, if ever anybody saved another person's life. At least, she is happy and content, not the creature she became ... "

Again she paused for a long time before she went on and she was living it all over again.

"One day, the child wasn't well at all. She turned away from the bottle, and then she brought up the little she took, and blood in it. The doctor came and he asked me if she bruised easy and for the life of me, I couldn't think what he was on about. He took out a syringe and a needle and he drew some blood from her and put it into a bottle, took it away with him and made none of us any wiser — only for your father, your foster father, I suppose I should say. He went downstairs with him and they had a talk — a long talk, but the Master didn't let on what he said, but there was no smile on his face. The blood had to go somewhere to be tested. I don't rightly know about such things, but the answer was a long time coming and when it did come, the news was as bad as if the devil himself had sent it. The four sons had been stillborn. We could work it out for ourselves. It was highly likely that there was some flaw in the new child, even if she had held on to life a bit. God help us all! She had no more life left to her than a sand glass might have sand and it running low. She had a blood disease . . . a kind of cancer and there was no cure, only to put fresh blood into the child and in a day or two, the blood would destroy itself and no power in this world to save her, but for a few weeks. The doctor broke the news to the Mistress at once . . . said it had to be done and not come sudden. She went crazy . . . not wandering a bit like she is now but to the edge of death. She wouldn't sleep, nor eat, just lay as if she was dead herself, sank down and down as the baby sank down and down. They gave the child blood, but whatever evil thing she had in her body destroyed every drop of it . . . I was there all the time . . . and the night the child died, I wished I could go with her and get away from the sorrow, that had come down on Lissarinka. She was like a small wax doll and the beauty of her broke our hearts for us, and her mother just turned away to the wall and gave up the will to live. Thank God we had told nobody in the parish! We didn't want friends and neighbours coming in and coming in to comfort us, for there was no comfort in heaven or hell. I saw the doctor to the door the day he came to give the child her death certificate and he was in an awful way. At the door, he said to me that the Mistress would have the baby in her own coffin, for there was no saving her either. Then in the hall down below, who should come marching in, but Morag Cameron all the way from Scotland, and a basket in her hands, the sort of thing you'd carry clothes in for the wash."

"Morag. Our Morag!" I cried and she nodded her head . . .

"Mistress Morag Cameron," she said.

Bessie had written to her that the baby was dying. She arrived without a telegram or a letter, stepped over the threshold of the front door.

"God send I'm not too late!" was all she said.

The doctor did not know who she was at first. Then he remembered her, told her sadly that she was indeed too late.

"The baby died just now, and worse than that, her mammy will follow her. It's a house of sorrow you've come to and there's nothing any of us can do."

That was what the doctor said and

Morag clasped the basket more tightly in her arms and asked if there was somewhere private they might talk. The master turned into the study, Bessie told us.

"It was this very room we're in today. He snapped on the light. We all stood here staring at her for maybe we thought she was cracked. She was smiling. She turned off the bright light . . . knew the place of old, turned on the desk lamp, set the basket down on the table over there."

Fergus had gone to sit at the desk and he turned round and looked towards the table and it seemed as if it was all happening over again, so vividly did Bessie call back time.

"Maybe you're wrong about it being too late, Doctor." Morag had said. "I've brought something with me that might do what nothing else could do. There's no saving the wee bairn upstairs, but I have a baby girl here, that's lost *her* mammy. What's there to stop you taking her in?"

Bessie's hands were clasped in front of her breast and she looked at me and her face was soft and gentle.

"I stepped over to the table there and I lifted back the blanket. It was the first time I set eyes on you, acushla. You were like a little princess, as dark as the other was, had a look of her too. There was no going against it. Still, I thought to myself that a mother knows its own child. Besides, where had Morag Cameron got a baby so handy and there must be laws . . . "

They had talked for a long time and then Morag had gone up to see Mimsy, for she was 'Mimsy' now and far beyond any stage of Mimsy, far out past the border of sanity, not eating, not sleeping, near enough to dying. Morag had known her in the old days and Mimsy recognised her, listened as Morag told her that the baby was not dead at all. She had dried Mimsy's tears and tucked her up in bed, and all the time, the doctor and Bessie and I had waited and I still in the basket.

The Master came back with Morag presently and Morag made them listen to her.

"The bairn in yon basket will call

Herself back to Lissarinka."

"That was what she said." Bessie went on. "She said that it was the hand of God had sent the baby to her croft on that out-of-the-way island. She reminded us that we were all farm folk."

Had not Bessie just said the same thing to Fergus and myself?

"I can hear Morag again," Bessie went on. "As if she stood and spoke to us, her voice all broad Scots again, with the feeling in her heart — telling us that we had only to dress the live baby in the clothes of the other."

"Put this bairn in agen her side. Whisper it's time the wean had her bottle. Is there no faith in Lissarinka any mair? Tim-Pat would have kennt how a shepherd puts the skin of a dead lamb on another ewe's lamb, that's alive. The ewe puts out her nose to smell the lamb and tak's it, as her ain?"

Fergus had come to stand at the table and he shook his head.

"So that was how it was done," he said quietly.

"That was how it was done, Mister Fergus."

There had been a deal of discussion before they took me upstairs all the same. The rector came and the solicitor and they talked the hours away. Lissarinka had kept the sorrow close and nobody knew about the tragedy, only a handful of people, who had served the family for years. Plans were laid and no voice above a whisper, but before they were finished Bessie had taken me to the bedroom, 'dressed in the fine lamb's fleece', as she put it. She drew the shawl down a bit on my fore-head, but there was such a likeness, that nobody would ever know.

"Your little mouth came out searching for the teat, good as gold, suckling the warm milk down, as if you hadn't been fed for a month of Sundays. She put you up against her shoulder to bring up the wind and then she finished off with the feeding, asked me if she couldn't keep you in bed with her for a wee while. You slept against her side and she slept. Aye! That was how it was done."

It was a conspiracy that save Mimsy's life, and some of her reason. It was all within the law and it was done deliberately, step by step, with a white coffin, made in secret by Joseph Byrne. Constance-Tenacity slept her last sleep in the room at the end of the passage, with the key turned in the lock. I took her place in Mimsy's room, in Mimsy's baby's cot.

Morag lived on an island in the Hebrides, so remote that the clergyman rarely visited it. I had not been baptised, but I was baptised now. The rector of Killeen Church baptised me here in the study again, where we were now, drawing his finger in the sign of the cross on my forehead.

"Constance-Tenacity, I baptise thee in the Name of the Father and of the Son and of the Holy Ghost."

"It was a strange kind of magic, as if God fitted the prayer to the miracle," Bessie told us. "I'll never forget the prayer he said, not to my dying day."

She took a prayer book from one of the shelves and found the place she wanted . . . read out the prayer to us. She said, "It was like it was meant."

"We yield thee hearty thanks, most merciful Father, that it hath pleased thee to regenerate this infant with thy Holy

Spirit, to receive her for thine own child for adoption and to incorporate her into thy holy church. And we humbly beseech thee to grant that as she is now made partaker of the death of thy Son, so she may be also of his resurrection, and that finally with the retinue of thy saints, she may inherit thy everlasting kingdom, through the same Son, Jesus Christ our Lord, Amen."

I became Fitzgerald by deed poll. It was only the matter of a signature on a piece of paper and by the signing of a will, I became heiress to Lissarinka, but that was weeks later.

It was all so simple and it all went well but running alongside it at the beginning, was the unhappy shadow of the funeral of the real Constance-Tenacity, in secrecy with nothing out of the usual happening at Lissarinka, except that a baby had been ill and was well again . . . with the mother a bit strange in the head, for all the worry and fretting she had been through.

"The funeral wasn't like any funeral that's ever been," Bessie told us. "Afterwards Morag went off home to her croft in the Hebrides, but she left her heart behind her with you, Honey, and it's been here ever since. Have you never wondered why she remembered the birthdays and the Christmasses and why she took such delight in the photographs . . . and in the little notes that you wrote her at the end of mine?"

Fergus came over and put his hand under my chin and lifted my face, kissed me on the mouth with a kiss as light as a butterfly's wing and Bessie took no offence about it and that surprised me.

"Isn't that what life is all about?" he said, almost to himself. "It's love that's important, for it spins the world around a day at a time . . . the love of a mother for her child and the child for her mother, the love of a man for a woman."

Yet the love of Richard Fitzgerald had not brought Moll back to her senses, even though they loved each other more than most husbands and wives. The loss of her sons had turned her into a gentle shadow. There were times when Bessie thought she knew about her daughter . . . she had lucid days . . . said strange things. Well I knew that she could never have had more love from my foster father nor from Bessie, nor yet from myself, and she was happy . . . hardly ever anything but happy.

Bessie seemed to have taken herself off into a world of her own, remembering the funeral of the baby, the Gothic door, the white coffin, the flowers, that had lasted down eighteen years.

"The funeral was late into the night and there was no moon. The rector had no surplice on him — just the cassock, black against darkness and the sadness and the farewell. The service was said in the small room. Joseph Byrne was undertaker and carpenter and keeper of the vault. He had a still tongue in his head . . . has it now, just the same. Morag was there and Tim-Pat and myself and the Master . . . nobody else. Don't think we didn't give her a loving goodbye . . . didn't sweep her away without a care or a ceremony. The service was like a thanksgiving to God and a promise of happiness for eternity. "I am the resurrection and the life," "Though he were dead, yet shall he live . . . The Lord is my shepherd . . . Open our eyes . . . that we may perceive that thou has taken this child into the arms of thy love and blessed her . . . "

"It was such a small coffin. The Master carried it in his arms. We went in Joseph Byrne's big car and no sound in the stable yard, but the horses' feet against the cobbles in their stalls and the whuffling of their nostrils. Morag stayed in the house to be with the Mistress, if she woke up — and a bit to say goodbye to yourself. Constance-Tenacity . . . "

It was the first time she had called me by the name since she had told me my history and it sounded strange on her lips, but she nodded her head and said it again. "Constance-Tenacity . . . That's a good name . . . and it's yours by right and never doubt it. Morag was waiting at the front door when we got back from Killeen cemetery, and the lights were on in the house and streaming out into the drive . . . a great sheaf of flowers on the hall stand. The house was passing out of its sorrow. I don't think there was one of us, that didn't feel it. We were all waking up to a new life and big happiness. That was the beginning of it and the end of it too."

I looked up at her dully and saw the exaltation, that possessed her as maybe it should have possessed me. There was happiness about Fergus too, but I was far from content. It was as if somebody had given me a first taste of a great banquet and then withheld the rest of it from me and I was hungry, hungry for more information and may be there was no food for my curiosity. Maybe there was nobody to tell me what I wanted to know, what I was determined to know, which I was ready to die to know.

I should have thanked Bessie for the way she had gentled me with what the story she had given me, but I shook my head. I thrust the blanket off my knees and got to my feet.

"Of course, that's not the end of it," I cried. "Who was I, Bessie? Where had Morag found me? Where was my own mother and my father, where was he? Was I some relation of Morag, that she wanted to find a home for?"

Fergus put out a hand at that and pressed me back into my chair and his grip on my shoulder reminded me that I was showing poor taste. I shrugged his grasp off and went on, but I remembered that I had no right to be rough on Bessie, because I had had too much emotional disturbance and too much sherry. I grabbed Fergus's hand in mine and kept a tight hold on it, to ask his pardon for shrugging him off.

"Are they alive or dead, my real parents? If they were alive, why did they give me up? Was I some foundling, whom nobody claimed? Morag comes from the Western Isles, so presumably I'm a Scot. Oh, God! Why didn't Father tell me about this years ago? I wouldn't have cared. I don't care now. They couldn't have treated me better, if I'd been their own flesh and blood. They chose me. That's what they tell adopted children, but I was forced on Father in a kind of way. He never held it against me. I just can't stand to know so much and no more. I must hear the rest of it, Bessie, I must."

She looked at me with pity in her eyes and with the same mother's love, that I had from her all the days, since she had looked at me in my basket, like the basket you might use for the wash.

"The time may come when you'll know everything that went on. I don't know if it ever will, or if you'll never know. Sometimes, there's no way of finding out the truth of a thing. Morag didn't know it herself, or she'd have told us. They weren't able to find out who you were, when you were born and that's long ago now. I'll tell you what she told us and I'd advise you to shut the story up in your heart and bide your time. The Master will tell you when you come of age and you're not to go laying more burdens on his shoulders with questions about what happened last night nor today or any day. Just go on the way you've been doing in this house for the last eighteen years. I'll tell you the wee bit more I know and that's all anybody knows, but when the Master tells you you're adopted and not his real daughter at all, just you go into his arms and thank him for the great kindness and love he's given to a wee pieceen of a baby, brung to his door in the night with a head of hair on her as black as a crow."

"But my real father?" I whispered. "My real mother?"

"Her name was Claudia," Bessie said. "I don't know the rest of it and I don't know that anybody does. She wouldn't say what her surname was, but perhaps there was no time left to her, when it came to the telling."

My father must have come into the room some time in the last minutes. We all became aware of him, standing over by the door. There had been no sound of car engine, nor yet of his footsteps against the soft carpet, no banging of doors. His face was sad and silent and closed, lined with the years too. We stood like a living tableau and looked at him, wondered how much he had heard, waited for him to speak, were every one of us aghast that he had come in and heard what we had been saying . . .

I can see him now, his head bent a little and his eyes deeply intent, his hair greying at the temples, his shoulders braced against the sorrows they bore, his face clean cut and handsome. He might have commanded an army battalion. He might have painted a great picture, made a mark in history. He was the ideal film hero, ageing a little but gracefully, voice pleasant, manners impeccable. I had been so proud of my father, who was my father no longer. We stared across the room at each other for a long time and the thoughts whirred through both our minds, like the panel in a fruit machine. There was no telling what way the fruit would turn up, in rows winning a prize or in useless lines, that could only condemn the stake to be thrown away into the cash bank for collection by the hawks that prey on foolish birds and that is a mixed metaphor if ever there was one, but I was past caring about mixed metaphors even in my thoughts.

How long had he been in the room? At least he had heard me demand who my real father was. I think he had been there a long time. There was a sadness about his eyes and in the white face, and he must know that the news had broken at last. So we looked at each other across the room and there was nobody else in the room, but he and I and our eyes interlocked, one with the other's. I thought of the past eighteen years and what he had been to me . . . of all his tender loving care of me and how we both protected and loved Mimsy. I thought what we three meant to each other and knew that no accident of birth could ever change the feelings between himself and me.

Bessie was not the least part of the whole thing and Tim-Pat, for we had united against the whole world and dared people to think Mimsy was different. With us as a phalanx about her, she lived a full life, but Bessie must not be ignored, nor Tim-Pat, with their loyalty and the love they bore us, with all they had gone to pass the counterfeit off as the real, for the sake of a person who might have died, else.

So he and I stared at each other and the others were shadows and then I drew my hand away from Fergus, for he held it still. He was another such as Father. In that second, I recognised the fact and then forgot it, went running across the room and into my father's arms. I think that neither Father nor I had any realisation that we were not alone in the room. I spoke to him, in little sentences, disjointed and sometimes without much sense. I told him I knew what had happened and how he had joined in the great conspiracy to make the daughter of Lissarinka come back to life. I poured out my heart there and I was far past caring who heard what I said. I thanked him for his love and his tenderness and for all the material things he had given me, but more for the spiritual things, the things that only love could repay. My voice went on and on and he held me tightly against his chest. I got the tobacco and saddle soap and safe secure smell of him, that had comforted my child days. He was like a rock in a storm and I was in the eye of the wind now, but he said nothing, just held me far too tightly for comfort and kept his face pressed against the top of my head.

There was a silence when I had finished it all and I had gone through the story of the vault again and he winced at the pain I caused us both. Finally I ran out of words and Fergus and Bessie were sitting there like extras in a great drama, that maybe was approaching its climax.

Then at last I finished. I had emptied

myself of all emotion and there was no more to say. Yet I broke out with more.

"Phil's people will have to know. It's likely he won't want to marry a lass with no pedigree. I know his mother won't want it."

"It's not for his mother to decide. Surely it's for Phil? Surely it's for you?"

Fergus put in from across the room and he was like any foreigner, that interrupts at a family conference, and we hardly heard him.

"The old lady McCracken will probably jilt you," said my father and the humour had come back into his eyes. "She wants nothing but the blood royal for her darling, but I didn't think you're all that taken with him yourself? Are you, Constance-Tenacity?"

Now he was giving my strange name, which I had thieved from a dead child and there was no strangeness about it. To him, I knew well that he was my father and I was his daughter and there was nothing that would ever change the love we had for the other.

"But I'd best be telling you about

Morag. There may be bits you don't know."

It was very silent in the room as Father filled in the gaps in the story, and when he had finished, it was still a far from complete piece of tapestry, yet it had the grace and the beauty of an old battle banner, that had seen victories and defeats and hung on a church wall to the glory of men, who had fought and won and lost.

"Bessie will have told you most of it, but maybe there's more to Morag Cameron, that you don't know . . . "

He had walked over to the window and stood looking out into the garden and the smell of the lavender bed was sweetness and a memory of cool sheets on a warm summer's night.

Morag Cameron had been at Lissarinka for many years. She had come when Father was a boy and she had seen after the whole place.

"Good Lord, I can't call you anything but daughter and you mustn't start saying 'foster' father. There's truth in it, but no comfort and no real daughter could ever — "

He broke off suddenly, his back to the room still, and returned abruptly to the story of Morag Cameron.

His mother and father had been alive and then after a while, they died one after the other. "Too wrapped up in each other to wait long," was the way he put it. Then Morag took full charge.

"I grew up and got married and there was a change for us all. Morag had people on a 'wee croft' as she used to call it. It was on one of the Outer Hebrides. One time, as a boy, I went there for my holidays and I thought it was maybe paradise. It's at the end of the earth and it's all mountains and heather . . . and sheep with curly horns, Highland cattle. There were stone hot water bottles in the beds on Morag's croft. She called them 'Piggies', and a time or two, she called them 'Curates'. It's funny how the little things stick in one's memory."

He kept wandering off the subject and back again and hither and thither through the days, that were gone.

"Morag was housekeeper at Lissarinka and then her mother took ill and she had to give up the job, go back to the farm on the Hebrides to look after the invalid. Then after Morag's mother died, there was still her father to see after. There was no escaping back to Lissarinka. Bessie was housekeeper there by this anyhow. Life had moved on. By the time Morag's father died, Morag herself was too 'fixed' to want to change. She had got settled in her ways and she knew that Bessie and Tim-Pat were 'managing fine'."

Fergus was thoughtful about that.

"I've often thought that death may have that sort of thing about it. When a person is dead, it's a short time, before his place is gone. It's not right. People are mourning and wishing a person back, but his possessions are scattered, his house is gone, his will has been proved and his goods shared out. God! Even with a dog, there's another dog in his basket and his place on the hearth rug taken."

"You're a philosopher, Fergus. There's your father's thinking all over again."

Father liked Fergus. I had always known that. They looked at each other now, for Father had turned round from the window.

"Come and sit down, sir. Let me

pour you a drink in your own house," Fergus said.

The story went on its way and we were all very intent on it. Bessie had taken a chair and sat very primly with her hands folded in her lap. Fergus and I were side by side on the sofa and his hand took mine as naturally, as if he were the one picked to wed me and not Phil McCracken. Father was at the desk nearby, his eyes never leaving my face, as he went on with it.

Morag was a very religious woman, he told us. She read a chapter from the Bible every day, even if she was tired from the work on the croft, for it was hard, when her father was dead. It was all left to her to do, not but that the neighbours helped each other, the folks from the crofts around.

"You couldn't picture it in a hundred years. It's so lonely and quiet and beautiful. The house is grey stone with a window at each side of the door. You'll maybe have seen snaps of it, but I hardly think Morag goes in for a camera. It's a different world from the mainland. There are a few small crofts round about, of course it's like the Highlands. The cattle roam free on the mountain, the sheep too. You have to go walking up the hill in Corran when you come to milking time and maybe for a mile or two ... but I'm off on another tack now. I was saying about Morag reading her Bible. If she hadn't been reading it on one particular night, and if she isn't as superstitious as Bessie, you'd never have been here today."

She had been sitting in the living room with the Bible out on the scrubbed table and she had been reading a chapter from St. Matthew.

"It's the part about Christ picking his Kingdom and dividing the sheep from the goats. The sheep were for heaven but the goats were for hell."

"I was hungered and ye gave me meat. I was thirsty and ye gave me drink. I was a stranger and ye took me in. Naked and ye clothed me ... "

Of course, I knew it. I knew the next bit too, for it was the picture of the day of judgement and it always filled me with horror. The righteous or maybe the unrighteous had said that they had never known our Lord.

"When saw we thee sick? When saw we thee a stranger?" and so on and so on. Christ had given the answer with no hesitation, that St. Matthew admitted to.

"Inasmuch as ye have done it to one of these the least of my brethren, ye have done it unto me," I whispered and Bessie nodded her head in agreement.

"Then your mother came walking down the glen, your own natural born mother, not Mimsy," Father said and I snatched my hand from Fergus and jumped to my feet.

"Mother!" I cried, but Father put me back in my seat and hushed me and Fergus recaptured my hand and I listened to the rest of it.

It was a place where strangers never came. If a stranger appeared, people would come to the door of their crofts to see who it was. Morag went to the door, when she saw the girl appear at the top of the rise. She was a young woman and she had nothing but a smallish bag in her hand, no suit case. Her shoes had not been made for walking mountains and they were worn through. She had a dress and a coat, but no hat . . . just a scarf in her hand with some things wrapped up in it. She saw Morag at the door and she came over and after a while, she asked for a drink of water. That was the moment, that Morag decided, that 'the stranger' had been 'sent'.

"By God! She had been sent too. If ever any person was sent to any place, that girl was sent to Morag's door!"

He cut a long story short. Obviously, if I went to Morag, I would get more detail. Even before I heard the rest I decided to go to her as soon as I could.

Father went on with the story. Morag had taken her in. She was a secret lassie and Morag wasn't one to pry. 'Claudia' was her name and that was about all Morag got out of her. She came from a long way away and she had had a bad time. Of course, Morag had taken her in and she had given her a drink of buttermilk and something called a 'stropack', which was Scots for anything from a cup of tea and a scone to a dish of rashers and eggs. She had stayed on. She had helped with the croft and Morag had been delighted with her company. Then one day, she had said she was expecting a baby.

"And that baby was yourself."

I cannot express the intensity of my interest in this most gripping of tales, but it was soon over and already I knew the end of it. It was an isolated place. There were no doctors and nurses on the corner of every street. There were no streets. The doctor came once a month, if the sea allowed him. There was a helicopter now, but in those days, people made do. I had been born and my mother had bled and died. She had died with her secret still closed in her heart. Morag had seen to her burial and there had been an effort to find out something about this young girl, obviously well-bred, who must have got herself into trouble.

Then had come the tragedy at Lissarinka and Morag had been expecting the news. Bessie had told her how ill the baby was. She already knew the tragic history of the four lost sons. Morag knew everything, that went on in Lissarinka. She was familiar with every step in every flight of stairs and every window and plot of grass and every move anybody made. So closely had she and Bessie kept touch one with another. She knew that Constance-Tenacity must die. She gave it a deal of thought and read a deal of the Bible, opened the pages and searched them for messages.

"Suffer the little children to come unto me . . . " she had read and a whole score of other messages beside . . . and the baby at Lissarinka was fading. One day, Morag found a basket just right for what she wanted. I was a fine baby and as good as gold and I had not cried all the rough journey across the Minch nor down the length of Scotland, nor across the sea to Ireland and all the time, the people had been slow and gentle and delighted to help a poor lady, with a baby, along on her journey, and so she had arrived at the front door at Lissarinka House . . . hoping she had not come too late.

There was silence for a while. We all sat with our thoughts and I had a great section of the picture clear in my mind. Then, as in such affairs, we started talking all of us at once and we talked for a long time and not much sense out of any of us.

After a while, I knew what I had to do. I wanted to go to Morag, wanted it more than anything I had ever wanted before, but Phil was on my conscience. I got to my feet and walked to the window to look across towards Puck's Castle, where the rooks were circling the tower.

"The first thing that must be done is to tell the people over there, that I'm not who I'm supposed to be. If Phil and I get married, we get married. If we don't, we don't. They must be told so much and the whole thing must be straightened out. It's too much of an arranged marriage ... and there's something with priority, Father. Please let me go ... go and go quickly to Morag, dear faithful Morag, who saved Mimsy from death and brought us all happiness. I want to go to her, but not with a beating of drums and a playing of fifes."

They looked surprised at that and no wonder, so I went on to interpret it.

"I don't want to travel in richness in a white sports car with all the trimmings.

Maybe I want to go a bit like my mother went — travel to the Outer Hebrides with the minimum of possessions. Maybe I want to come to Morag with my shoes worn from the walking, hungry and thirsty and glad of a drink of buttermilk."

I sat down again and clutched at Fergus's sleeve.

"It's hopeless to explain. Mimsy is my mother and I love her, but what about Claudia. There's a skein maybe tangles beyond unravelling. I'm being very dramatic about it. I want to go looking for Claudia. I can hear her inside in my head. I don't mean that I want to go and kneel by her grave, but that too, of course. I want to creep into the past and maybe solve old unhappy things. I want to know who she was and how she ended up the way she did."

I turned to Father and tried to explain to him and thought that I made no explanation whatever.

"It's since you told me and Bessie told me and I found the vault open and the white coffin. In the last few hours, I've had the strangest conviction.

It's as if something sad possessed me . . . somebody. I know it sounds crazy, but I have the thought that maybe Claudia is standing somewhere a long way off, with her arms out to me to come to her. It's the same thing all over again, like 'boys and girls come out to play, the moon doth shine as bright as day . . . '"

I stood up and went across to Father, begged him not to be angry with me. I would never regard him as anything but the most loved father in the world.

He understood what I was trying to say. Of course, he did. Then I suggested that I go over to Mrs. McCracken and tell her who I really was and he smiled as sad a smile, as I have ever seen.

"If you're set on self-destruction, you can try it. I'd rather you left it to me."

I shook my head and he let me have my way so far but no farther.

"But this talk about the trip to the Hebrides. You can go there too, but with the normal means at your disposal. We'll tell Mimsy you're taking a holiday. You'll travel in comfort and of course, somebody will go with you."

There was a long argument about this. Fergus went in on his side and said that I could not possibly be serious in considering setting out on such a long journey by myself and without proper arrangements. I must have somebody to look after me.

"I'd be making a pilgrimage," I said and Fergus snorted that out of court and we argued on and on and on, Father and Fergus and I. Bessie was dead against any idea of my travelling anywhere by myself and advised that I wait till I come to my senses.

"And if we are going to the Hebrides, in the name of God, leave the McCrackens till we come home again," she ended. But I knew it all, or thought I did. It was no good standing on the edge of an icy pool. It was best to dive straight in.

"I know where I'm going," I said as many a young person had said before me, and I believed it too, like we all do.

I think that perhaps I took it for granted that my mother had travelled to the Hebrides from Ireland. I was so thoroughly Irish myself that I worked it out that she must have been Irish too.

I hoped to pick up pieces along the journey that she must have travelled. I was quite certain in my mind that I would discover more about Claudia. Certainly I knew that Claudia called me with all the strength she could summon up in her soul, wherever she happened in the long stretch of eternity. When I had finished my pilgrimage and I was set on it, if they but knew, I would come home to Lissarinka. It was the only home I had ever known. I could never pay off the debt I owed to Lissarinka and all who lived there, not if I lived for ever.

There was a long silence in the room when we finished all argument, but nobody in the room could have understood what the impact of the news, I had had, had done to me. I had stood on a firm high foundation. All my life, I had been secure. Now my foundations were gone and I was nothing . . . nothing real, nothing but a nothing. I had no father nor yet mother. Almost certainly I was bastard. I had no proud line of heritage. Lissarinka might be mine one day, but it would be mine by charity. I had no right to it. Down inside me, in the very deep secret places of my soul, there was a small girl, who wept and would not be comforted.

"I'll tell them at Puck's Castle. Then I'll go over and see Morag," I said almost to myself and Bessie told me sharply that I was out of my mind and I wondered if she was right.

"Don't worry her, Bessie." Father said. "It's something that has to be done and we'll get to it in time. Let's leave it for now."

He took my shoulders in his hands and his eyes were soft with the love he had for me.

"Perhaps you don't know what Lissarinka House owes you, Honey . . . will always owe you, till the day we're all dead and gone and after that."

I kissed him and got myself out of the room, for I was not far from tears, that would have spoiled all the show of courage I thought I was showing, when I knew I possessed none.

Of course, I had no idea of inflicting any formal family meeting on anybody. I slipped out of the house and made my way to the Castle in the white car . . . found Mrs. McCracken tending her bees in the garden and laid all the facts down for her to see, when she had discarded her bee-armour and folded her hands to listen to me. She knew by my face that there was something seriously wrong. The garden was just right for plotting and intrigue, for it was pure Tudor, with rose beds and a maze and avenues of yew trees and of course, the bees in a row, making heather honey from the near mountains.

We went into the avenue of limes and the odd bee came with us. I thought there in that historic looking setting that Mrs. McCracken was a strange lady, so well she fitted to the picture. There was something of the cruel Queen out of Alice in Wonderland about her. Her chin would be sharp on my shoulder, if I let her close to me. She would cry "Off with her head!" as soon as look at me, by the time I had finished my tale, but for the moment I was in high favour.

"Why isn't Phil with you today? He shouldn't leave you gadding about on your own."

She was as 'mimsy' as Mimsy, but not in a gentle way . . . in a sharp cruel way, a sadistic way, when she wanted to be.

"I'm so glad that you're going to marry him. He needs stability and you'll give him that. You have it on both sides and back down the generations. Oh, yes, I know your mother was affected by childbirth, but that's not mental disease. That could happen to the best of us, and she's not anything but a teeny teeny bit vague."

I wondered how to break it to her that I was nothing but a nothing.

"Your father's line goes back six generations and all sound, and hers too. You'll be an anchor to Philip, for he needs somebody to stabilise him, like a ship on a rough sea. You'll cancel out . . . "

She went rambling on and on and her voice was like the buzzing of the bees in the heather. I let her buzz to a finish and then I told her quietly and with no dramatics the story I had heard, or some of it, asked her to keep it secret, between the two families. I sat on the seat at her side and I might have been a wandering bee, that had stung her. I was no daughter of Lissarinka. I was a foundling for all I knew. I had been adopted with the utmost secrecy and with careful planning. I might appear to be a high-born lady with a long pedigree, but I was nothing of the sort. There seemed to be no way of telling who I was or where I came from, nor who my parents were. I had been brought to Lissarinka in a basket, the sort of basket you'd carry washing in.

"Washing!" she exclaimed in a shocked voice, just like Lady Bracknell, and I managed to smile to myself.

"My foster parent, my father, would have told you, would have told me, when I came of age. He had no intention of letting me marry Phil, without your being agreeable to the marriage, all truth being known."

"About time too," she muttered, and "Quite right," and "It's a blow to me ... a dreadful blow. You can't understand. You're only a child, but Phil has wildness in him and I'd hoped we'd breed it out of him with your blood ... and now it seems you've got no breeding and no blood ... "

It was turning to pure farce and I had no sympathy for her. If anybody could be inhuman, she could, for she had no thought of me, nor what I must be feeling about the whole affair, no care whether I might break my heart if Phil turned me down, and of course, he must turn me down. She would make him.

"They hoped that we never found out," she muttered to herself and I shook my head and assured her that this would never have happened in any circumstances.

"I was to be told on the day I came of age, but I stumbled on a secret."

I knew quite suddenly that I would never have married Phil in any case. I felt a lift of my spirits, when I thought of ridding myself of such a mother-in-law, yet I took her hand in mine.

"I'm going to Scotland almost at once. I must see if I can trace my identity. In the meantime, of course, I release Phil from his engagement."

It was all so formal. It was as if people played on a chess board like pieces, yet well I know that there were no ivory figures involved, but men and women with hearts to be broken. There was no hint of emotion in her face. She was far too well bred for that.

"The marriage will not now take place," she announced with as much grandeur as if she were the English Times making the statement. "I can't have my eldest son, my heir, my first born, married to a person who might easily be a . . . "

She stopped up short but I finished it for her.

"A bastard!" I said and her mouth puckered in, as if someone had drawn it on a string.

"You said it my dear, not I."

That broke off all negotiations. She remarked that the roses in the garden were wonderful this year, but quite clearly and with no doubt about it in the slightest, she jilted me on Phil's behalf, kissed my cheek with no pity in the world, for what she might be doing to me.

She walked with me across the croquet lawn and again I thought of Alice in Wonderland and smiled at her.

"I'm sorry you can't say 'Off with her

head'," I said and that startled her.

I let myself out of the wicket gate and sent a last shaft at her.

"Besides, there are no flamingoes, so we can't play croquet."

Then I was into the car and away in a shower of gravel, that would do the tyres no good. I did not care, I told myself, but I cared very much indeed about not being Mimsy's daughter, not being Lissarinka's daughter.

5

Flight To The Western Isles

I HAD to get out, at once with no delay. There was no hope of formal goodbyes. Back at Lissarinka, I packed what belongings I wanted into a haversack, put on stout shoes, took a change of canvas slacks and a sweater, two pairs of socks. If I had delayed five more minutes, I must have been lost. I kissed Mimsy goodbye and told her I was off on my walking trip and she pretended she knew all about it. I left a note for Father, another for Bessie. I wanted to get in touch with Fergus, wanted it very much indeed, but there was shame in me for the way I had exposed my thoughts to him. I wanted no passage of arms with Phil. I would not admit it even to myself, but I cared not a jot if I never saw him or his mother again.

The same day when so much had happened, I set out on the evening train. I had Morag's address and that was all I wanted. I just must not allow myself the chance of changing my mind. I sent no word ahead of me to Corran in the Outer Hebrides. I must arrive as my mother had arrived. As the train drew out of Ballyboy station, I wondered if any of them would ever speak to me again, for what I was doing.

I was a dog with a tin can tied to my tail. I had no excuse for the pain I must be inflicting on Lissarinka. Then a thought came from nowhere swift as an Indian arrow. Was this how Claudia had started her journey? Had she felt the tears wet on her face as a train to somewhere gathered speed and she wondered if it were too late to go back to the place from which she had fled? If I ever hear the word 'pilgrimage' mentioned, even now, there is a sick feeling in the pit of my stomach and I think of the privations the old pilgrims must have suffered. Of course, my own pilgrimage could bear no comparison, but from start to finish, it might be classed as disastrous. If I had had any sense, I might never have attempted the humility in the first place. After all, there was not much point in it.

I arrived in Dublin after a journey in which the train seemed to stop at every station. I had a fine carelessness about routes to places, so I wandered down to the quays and found myself on a boat to Greenock, found myself a place in the steerage, with no comfort in the world, curled myself up in a coil of rope and was horribly sick on a rough sea. I was not surprised when two rather intoxicated passengers stopped to look down on my 'lifeless' figure, still in its coil and wondered between themselves, if I were dead. Then I had another bout of sickness and ran for the rail and demonstrated the fact that indeed I was not dead, only in my own mind, swiftly approaching the point of death and the sooner the better, as far as I was concerned. Arrived in Greenock, I took a bus to another part of the coast and crossed in a car ferry to Dunoon. There I found a bus bound across country to Obaig, where 'the island boats went from'. I do not know what type of bus it was, but it must have been privately owned, for there was a personal character to it and it had the habit of stopping very often, on the drive through the mountains, sometimes at a farm and sometimes just at the end of a lane, to pick up maybe a pair of fowl in a crate, a child, an old Highland woman. I could not understand more than one word out of four of anything anybody said to me, and sometimes they tried Gaelic in case I had not the English on me. I was so lonely for Lissarinka and sick in my soul that I was what might be called a foundling. I had not slept and sometimes, I wondered if there was any chance of ever finding myself alive by the time I reached the Inner islands, let alone the Outer. They sounded a very long way away indeed, judging by my progress this far.

I had not provided the hundred and one things I needed for such a journey. I had a comb in my pocket and a compact of foundation powder, a lipstick. It had rained a deal all through my journey, and I thanked God that my hair was curly. If I had been dependent on hairdressers, I would have looked like one of three hags in Macbeth and maybe I did at that. Yet there were moments, when the beauty of the land lifted my heart. There was a dawn, when the sun came out and chased the night clouds away and the mountains turned from pink to clover to topaz to blue and there were rowan trees and peat and small pools, big enough 'to bathe a star'. I had learned that last bit in an Irish school and I thought more longingly of home and the journey went on and on. I was fast asleep when I arrived in Obaig, in the early morning — "Obaig, where the island boats were to be found."

I had to wait two days till the boat left for Corran. There was a man on the pier and he filled me in on Scots island travel. It could be a rough passage and I might want to book a cabin. It took 'an awfu' lang whilie' for the boat was for stopping at every island that it came by.

Where was all my luggage? No doubt I had mislaid it on my way north, but I was not to worry about that. They were all honest folk in Scotland, not like the ones further to the south. My trunks would turn up before the boat sailed and there was plenty of time. It would leave when we were all aboard and not a moment before . . .

It served me right for rushing out of the house like an hysterical girl. If I had waited, I might be staying at the four star hotel down the front, with the white car parked outside. Maybe Phil would have driven me in the Lagonda, but I did not want Phil. I tried not to think of Fergus and his quiet kindness. He had no reason to come after me, not to offer to come with me, but I confessed to myself that I would have given much to see him waiting on the station platform at Obaig. I pushed away all thought of Fergus. Maybe I was infatuated with him, I half admitted that. It was no real lasting love and even if it were, who would want to marry a nothing, but a nothing? I turned myself back to my pilgrimage and then, as if heaven wanted to reward me for I don't know what, I got a message from Claudia, though I had no idea that was what it was.

There was an old man behind the ticket office on the pier, who looked at me and looked at me and came out through the door to look at me again.

"I've seen ye somewhaur 'fore."

I could scarcely make out what he said, for he spoke broad Scots, but he was fumbling in his pocket and he brought out a metal gadget. I had no idea what it was, and still he looked at me.

"Ye giv' me something years ago. I never forget a face. I'd thank ye to ken I hae it still and it's as guid the day as it waur then."

He was muddled suddenly for the years were going back on him. It was impossible he told me. I was a young leddy that day and I should have been a well grow leddy now.

"It's a slip of the mind."

Years before a young girl had come through the Pier and taken a ticket for the Isles. It might be for Corran too, but he could not recall. The big boat did na rin tae Corran.

His pipe had been blocked and she had given him a thing she had had wrapped in her kerchief . . . He showed it to me now . . . a metal pipe cleaner, showed me the way you could clean the pipe out or tamp down the baccy with it. He had had it nigh on twenty years and he never used it, but he remembered her bright face, not that she had been bright that day. He had often wondered what became of her.

I could make him no wiser. I did not even connect him with Claudia, till a ship came round the point of an island opposite Obaig on the way in to the fish quay. Then I asked myself if it were even remotely possible that Claudia had come along this way and given the man the pipe cleaner. Yet what would she be doing with a pipe cleaner? We were like twin lassies, he assured me and now he had it back in his head. She was on her way there to Corran too. The man in the office had told him that I was upset about having to wait till the boat sailed in two days time. If I was in haste to get to Corran, there was another way I might go. Young Lachlan McLachlan was taking his craft out to Corran to deliver some important mail, and it was a fine strong craft. He would be away within the hour and seeing I was such a bonnie wee lassie, Lachlan would be glad to give me passage. 'I need na be feerd of him' and it would cost me nothing, for Lachlan was no man to be grabbing siller from wee girls that wore hard up.

I wondered if my luck had changed. I was introduced to Lachlan and he knew Morag well. It seemed that everybody knew everybody else in the Isles. Of course, he would be glad to have me aboard, but "there might be a wee bittie swell." He went, rough or smooth, when he had important stuff to carry.

He was tall and handsome and he looked quite something in his fisherman's kit and the pink wool cap with the bobble. The boat was the sort of thing they used for lobster fishing, a long strong sea-going boat with a winch 'to be lifting the pots' ... and that meant lobster pots. The old man saw us off from the pier and Lachlan gave me a tarpaulin for protection against the Atlantic. My luck had changed or I thought it had. Of course, it had done nothing of the kind. As we glided out across the bay I looked back at the promenade where the big hotels were. The air was so clear that you could see the people, who leaned against the rail and watched us go, see them, as clearly as if you had a spy glass. There was a big hotel, near enough to the Cathedral, steps up to it and a car that drew into the steps to park. I knew the sort of car it was for Fergus had one the same. Then Fergus got out of it and walked up the steps, turned to survey the sea with all the small boats bobbing on its poppling surface. He did not even notice the strong sea-going lobster fishing boat nor the bedraggled girl amidships with the tarpaulin draped across her knees.

I spun round to where Lachlan stood in the stern, almost cried out to him to turn about and put me ashore. Then I realised that I could not afford the comfort. Besides how did I know Fergus had come after me? ... I turned back and settled myself down, tucked the cover round me and tried to shut in the warm feeling that possessed every part of me. Of course, he had followed me. Of course, he cared about me. I held the thought tightly against my heart as we met the Atlantic swell and the bow began to lift. It was a frightening journey part of the time. There were squalls that swept down out of nowhere and disappeared again and the sun came out. I was cold, but thank God I was not sick. I had no wish for death now. Had not Fergus come after me to see that I was not unhappy? Perhaps? . . .

The crossing lived up to its reputation and there were times when I wondered if we would set foot on dry land any more. If only I had waited for the Garrymore! I would have met up with Fergus and almost certainly he would have insisted on my staying in the hotel. He would have insisted on my getting dry clothes — new socks at the very least . . . and food. I would have had a fine dinner and Scots salmon. My appetite was returning when I had never thought to be hungry again, I could have eaten hors d'oeuvres and Scots salmon and maybe a steak to follow.

As it was, Lachlan lent me a fisherman's jersey and wrapped me very kindly in the tarpaulin, covered me in completely so that the spray lashed the tarpaulin and not myself. He gave me sandwiches and tea laced with whisky. The sandwiches were of cold mutton and home-made bread. They were his provisions and I was guilty at eating some of them, but I was starving and he told me he had enough and to spare.

"Sure! The weather's nothing to fret aboot, it's no but a wee bittie blow. The women in America are aye shaking oot their blankets at the sea to be airing them."

We talked sometimes in the hours, but mostly with the howl of the sea and the throb of the engine and the whistling moan of the wind, it was not comfortable conversation, but rather shouted words, that passed between us, with intervals of long silences. He knew Morag Cameron well. Everybody knew everybody else on Corran and he had an aunt with a croft on the north end, Miss Cameron lived to the south. There weren't many people left on the island. The young ones had all gone off to the towns . . . more sense than to stay lifting the peat with the old folk. There was no fishing to speak of, mostly lobsters, and by the time you got the beasties to the mainland, if there was a glut of them, you got damn' all. The lassies went into Obaig for the season and did hotel work, serving the tables and making beds. Sometimes they came back in the winter, but often they didn't want to leave the picture houses and the Bingo. They drifted farther to the south . . . to Glasgow, even over the border.

It was a rough tough journey and sometimes the rain came down and closed off the sight of the lovely mountains on the islands. We stopped off at some of the small ports, but nobody took any notice of any passenger in any boat. There was a strange intrigue about the whole journey, that I was at a loss to understand. Lachlan brought food out to me, but he said nothing about what he was carrying as cargo, and I wondered for a while, if we were not engaged in smuggling. Later on, I discovered that we were smuggling myself.

There was hardly any night . . . only a few hours of darkness and we drew in and slept in the lee of a harbour, that was surely the smallest harbour in the world and not a sight of any person about, nor any boat either. Then on again through another day and towards the evening, with the sun still bright, we came in sight of Corran.

"Yon's Corran at last and Morag Cameron's croft is at the south end. I told you. I'll take you in close by the rocks and you can jump off near enough her front door. It's no good taking you up to the north landing, for it's a good step back. There's no car on the island, only a man's two feet."

It was a beautiful land in miniature, with a mountain that was a patchwork quilt of fields. The white-washed cottages were toy houses that dotted the hills and the sheep were a child's sheep out of Noah's ark. The air still so clear that you could see each thing with a great distinctness. The water was like crystal and as we neared the shore the dark sage green seaweed fronds came waving out to greet us. There was a small hill, that was divided in the middle to make a glen and down near the shore, gunmetal rocks and one flat, that must do for my landing.

I had hardly time to thank him, offer to pay him, but he shrugged that off.

"Maybe you can do me a good turn one day. Ye've been great company and good luck to you. Tell Morag Cameron

I was asking after her."

"Now get your things ready. Make the haversack fast on your back and get set. Don't be afeerd. Take a good leap for the rock. Walk up the hill and on the other side, there's this wee glen. You'll not get lost. It's only a wee jump and if you were to fall in, I'd pull you out in less time than it took you to fall in, in the first place . . . "

He turned the boat with great skill and held it off the hardness of the rocks and I shut my eyes, jumped and landed, got to my feet and saw him backing out and away from me. Suddenly I did not want him to go and leave me all by myself on the empty island, for there was an emptiness about it for all the fact that I had seen the cottages on the hills.

"Lachlan," I called and the wind caught my voice and carried it maybe to the reaches of the Atlantic beyond.

He cupped his ear with his hand and I waved to him.

"Thank you," I shouted and managed to smile at him. "I'm might obliged."

I watched the boat till it disappeared from view round a crab's claw of land, that enclosed the small bay where the landing was. I felt very alone. I would have given much for a glass of sherry, like the one that Fergus had given me such a short time ago. I was lonely for Lissarinka. Yet had I not arrived, or almost arrived at the place I had so obstinately insisted on going? I tidied my hair and straightened my clothes, looked with misgiving at my shoes, for one of them was casting a sole. Then I faced up the small rise, after negotiating some rocks and came on the hungry sea grass. There was a little hill that hid a valley and come to the top of it, I saw, that it divided into a glen. That was what Lachlan had called it. I went walking down the glen and my loneliness was over in a flash of sunshine. I admit I am superstitious, as most Irish people are. Anyhow, there was all that influence from Bessie and Puck's Castle and its ghosts. Suddenly, I could feel Claudia all around me and in every part of me. It seemed that she had been waiting for years for my coming, maybe by herself down on the flat rock, watching the sea. My whole spirit was uplifted and my heart filled with singing. There was no sorrow to be found anywhere in my whole world, as I went tramping down the glen on the sheep track and over a small rise and here I stopped again, for the last shaft of sun had spot lit what had once been a thriving community. There were grey stone cottages spaced out in a sheltered dip in the hills and some of them were occupied still, with smoke curling up from their chimneys. There were small whitewashed cabins. At the head of the glen was a bow-fronted house and it was a little grander than the others, with its brass knocker shining out at me, with its two windows below and three above and the blinds all half drawn down to the exact distance for one to match the other and the curtains as white as bleaching in the sun could make them. There were other buildings, but none so grand. Sadly there were empty dwellings with a foreign look about them, with no glass in the windows and with the doors open for the sheep to shelter in them. Above all, there was a silence and a peace, a tranquillity that seemed impossible to find in this day and age.

There was nobody about ... no living creature, except for the animals — a cow, that waited with its calf half way up a nearby hill, sheep, scattered about the mountain at the back, like dice thrown down on a purple cloth. Then the door of the bow-fronted house opened and Morag came out on the step. She stood there and looked at me and I could see her, as if I had opened the album and looked at the picture of her.

Again, I got the strong conviction that here was somebody, who had waited a long time against my coming. The sun shone on her white hair and her calm face. There was no change in emotion as she stood there and looked at me, her hands joined together in front of her spotless apron. I went walking towards her and still she stood as quiet as ever her photograph had been. Only her eyes took in every last detail of me, from the top of my head down to the flapping sole of my shoe. Then I was nearer and still she did not move. She seemed unable to take a step to meet me, yet I knew she wanted to run to me. I was near enough to see the dark blue of her eyes, before her arms came out to me and I ran the last steps to be closed to her breast.

"If you knew . . . " she started and then stopped again hugged me more tightly still. Then her hand held my chin and my face was tilted up to look into hers.

"If you knew how I've wished for this day," she said. "It's as if she came back to walk the glen again, to come to my front door and the shoes broken on her feet too . . . the same eyes and the same face and the raven hair, but not the lost look. Thank the good Lord . . . not the lost look!"

"I've come to Corran, Morag," I began, my voice was husky with emotion. "I'm sorry that I did not send word on before me, but it was a thing I did without thinking much. I just wanted to see you, couldn't wait anymore."

She lifted her head and took an eagle's glance about the little hollow in the hills. There were the few inhabited crofts and the dozen or so grey-stone ruined cottages. There was a small graveyard half a mile off with a lichened wall about it, but no church nor school nor anything else. Morag scanned the view for anybody, who might be surveying my arrival and seemed satisfied that there was nobody about. Then she drew me in by the front door, paused at what must be the parlour door on the right and went straight through the small hall and on into the heart of the house, which was the kitchen.

"Come on away in and not a sound out of you till you have food in your mouth and dry clothes to your back and a wee while to rest. Not a word now. I heard it from Bessie."

The kitchen was the cleanest plainest plane I had ever seen, but there was comfort in it and a refuge, yet why I might need refuge, I did not know. I sat down in a big wood chair with a cartwheel back and leaned against a blue padding, she had stitched to the back of it sometime in the past. There was a bowl of broth in my hand and wee squares of fresh yeast bread floating on the top and I thought I had never tasted anything so delicious.

"I had to come to you, Morag. I heard Claudia calling to me to come and I knew she was here."

"Och! She lies in peace on the green hill yonder and you'll pay your respects to her as soon as maybe."

"I should have asked you if I might come. I should have let you know."

"Bessie let me know."

She was kneeling at my feet, slipping off the broken shoes and she looked up at me with a smile.

"And have you never heard of the Highland Telegraph? Do you not know that everybody in the isles knows everybody else's business? I knew you were due in here with Lachlan, before you had long put foot in Obaig. We all knew. My eyes are worn out with the watching for you. He's off to the north of the island now, but the people will keep still tongues in their heads. I'm afraid you'll have to lie low here for a day or two, for some things have happened that you don't know. That's how you were smuggled out so handy."

She was so pleased that I had come to see her that there was a light to her face and a joy that glowed all about her.

"Maybe we people know more than

you do for yourself about what's been going on. We have aye thought of you as the daughter of Corran herself, sent to us, out of no place and blessed. You're a kind of a good luck piece in the island. There's a great importance to you."

I had finished my broth and she took off my damp dry clothes and wrapped me about with a plaid, bathed my feet and tut-tutted about my general condition and was very like Bessie.

"Why you couldn't have travelled up to Dublin in that fine car of yours and come across on the boat, I'll never know, but to go half way round the world for sport, but then I suppose *they* were trying to catch you?"

She put a glass in my hand with whisky and hot water and I took a good drink from it and thought the roof of my head was flying away. There was lemon and clove in it and a piece of loaf sugar, and she begged God's forgiveness for destroying a toddy of such a splendid malt whisky with the taste of lemon and cloves.

"I worked a long time out of Scotland. It's my foreign habits," she explained and there was no idea in her head of talking a word about Claudia, till I had completely recovered from my rough trip and the emotion of my arriving.

"Trying to catch me?" I said, trying to catch my own concentration against the influence of potent brew.

"There's none on the island that's not for you," she explained. "They know what's happened, aye, back for near nineteen years, but what none of us know is this. Which one of them is the one you want, for both of them wants you? They've made that clear. They're both on the island this minute. One chap came in a speed boat from the West Highland Hotel and he took his life between his two hands when he did it. The other one is a big bullying sort of man, that maybe thinks he owns the whole world. He bribed mad John Russell of Liss to drop him off in his plane. If it's first come, first served, he'll have won you for himself, the bully boy. They're both here, but we want to know which one's your man."

I got it sorted out at last. Phil had flown out or been flown out by a man called Russell in a small private place. Fergus had borrowed the hotel speed boat. They had both arrived and the island folk had drawn a web of secrecy about the fact that I was expected. Bessie had been on the phone to the Post Office, not half an hour after I had left Lissarinka and it seemed that the island folk had been scanning the horizon for the arrival of Claudia's daughter. It was imperative that they find out which was the prince and which was Dandini and that was what Morag must find out, before she tucked me into bed and let me have the sleep I craved. She tucked me into bed anyway and perhaps it was the whisky that spoke to her, for maybe I said a deal of things I might not have said, if my head had not been tipping me over, as if I went down the glide on a roller coaster. I had to keep my eyes open and then I was fine.

"I was engaged to Phil, but you'll know that. His mother jilted me. That's news for you, but she hadn't a set to play croquet, for there were no flamingoes," I started and I imagine that was how I went on. I do not remember much of what I may have said. "They had flamingoes in Alice in Wonderland." I paused to try to sort out my thoughts . . .

"It's an arranged marriage . . . well not that now, for the McCrackens won't have it. 'A made match' that's what we say. I don't want it . . . don't think I ever did. It was a kind of drift for both of us. It would have suited both families, but Morag, he was cruel . . . "

Here I let slip a great deal of my secrets, that I had never breathed to a living soul. Phil was unstable, his mother had said, and I had wondered if she knew how unstable he was. He was a sadist. Maybe I did not recognise it, but I knew his great pleasure was in the pain of another. He had given Connor a cruel childhood. The twins ganged up against him but Connor had been quiet and defenceless. Even with me, he was cruel. As a child, he twisted my arm, tried to twist it, till I screamed and I wouldn't scream . . . and I had often wondered if my joints would grow out of the true because of it. Then when we were older and the strange phenomenon of 'love' had appeared, his passion was fed on pain. With this kisses, had come pain, pinches and bites and things I could not even understand. I had looked in his eyes at such moments and seen the devil that tormented him. He did not want to inflict hurt. It was something he must do to achieve some fulfilment and it had frightened me, yet it was something I had never dared ask anybody about. One night, he had noosed his tie about my neck and had pulled it tighter and tighter as he kissed me, had held my limbs down with the weight of his body, till I remembered no more . . . and when I woke up, he had been Phil McCracken again, returned to his bold piratical self, full of fun and laughter. Now Morag had it all, the things I had told to nobody and maybe it was because I was tired and more than a little drunk. I did not want to marry Phil or have any more to do with him. This whole affair had been a let out for me and it was not because I had fallen in love with Fergus, but I thought I had.

"And Fergus is the son of the Tribune?" she said with a smile. "A dark young man with a shy way to him and lock of hair as black as your own, that falls down over his forehead. He took his life in his hands to chance the Little Minch in the hotel speedy boat, but it was no harm. If a storm blew up, he could steer for the nearest bit of shelter. He has the speedy boat hid in a wee creek near the Widow McKay's croft and he's staying there, like a hare sitting in a form and no sound out of him. Master McCracken has camped out under a tent on the north side of the island. Neither of them knows the other is here, nor yet that you're here, and they won't know you're here till you're good and ready and rested . . . and sober with it. The whole island knows, but it's a tight little place and we're not all that keen on trippers. We held a kind of what you might call a parliament . . . " she pronounced it parliament too. "We thought we'd wait for yourself and before you go to sleep, maybe you'd give me the casting vote. If you want to marry one of them, which one is it to be, if you know it for yourself and it's a thing you'd want to be sure of."

I betrayed him and felt as guilty as

Judas. It was not his fault if he was what his mother called 'unstable'.

"I don't love Phil McCracken. I love Fergus, or think I love him. Maybe he doesn't give a tinker's curse for me. He's a newspaper man and he's likely here after the story, yet he kissed me. I think he said he loved me, but I'm confused. Maybe he said nothing of the sort, but he was so understanding with me . . . and he must have kissed me, for when he did, it was like as if I stood in the burning fiery furnace, with the way the flames devoured me and scorched me up and I thought maybe I was on a rocket half way to the moon."

And that shows that a strong drink of hot malt whisky can do to an innocent maiden, but even as sleep drooped my eyelids I knew there was truth in it.

"Then Fergus shall have Scots hospitality," Morag said. "And Master McCracken can get back to his own wee island and put chicken's blood on the hall flags to frighten the kitchen girls out of their wits."

Her voice sounded as if it came from another sphere, but I could hear it clearly on the edge of consciousness.

"The McCrackens were aye after the lands of Lissarinka. The Tribune's son had no axe to grind. That's what I told them, but they said the choice was yours. You were the one that had to be bedded with the one you chose. Take your ease now and in the morning, the sun will come up the sky and there's a deal to be settled between yourself and myself, for maybe I did you a great wrong. I wanted you for Lissarinka. I wanted you as nobody can ever have wanted anything in all their lives. You were mine and it was I had to chose who you went to. It was I, who had to give out the facts and the figures and show people where she lay in peace at last. If she ran away, there was a reason for it and perhaps her man was another like Phil McCracken. She was such a sweet lassie. She'd not put out her foot to crush a keerogue on the floor . . . a beetle. It had feelings, she'd say, and death is as cruel to a mouse or a beetle, as it is to you or to me. Let it go, Morag. Maybe it has children to go home to. She was lovely and sweet in her ways and she lies at peace above.

In a way, I thought that was the end of it, but there were things I told nobody. You've come, like the wrath of God maybe, with the right for the whole of it. My heart is full of trouble that it was wrong I did you, but I don't think it was. She was a poor lassie that had got herself in trouble. That's what they all thought, but not the folk on Corran. They saw the mark on her finger where the wedding band had been. They saw her for what she was. In a way, we adopted her. She could have lived happily ever after and the love of the people for her would have been something for her to cling to. The child would have been taken to our hearts. Marriage and the presence of a man in the house, isn't counted all that important here, the way it is in the south. You'd have had a happy life here with Claudia as your mother. Then she lay in her grave. She bled, because the sea was rough and the boat couldn't put out and there are folk like ourselves who bargain against the facilities of civilisation for the beauty and the silence and the peace. She bled and then she was like a wax doll and no life left to her. You were a lusty child. You seemed to have grasped the life and refused to give it up and you were the bonniest wean. You were like a princess of the blood and the black hair curling into wet rings on your head . . . and she had a broken heart. It was a release for her and we let it lie the way it was. The polis came. Of course, they did, but we closed the ranks again, like we're doing now. It's a bit of habit with us . . . independence and self-reliance and that. I sometimes, think we're an outpost of that sort of thing, but it was myself that did the wrong . . . Ach! there's more to it . . . "

I woke in the morning with the sun streaming in on the patchwork quilt and there was Morag with a cup of tea for me. She had washed and ironed my slacks and sweater and my stuff was set out for me to put on. I had only to drink the tea and wash myself at the basin. If it was not for the fact that I was being held in secrecy, I might have gone for a swim in the sea, but they must take no chances with me.

The island committee had met in the night and soon, Phil would be told where

I was and I must settle my affairs with him. After that, there were things to tell me and after that, Fergus would be brought to visit me ... and what I did, in any part of the day was my own affair and no business of the folk of the island at all, at all ... and that was to be the way it was supposed to come out, and every man, woman and child on Corran in it, up to the eyes.

In the morning, they came slipping along to Morag's house, mostly along the dry stone walls at the back of the crofts, dodging the main path up the brae. They were back door company at least for today, for Morag's front door was shut fast and it seemed to me that this was some sort of signal to them. There was Alastair Beg with a sack swinging from his hand and two fresh sea trout in it and a lobster as big as a dog. There was Kirsty and a batch of new bread and a fresh-killed fowl. There was Kate Ann and eggs gathered that morning and the hens laying fine. There were a great many secret callers and each with a sideways look at me and the women folk with a kiss for my cheek and they all talking awkwardly in English, because they knew I had not the Gaelic on me. I stood up as they came in one by one, but my throat was too full for words. Morag had passed the secret answer to the question in everybody's eye, though I never heard her do it. I was conscious of their comments, that whispered round the room and were surely never intended for my ears. They seemed to swell up and fill my brain, as Morag's words had done the night before, when she had spoken of Claudia. Now there was Big Jack and Janet the Post and Lachlan himself, who had brought me to Corran in his boat. Maybe I could understand some of the Gael's tongue for had I not learned Irish at school, but always when they spoke in Gaelic, it was not to me, but among themselves, but they whispered among themselves in awkward English too and my ears were antennae, posed to catch the slightest impulse.

"God and Mary be praised that it isn't the bully boy she has her heart set on. His mither is as mad as a hare in March, with the way she puts blood on the stones and says it's the fairy people. If the fairy people wanted blood on the stones, aren't they well able to do it for themselves?"

"He's a hard man . . . a mighty hard man and no thought for the widow of the man that flew the plane in, if he had been kilt . . . There's no landing place on Corran, except what a fly might light on, but he bought John Russell of Mull for gold, like another man might buy a bull at the Highland show."

"So the one from the speedy boat was her heart and small wonder!" (This was Fergus of course.) "He has nothing to say for himself, but maybe he thinks the more. He was a brave man to breast the Minch and he not knowing the tides . . . and nothing he does, but hang his head and the smile on his face would draw the heart out of any lassie . . . and 'it was nothing,' he says. "You want to try the Atlantic out beyond Galway on a rough day, when you'd not be certain, which was the sky and which was the sea."

"Have you ever gone out in a corracle?" he asks me. "The kind of craft they use off the coast of Ireland in the big ocean and it just the skin of an ox stretched out on wood struts. That boat from the West Highlands Hotel was like the Queen Elizabeth on a calm sea. I'm not a man to take a risk, even if I'm trying to capture Maeve, the Queen of Connaught . . . and what the hell could he be meaning by that?"

The ladies were softer and more confidential still and they admired the dark good looks of Fergus, but first things must be done first. Wasn't it high time that I saw the place where Claudia slept? There was nothing to fret about. There were plenty of islanders to guard the glen against intruders.

It was all like some play that had never been, except in the imagination, something that had been dreamt out between the night and the morning, with the islanders disappearing as swiftly as they had come and not a move to be seen on the hillsides, only myself and Morag walking quietly up the grass hill to this other cemetery, that was surrounded by a grey drystone wall to keep the sheep out. The women had vanished into their crofts and Morag and I walked on past the noise of clucking fowl and the bleating of sheep. There was no need to open the door to the graves. One had to go through a little stile and use a stepping stone set in the wall and straight away we came on a small line of military graves, with stones, that matched each other in simplicity.

I stooped to look at them and saw they were the sailors' graves from the last war, unidentified sailors that had been washed ashore on Corran, unidentified and buried here in this lovely quiet place.

"He is known to God."

That was the inscription on each oblong stone and again, my throat was too full for speaking. Then I was beside a plot that was gay with flowers, such flowers as might be come on in an island garden on the edge of the world. There were bunched sprigs of white heather and yellow daisies and branches of the rowan heavy with berries like sealing wax. There was a small wreath of everlasting flowers and my heart missed a beat when I saw it, for I recalled the white coffin and the flowers, that had lain in my pocket. I knelt by the grave and put a finger out to touch the flowers, first one and then another, wondered if every eye in the croft was upon me, though they all stayed indoors, the women. The men would be guarding the place against the coming of strangers.

"I'll leave you by yourself with her, Honey . . . just a wee whileen," Morag whispered. "She'll be so happy you came. She'll want it to be just the two of you together."

She turned away, but stopped short and came back again.

"It's been worrying me, the day," she said. "I might have given you the idea that the whole Western Isles knows your story and that's not the way of it at all. The Highland telegram, I said, but that's only the way news travels fast and one island helps another. It's only here on Corran, where the secret is tight known and kept in the fist. For all the others knew, you were contraband, that had to be brought here, fast and quiet. It had to be as quiet as if the Excise men were at your heels and that was the way it was done, but there were none to know the reason for it, only the ones that live in Corran . . . "

I knelt by the grave and could think of nothing, not a prayer, not a tear, not a sigh, only a great emptiness, that I had come too late, that I had never been, for her . . . and the time passed as slowly as honey dripping from the comb. There was peace and I knew she lay at rest, but still there was something she wanted me to do. I concentrated with all the power of my brain and wondered if I could bring her walking down the planes of heaven. She had something to tell me. Now strongly and more strongly, I could feel her coming to me, as if she was just going to appear in front of me. I imagined her as she must have been and knew the dark hair, the slanted brows, the peak of widowhood on her forehead, when maybe she was no widow, but a woman wed to a man, or maybe not wed.

They had guarded the glen against the stranger, but they had forgotten that strangers might have entered the fort before the guard was mounted. I looked up from the grave and saw

Phil standing there in the shadow of a tumbled-down stone cottage on the edge of the graveyard. God knows how long he had been there, but he looked as if he had slept rough. He had a stubble of beard on his chin and an unkemptness about him, so much that I could scarcely know him, only for the bright hair and the familiar voice, even though he whispered.

"Don't call out or make any cry for help. I want to talk to you and they're all against me. Just stay kneeling where you are and I'll stay here and we'll have the matter out between us with no interference from foreigners, why you think you can throw me over like an old suit of clothes?"

I looked down at the quiet crofts and knew that there would be people behind every window. I looked at the foothills of the mountain and knew that there would be island men on guard for my safety. I looked back at Phil and my heart dropped at the knowledge that what people said was maybe true. He looked mad. I cannot describe the thing that watched me out of his eyes — an evil thing, if ever I saw one and there was no softness nor love there now, not even liking. I had once seen liking and admiration there, but it was gone.

"So you and my mother think fit to put us asunder as they say in the prayer book. Just between the two of you, you throw me overboard — and away you run, with your scut between your legs — and not even the decency to face up to me and tell me for yourself, not even the kindness of a letter."

"I wrote you a letter, Phil . . . a little note — gave it to your mother — just a few words," for I had done so.

"Well, then, the old rip tore it up."

He wanted to pace up and down, but he had his one patch of shelter and I think he knew he was under guard, for he must have tried the cordon before and got nothing but polite refusal and a mulish blocking of his path.

"I risked my life for you. I let a crazy devil take me over the Minch in a plane that wasn't fit for scrap and do you know why I did it? Do you think I want you back?"

I shook my head and he told me. He had no intention of being jilted by a bastard. *He* was throwing *me* over. He wanted no part of me. As far as he was concerned, I could go jump in the sea off the rocks. He could marry any girl he chose to reach a hand out for but he would not have it said that I had jilted him. In fact, he would not have me get away with anything, not with any bloody thing.

"That newspaper chap has come after you, or has he? He won't get you, if he has."

I told him that I had not seen Fergus, which was quite true.

"Back at home, they said he was breaking his heart for you. Listen to me, Constance-Tenacity or whoever you are, you and I have been tied together for years, like a pair of spancelled goats and there's nobody at home that would believe you'd ever have been left at the altar by me. I don't care about you and I never will, but I'll kill you sooner than let another man have my girl and you were my girl . . . You were my girl. It's common knowledge now that you're bastard, or will be . . . false coin, if ever there was forgery. I want to make it clear that's not why I object to you. If I wanted you, I'd take you. Keep your head down, you little bitch. You're supposed to be praying."

I had only to get to my feet and run as fast as a deer. I owed him an explanation and I tried to give it to him, God knows what I said and the islanders must have been thinking that my prayer over the dead was long.

"I found that I didn't love you. I scribbled a note and took it to your mother. I ran away to come here to try to find out who I am. I can't live with thinking I am a girl that came out of Nowhere, Phil, but I'm sorry . . ."

"And Fergus?"

"If Fergus followed me, it's likely he came for a story. No, that's not true, Phil. I think Fergus likes me. I love him. I'm sorry. I can't help loving him."

He took a stride forward and he lifted me up in his arms, went across to the stone wall, where there was a place, that ran down twenty feet in a scree. He put his mouth down over mine and kissed me savagely. Then he ground his teeth into the side of my neck as if he meant to suck the blood from my body.

Then he put me down on my feet and took my shoulders in his hands, pushed me towards the wall.

"That's where they dump the rubbish off the graves. I'll dump you there and I hope you're dead by the time you hit the bottom of it."

I went slithering down the scree and through brambles and presently I came to rest against a rowan tree, which caught me in its mercy and held my body. Looking up, I saw that there were dark faced men circling Phil on every side, men who treated him with no kindness in the world and took him up and away from my sight. There were others who climbed down and retrieved me like a gull and there was talking in Gaelic now with a vengeance and I could not convince them that I was unhurt. I looked up at them as they lifted me back over the dry stone wall.

"Please don't hurt him. I think he's mad."

Then I was in the bow-fronted house and the talk was fast and furious and it was clear that Phil was on his way out of Corran, but if I wished it, they would let him go alive. I had to laugh at the seriousness of their faces, for I think they would have thought nothing of burying his body in the scree, or of throwing him into the bay with an anchor round his neck.

"But he's as mad as his mither, poor soul, and she to be putting chickens' blood on the hall stones. Maybe we should be asking the Almighty to pity him!" said Morag.

Finally they were all gone and Phil gone with them, I supposed. Then a long time after, I was allowed to get up and explore the life of the dip in the hills. Over the next day or two, they allowed me to settle in and always I thought of Fergus and wondered where he was and what might be happening to him at the hands of rough justice.

There was nothing happening to Fergus, that might be in any way called rough justice. He was experiencing Scots hospitality. He said afterwards to me that if he had been 'visiting royalty', he could not have had more kindness. He wondered, if they had mistaken him for a prince of the blood royal and the fact that there was being a little dust thrown in his eyes was not allowed to incommode him in the slightest. He got the news of me from the Highland telegraph, perhaps a little slant-wise from the truth, but the islanders were determined that I should have time to settle in. They were wise in their isolated self-contained community and they believed in the old ways. 'Marry in haste and repent at leisure'. They knew that I was in high excitement and under great stress. They knew what a strange experience I had had at Lissarinka and then there was the arduous journey. Then a while after had come the traumatic experience with Phil. So Fergus was told that I was on my way and would meet him very soon. I was safe and well, but pace was slow when a body travelled in the ways I had chosen. Would it not be a good idea to go out fishing for the day, or maybe help the men with the lobster lifting? It was a grand day for a sea trip.

Or perhaps he might like to go up the crag. There was a golden eagle and two young in the nest half way to heaven.

It was a stiff climb, but hadn't he the limbs for it? It was a thing he might never see again and Rory was going up and would be glad of the company. It would take most of the day, but it would pass the waiting and two to one 'Myself' would be at the house tomorrow or the next day with the heart bursting out of my chest at the sight of him . . .

'Myself' certainly could feel some strange sensation in the region where I thought my heart should be, though sometimes my heart might move up to block my throat. Morag was so patient with me, not rushing me into talking about Claudia, till I was ready and till then there was the work of the croft. I had always thought it might be a wonderfully lazy idle way of life to have a croft in the Outer Hebrides, but I found it quite different. The long days were just not long enough to do the work, that must be done. I helped automatically, watched what Morag did and fell in beside her, with my sleeves rolled up and my gum boots on, when they were essential. I had borrowed a pair from some unknown benefactor and they fitted me well, with thick-knit socks worn inside to keep them from slopping up and down. So Morag and I fed the hens and cleaned out the shed where they lived. We walked the hills till we found the cow, if she had wandered. Sometimes, she came to the house for the milking, but she had an unfortunate habit of taking a stroll. With time, she might come when she was called, but she was a new cow and Morag said that given half a chance, she would be on her way back the ten miles from whence she came. At any rate, when we found her in some dip in the hills, we put a rope on her and led her home with us. That saved us from carrying the milk pail. On a fine day, it was a leisurely relaxing pursuit and there was time for talk.

"What was Claudia like, Morag?"

"If you stand in front of a glass and look at your reflection, she's there and her eyes holding yours."

Back in the shed where Jersey Lily, the cow lived, I would sit with the milk bucket between my knees and my cheek against the honey-coloured side of her. "I'll have to mind her well in the hard days. A Jersey cow is a rare sight in these parts," Morag said from her perch on a rail we tied the rope to. "It came into my head that I might get a coat to put on her in the night and when I took her out. Alastair Beg has an old coat that he bought with a horse once at Obaig Sale. Leastways, he didn't buy it. It came with the horse and much good it did, for the beast died on him. He'd give it to me and welcome."

I thought of the cow in Cranford and how she fell in the lime pit and had to have a flannel coat made for her and knew that there was an element of Cranford in Corran, yet a tough cruel Cranford, where folk forced a living out of a lovely land, that had no richness except in its beauty.

We carried seaweed up from the shore and spread it on what growing land there was. We cut peat and stacked it to dry and carried it home in creels on our backs. We searched the heather for the eggs of a hen, that was 'laying away'. We fed the pig and the hens and the cow. We shut them up safe at night, for there were foxes and wildcats and all manner of predators. We chopped wood and cooked and polished and scrubbed. We cleaned every window of the salt from the sea, but of course, we did not do it all in those first few days. I got the impression that we were never idle. There was knitting for fingers and mending and sewing. Talking about knitting, there were sheep out on the mountain that were ours and when the time was right there would be the dipping and the shearing to be done and then the spinning. In the meantime, there was sheep-dogging to be seen to, for the flocks had to be watched in case a lamb fell into a gulley. The sky must be scanned for buzzards or eagles. It was a completely foreign land to me, yet there was no strangeness about it, for there was the smell of the turf smoke and did I not know how to milk a cow and make butter? Did I not know how to make bread and pastry and cake? Then conversation dripped slowly . . . a sentence at a time, and one day followed another.

"Your mother was just such a lassie, not one to sit with a trash-magazine in her hand."

"She hadn't the milking though. She

had a fear of cows, but I had an old cow those days, that was as easy as a cat would be to milk. I went in to the shed and there was Claudia, struggling with the udder and the old cow fast asleep and her whole weight down against your poor Claudia's head."

I went up to the grave every morning and left some wild flowers and sometimes, I would find other blooms there, maybe a precious cultivated flower like a single rose, that I knew would have come from a rare garden down the brae.

There was very little said in the island, but there was a depth of feeling, that I had rarely experienced, and little by little, I got some more of Claudia's story.

She had come in out of the evening with the shoes broken on her feet, but her clothes were good. They were the worse for wear, but they were not the sort of thing a beggar woman might have. She had had a suede coat, with a rent in the sleeve where it had 'caught on barb' wire' and a tweed skirt. We were out looking for the eggs of the 'the hen, that was laying away' at the time this piece of information came out.

"It wasn't Scots tweed — that skirt she had and it hadn't stood up to rain pelting down on it. She had a wool jumper, but not hand knit. It had come out of a shop. It was white, I remember, with a high neck to it. She was glad to be able to get the chance to wash it, but it went shrunk on her and she knit up another. She hadn't much hand for the knitting though, no better than you have yourself."

The facts were brought out, one by one, and neither of us needed to know whom we were talking about. I was there for a time before Fergus came to the house and always I thought that Morag wanted to tell me something of vast importance, but could not bring herself to do it. She caught me scanning the sea for Fergus, the mountains too. Then at last, one day she put an arm round my shoulder.

"He'll come tomorrow. Don't be impatient against his coming for you've had time to get straight. So has he maybe. It's better that way, with all your lives before you, but you're a bonnie lassie, Constance-Tenacity. It's sadness on me that he'll take you away and leave me lonely after you, for the happiest days on the island for me were the times when Claudia was here and the sun shining out of her and her eyes like the stars of heaven."

"Fergus is coming for a story, Morag. Don't you know he's a kind of a Press reporter. He'll be after the story for the *Leinster Tribune* — or maybe to scoop it for the National papers."

She looked at me with scorn, as well she might, for I only wanted a denial.

"It's yourself he's after and in your heart, you know it. It would serve you right justice, if it was the story he took away and left you behind on Corran, but there's no hope of that. Don't I heard what goes on in the rest of the island and he on fire with the wanting to get to you and tell you he loves you and know you love him? Get on with you out of that and stop teasing an old woman!"

The next day was when she had promised me that Fergus would arrive. In the morning I looked out through my bedroom window, down across the crofts, that clung together at the edge of the sea, with the mountains behind for protection. I might have thought it was a deserted place, but now that I knew it, it seemed as animated as one of those Dutch paintings, full of people and life. There was a straight plume of peat smoke from each dwelling and that meant that the people were up and I was not as early as I had thought. The hens had been released from their safety of the night and were clustering round, near as they could get to their owner's door, waiting for the scattered food. There were cows on their way out after the milking and sheep, that dotted the hillsides, their lambs at heel.

Alastair Beg had his boat ready for going out to pick up the lobster pots, or maybe he had just come in. He had collected his friends, like a flock of hens and they were gathered round the rock, where the boat was moored. There was conversation amongst them, but not the quick cackled talking of the hens, but slow considered speech and everything well thought out in the mind, before it came a-lilt through the mouth. There were women, who shook mats through doorways or passed leisurely along carrying buckets of water. There were black and white sheepdogs, sitting in the cool early sun.

I knew most of the people now, Big Jack and Alastair Beg and Janet, the Post, and Lachlan and two dozen others and they never failed to stop to pass the time of day, when we met. Often they dropped into the house for a strupak . . . a cup of tea or a dram, a plate of scones dripping with butter, even a plate of rashers and eggs, but that was later in the story. There was something more important today. There were voices, that reached me through the ceiling of the kitchen and perhaps Fergus had arrived. It was Janet, the Post. Morag and she had their heads close together, talking animatedly, but they stopped up short as I came down the stairs. Then Janet's face lit up.

"Sure Constance-Tenacity could mind the house for you and you'd not be gone long. She's as good a hand with a croft as any of us, by what I hear . . . "

It seemed that an urgent message had come into the Post Office for a woman that lived two miles north up the coast. Janet couldn't leave her counter in case Her Majesty's Mails wanted attention and Morag often did this sort of thing for her. I did not mind at all. I was quite content to milk the cow and get on with whatever things had to be done, and Morag would not be long. It was just a walk of two miles there and two miles back and maybe she'd just stop for her elevenses, as the English called something similar to the strupak.

She was gone and so was Janet, the Post, and there was something between them that I could only guess at, but must not be told. I worried a little in case I did not manage the croft as well as it should be managed and I worried more that Fergus would come and find me milking the cow, or forking seaweed or with my arms deep in dough and not dressed up in the best I possessed, with my face made up and my hair brushed. I need not have worried. I had plenty of time, for Morag was not back for hours. How could I know that she had gone to meet Fergus in a little bay, where the speed boat was moored — meet him by appointment and talk to him, talk to him long and earnestly and tell him the thing, that she had hesitated a hundred times to tell me. She came back in the middle of the afternoon and told me to put on my best skirt and a clean jumper and go and sit at the head of the pass. The skirt was one she had made for me in two hours the night before, but it had a Bond Street look about it. It was Hunting Stuart tartan and anybody had the right to wear the Stuart tartan, she told me, in case I was feared to wear a clan tartan without permission. I had my own green jumper to go with it and I brushed my hair till it shone, for I guessed that it was time for Fergus to come. I looked at myself in the little glass over the dressing table and I might have been another person for the colour in my face and the light in my eyes. Morag looked at me as I left the house to go up the pass.

"My! You're a bonnie, bonnie lassie. You deserve a life of happiness and I pray you get it, but God forgive me if through my fault . . ."

I half turned back to ask her what

she meant, but she waved me away and presently I sat on a stone at the head of the pass, high above the township and looked along the long sheep track that led through the green hills to the north. It was the way he would come and I was quite sure of it, quite sure too, that Claudia had meant it all to happen the way it was happening. In some strange supernatural way, her spirit had escaped the grave and she was nearby somewhere, watching me, helping me, willing good to me. There I sat with my eyes on the twisting sheep track. I could see a clear two miles down into a valley, so I must have good warning, but still he did not come. Perhaps he had forgotten all about me? Perhaps he had gone back to the mainland? He had just wanted a story and not found one and had taken himself back to Ballyboy. Yet Morag had promised me that he would come today and there had been an excitement about the whole place.

6

Signal Received

THE dead branch of a tree cracked behind me, where it lay on the path down to the houses. How could I have known that he would come this way, up from the crofts and not along the sheep track north? I had imagined Claudia had told me, but it was all a trick of the mind, just as it was a trick of the mind that she was nearby, watching me, willing me good. Fergus had come and that was all that mattered. I jumped to my feet and spun to face him and the moment crystallised in time. Somebody had stopped the clock and we stood there, almost toe to toe, our faces naked for the other to read. There was love in his, but maybe that was my imagination again. Perhaps his heart kept pace with the racing of mine. His eyes searched my face and then he looked down to my feet and up again, slowly, slowly, as if he was taking in every detail of me. I was certainly taking in every detail of him, the moleskin slacks, the old tweed jacket, the careless cravat, the deeper sun-brown on his face, the dark gravity of his eyes, the lock of black hair on his brow.

He held me by the shoulders and ran his hands down along my arms, took my hands into his and held them out from my sides, looking at me the while.

"You're just as beautiful as I remembered you," he said and no more for a while. Then he sighed.

"If you have any idea of the trouble you've caused me to run you to earth, just double it and square it, do whatever you like to it. Why did you run away from me? It would have been far better to run to me."

He sat me down on the stone where I had awaited him and squatted at my feet and I welcomed him and said how brave he had been to cross the Little Minch in 'the speedy boat' and he grinned at that and told me that that wasn't the worse of it.

"It was trying to find you on this very small island. You weren't supposed to be here. Phil had arrived but you were 'still on the way'. Then Phil was gone, silently and suddenly. There was a look in their eyes, that made me hope he made it alive. They didn't like him, the islanders, and there was a feeling in the air, that you didn't like him either."

"I don't love him," I whispered. "I don't like him even . . . not now." He just remarked that it was a very good thing Phil was gone then.

I was disappointed in his cool attitude to the whole affair. I had imagined he might take me in his arms and kiss me, but he did no such thing . . . just put a blade of grass between his teeth and said the words that rocketed my heart to the skies.

"It leaves the way clear for me."

Then he veered off that subject to another.

"I knew you had arrived, but they hid you. Damn it! Where could you be but in Morag's house, but could I get to Morag's house? I've had a wonderful holiday, climbing the mountains after eagles and taking passengers for trips in the speed boat. I've sat up and helped to deliver a cow of a fine bull calf. I've fished the seas and lifted lobsters. I think I've done Mistress McTaggart an injury with the way I made her laugh at my efforts to steer a pig into his sty. I've almost met my death at the horns of the local bull. There's only one on the island and he roams loose, or what I call loose. He hasn't even got a ring in his nose, but he's red and he has the biggest Highland horns I ever saw on a bull, even at the Obaig show. If you see him, run as fast as you can. Run like hell."

He was laughing at me, laughing at himself too.

"Every time, I turned to the south I was headed off. I made it here one day, but Morag's house was all shut up and there was no sign of you, or of her either and they all spoke Gaelic. They couldn't understand a word I said, but they were mightily interested in me. There wasn't a soul — man, woman or child, that did not come to have a look at me. Then some character called Alastair Beg presented my with a lobster the size of a lamb and saw me to the borders of the homestead. He 'rode me off' and I was picked out by the natives that were supposed to be entertaining me. Their hospitality has nearly killed me. They had celebrations — pronounced 'cayleys', that went on till dawn and you were supposed to tell stories and sing songs and drink Highland malt whisky like water, and the next day, up the sheer face of a cliff, with two eagles protecting their young . . . but every time I managed to get the boat out and turned towards the south, there was a reef that was dangerous or one of the passengers felt sick and wanted to go ashore or Mistress McTaggart thought she had left the bread in the peat oven and it would be destroyed on her, if she did not get home straight away. Don't ever question Scots hospitality to me. If I hadn't had my mind set on finding you, I'd have enjoyed myself more than I ever have enjoyed a holiday and at last they told me you were safe and promised I would see you when the time was right. Then Morag came, this morning. She had made some excuse to you, for she had to talk to me — "

"So that was where she went?"

"It's north up the coast a piece

from here. God! Constance-Tenacity! Everybody on this island knows everything about everything. They're all in it and have been in it from the start, and this part is serious, for perhaps the law was bent a bit. There's something I have to tell you and you may not like it. You may not agree with it. You may even think it was wicked. Morag is frightened about something she did a long time ago."

It had to do with Claudia. Of course it had. I got a hollow feeling in my stomach, that he was going to tell me something that would bull-doze my new-found happiness and make rubble of it.

"We talked about it for a long time this morning and I said you must be told. They left the decision to me. So I'll tell you tonight, or maybe she'll tell you herself, if she can bring herself to do it. Don't look as if the world is coming to an end, for it is not. She did the right thing all that long time ago. If she had not had the courage to do it, I'd never have met you, but we'll wait till the curtains are drawn and the lamps are lit. Just for now, I'm going to take you in my arms and kiss you. It may not have come to your attention, but we're sitting up here in full view of the houses. I'll lay a bet there's not one window without a face behind a curtain. Don't you think it high time that I gave a demonstration of the fact that I love you as much as Robbie Burns loved 'his red, red Rose' and that I will love you 'till a' the seas gang dry'?"

And that is just what he did — the demonstration I mean.

Yet for all I walked through the stars and with moons soaring round my head, I had to come back to earth again, find myself still at the top of the rise. We went together down the hill and came towards Morag's house and there we found the population had appeared again and were anxious to shake Fergus by the hand and bid him welcome. We progressed past the crofts, with many pauses for conversation and often with flocks of chickens round our feet looking for crumbs from the stranger's table. Even the cows out at pasture, turned their faces to watch our progress and the sheep gathered together on the hills as if they discussed all that was happening below.

We reached Morag's house at last and a great many people came in for a strupak, but at last they were gone. The evening had come down and Morag looked unhappy. I knew why. There was no longer any excuse for putting off what she thought might be a confession of wrong.

There is no place more comfortable than Morag's kitchen, no place more fitted to the telling of secrets, no place more secret, with the sound of the sea in your ears and the wind whispering at the window panes ... with the peat fire glowing on the flat hearthstone, sending its incense up by way of the wide chimney breast to the star-lit sky above, with the kettle singing on the hob, steaming a little but pushed to one side against the time when we might want a cup of tea. There was a wide chimney piece with hooks where the pots hung and standing on the stone was a three-legged pot, that any tourist would have gloated over. They might have bought a miniature of it any place in Scotland or in Ireland and brought it home to grace a foreign house in the Americas, attached great sentiment to the way their ancestors would have cooked in such an iron vessel, bacon and cabbage, or perhaps potatoes, in the lean days. Yet in a few days, I had learned how to pull the Scots frying pan over the fire and cook rashers and eggs. I had learnt a deal of things in my short visit with Morag and not the least was that to Morag, I was Claudia, come back to tread the earth again and she loved me and I loved her.

Now the curtains were pulled against the night and the round-globed lamp was lit and the hearth was tidied and Morag had pulled the chairs up to the white-scrubbed table. If she were facing her judgment, and it seemed that she was, for some strange reason that I could in no way understand, she preferred to face it sitting at the scrubbed table, her face sharp and sad and serious, her hands clenched. In front of her was the bundle wrapped in heavy rich white silk.

She had gone to the dresser and unlocked a drawer, in a house where nothing was ever locked, in an island where no door was ever barred and she had taken out a folded bundle, the sort of thing Dick Whittington might have hung on the end of his stick as he set out for London, but much more rich and costly in its appearance.

We sat about the table, one of us at either side of her and she looked at Fergus for help. He nodded his head and began the description of Claudia and her arrival at the island. Some of this I knew already, but I said nothing. Claudia had come from nowhere and she had never divulged who she was, nor why she came, nor whence, nor anything else. She had fitted in and all the people had come to love her, for she was made for love.

As Fergus said this, his eyes found mine and he told me with never a word between us, that I was made for love too and that he would love me till a' the seas went dry and the rocks melted in the sun . . .

Then the last hours of Claudia drew a sadness into the dim room. She had her baby and there were no ambulances, no nurses, no transfusions, no helicopters, no doctor for twenty miles and the sea at tempest.

Morag interrupted him then, but it was

no interruption just a soft plea for mercy from me.

"She gave you to me, acushla. I knew there was no saving her and she knew it too by then and she hadn't thought such a thing might ever happen. I don't think she ever thought of death and why should she? She was so young."

There was near silence. Only the sea murmured its eternity and the clock on the mantel ticked out the hopelessness of man, think he might live for ever. There was an ash log on the fire and it gave off a cannonade of grey smoke, as if it laughed at the foolishness of the human race. Morag was back nigh on twenty years in this same house and her fingers were caressing the bundle, stroking it and pleating the heavy silk of it, holding it between her hands and turning it first one way and then another, as she spoke. Her eyes never left it.

"She said very little. She was almost gone. I had bandaged her legs and arms to keep all the blood that was left, to go to her heart. The doctor from the other island told us to do it. He kept sending messages through Janet, the Post, on the battery wire down at the Post Office. He was the only help we had. It was like a devil's dream, yet it was real enough, with the blood running away and running away and nothing to stop it. There were other women with us, wise women, who knew about childbed. Then at the end, she sent them away, just for a whilie ... said there was something she had to say to me."

"They looked at her and they didn't want to go, but she begged them, said she knew there was no time left to her ... and they went at last. She had this bundle under the pillow and she asked me to give it to her. She had you in her arms still and I set the bundle beside you at her elbow. Then she gave you to me, Honey. Her voice was a whisper. I had to put my ear against her lips."

"You're to have her, Morag," she said. "It doesn't matter any more. Her father doesn't want her and I'll be away. Love her ... the way you've loved me ... best you can ... best you can. It's all I ask you ... do the best you can for her, for there's little I have to leave her."

"She pushed the bundle towards me

and I picked it up, pushed it under the bed and put my arm about her. She was almost gone, but still something troubled her."

"Hide it away in a drawer, Morag. Please . . . "

"I could not make her rest easy, till I did as she asked me and when I got back to the bed, she was on her way — away. She gave a long sigh and her eyes filled with tears."

"That's all I have to leave her . . . strange heirloom. Keep it safe for her, Morag . . . and don't tell . . . don't tell . . . "

Then she was gone and the other women were coming back into the room.

Fergus leaned across the table and lifted the bundle from Morag as tenderly, as if he lifted a new-born baby. He smiled encouragement at me and his voice was his normal cheerful voice, that drove back the past to its proper place, with all the dark things, that had come back to linger in the corners of the house.

"So there's your inheritance, Constance-Tenacity. I daresay you'll make no more of it than Morag has done, for she told me all about it and it's a mystery to me, just as it was to her, why Claudia kept the things and made a secret of them . . . only gave them to Morag when she knew she was dying."

I opened back the knots that held the rich white silk. There was a hand-made embroidery on the edge of the silk square, beautifully done with the initials C.C. I spread out the fabric and looked with amazement at what it contained and Fergus picked out a necklace.

"There's an heirloom for you," he said, "but the other things, there's no more sense in them than ''Twas brillig' and Mimsy or the blood on the stones at Puck's Castle."

I took the necklace from his fingers and it was round my neck, yet I could not remember putting it there, six inches past my waist and made of wood, honey-coloured wood, in beads . . . and a small ticket with MADE IN JAPAN. There were eight beads all told, and separated by a black chain and first came an egg-shaped bead and then a square one and each with a gold binding at either end. It was like a strange rosary, but there were only eight beads to it, so maybe it might be a prayer you were making to a foreign god. I took it from round my neck and wound it about my wrist and it went five times round that. It fitted my throat round twice. There was a beauty to it that was all its own and it clinked out a small sound and there was a happiness about it, out of all proportion to its monetary value, for surely it had no monetary value. Yet I loved it at first sight and I have loved it ever since, but now I was turning to look at the other things, I picked up a white bone-handled penknife, a good strong knife, 'MADE IN THE REPUBLIC OF IRELAND.' It was a weapon, that would have been without price to Robin Crusoe. Then there was a key-ring, white plastic 'MADE IN HONG KONG,' with a flower on the side of it and something that looked like a whistle ... a whistle for one of the Seven Dwarfs, but there was silence to it, only a tiny battery light that came on, when you pushed the flower that decorated its side ... still came on after eighteen years. "Curioser and curioser," I thought, and knew I was caught up with

Alice in Wonderland again and with the children that had sung outside my room at night . . .

"Boys and girls come out to play. The moon doth shine as bright as day."

My fingers searched with tenderness through the jumble of such things, that might delight the heart of any child. Here was a paintbox, in grey metal, a tiny thing, but quite perfect. Inside, the small oblongs of paint were as they had been when it left the shop, yellow and red and purple, brown and green and black and a tiny brush and under it was 'MADE IN ENGLAND'. It was such a thing that I might have loved at one time. Indeed, I loved it now. It was a paint box fit for a doll to play with. There were more sophisticated things too. There seemed no end to the contents of the silk square, but now I picked it up and looked again at the initials C.C. and they were done by hand in tiny stitches, each stitch perfection, worked by dainty fingers. Yet there was more richness. I spread the square down on the table and went on with my Aladdin's cave search.

"She left these things for you, my

darling. That was all she left."

Fergus's voice was in the background and I only half heard him, for now between my fingers was a black cigarette holder, tipped with gold, the sort of thing where the mouthpiece comes up to eject the spent cigarette. There was a metal gadget too and I identified it in a short while, as a combined bottle opener. It had three different shapes to it, so that you could prize the cap off a bottle or punch a hole in a can or just lift off the frilly top of a drink. There was a model racing car, two inches long and a driver with a red helmet, who sat at the wheel and he came from Israel. There was an Indian, fashioned in a marvellous way but not more than four inches tall, yet his limbs moved in any way you moved them and stayed where you put them and he had a head of Indian feathers and a tomahawk and a knife, a green painted centre to him, that would hide his nakedness. For all his savagery, there was a genial look about his face and no war paint. There seemed to be no end to the bounty of my heirlooms. There was a blue plastic case and in it there was a scissors and a nail file, even an eyebrow tweezers and the whole thing most neat and from *Hong Kong* again. From Hong Kong too came the red plastic container, dwarf sized, but beautifully fitted out with a handle and all the gadgets that screwed into it . . . the screwdriver, the plain probe and another thing I could not identify, that ended in a twist and I thought it might make holes and you screwed a screw in afterwards, if you wanted something like a cup-hook. Last of all, or almost last, was a text, two pictures back to back enclosed in a clear cellophane case with a brown ribbon to put round your neck, coloured like a brown shoe lace, pictures of the Madonna and child. In one she wore a yellow robe and in the other her traditional blue and the baby Jesus was sitting, proud in her arms. It was MADE IN THE U.S.A. and I thought that surely the gifts had been gathered from a wide harvest. Underneath the virgin was the same text, on each side.

PRAY FOR US.

I almost missed the last thing of all, for it was gilt and brown and there had been so many small things, but this might have fitted to the necklace as a pendant and it was beautifully contrived, though what it was for, I could not guess . . . another key ring, most likely.

There was a miniature strap, that might hold a key ring, sure enough, but it held a small gilt keg. The strap had a gilt buckle and a chain that suspended the barrel. There were leather looking rings that bound the barrel, and to my unsophisticated eyes, it looked like great craftsmanship. It seemed heavy and I wondered if it might be full of diamonds, but it was too small for that and there was no way of opening it . . . and that was the end of my treasure trove. I sat there and looked down at all the tiny, pretty things and could think of no reason why Claudia should have attached such importance to them. Presumably she would know the child, she was bearing, would like them, but what of bottle openers and cigarette holders? My mind searched round and found the memory of the man on Obaig Pier, who said a lady had given him a gadget to clean his pipe. He had thought I was she. There was a chance that she *was* Claudia, but a slim chance. Still, maybe Claudia had passed that way and maybe she had given him the pipe-cleaner, for it would match up with the array of things laid out before us on the table. He had the time right and she had been my twin, almost twenty years on, on the same path. Perhaps?

My mind was drawn back by the sorrow of Morag's voice, so filled with repentance and doubt.

"I locked that drawer up. I never told a living soul! Not for a long time, the silk handkerchief too. I folded it and put it away. She had given you to me and you were mine . . . mine . . . mine. Then the baby across at Lissarinka was sick and there was no God in heaven could save it. Her need was greater than mine. I was just a lonely woman, but with my health and strength — and friends and neighbours. It was the devil made me hide the things. I did it in the first to keep you for myself. When the polis came, I left the scarf and that, left them lie in the drawer. They might have traced the child. A picture in the paper of that scarf and surely, there would have been a person to come forward? I knew it was wrong, and I'd burn in hell for it. I decided to go into Obaig and tell the polis — tell them that I had told a lie when I said I thought Claudia had no people. Then the letter came, saying the baby was dying at Lissarinka and I saw that God had punished me in his own way. I had to give you up, no matter how I wanted a wean. You had a rich future there, past anything I could offer you, on this hungry coast."

Her words fell into the stillness of the room like black pebbles flung down into a well of loneliness, one by one and slowly now and she was back in the years that were gone.

"I called them here for a counsel, the people of Corran. They all loved you. I made a clean breast of what I had done — told them of the other wean and the way there was no years left to it. I said I must bring Claudia's baby to Lissarinka and there were plenty agen it. You were a fine bairn, whom the good Lord had sent, with good luck in your fist for the island. Then they agreed that you must go. Alastair Beg took me to

Obaig in the lobster boat and I got the train from there. You were as good as gold the whole way, not a peep out of you, but happy as a blessed creature. I loved you so much that there was a pain in my chest when I stood on the front step at Lissarinka . . . and now maybe you'll curse me for not trying to find out who your dada was, for Claudia was married. There was the scar of the ring on her finger and round her neck her wedding ring on a chain . . . buried with her. Maybe I broke his heart as well as my own, yet it's been a grand thing to have you back here, even if it's only for a whileen. Don't hate me for what I did, for there's no doubt, I hid out evidence that might have found your real folk for you."

Morag's hands were work worn and her fingers were sanded from the sewing and the knitting and the cooking and the weaving. Her face was as weathered, as any seaman's from the winds that blew in from the Atlantic, from the rains that beat across the island, from the Scots mists that hid the beauty of the mountains. Her body was leathered from the life she led. Her hair was white as the mountain caps in winter and perhaps it was sorrow that had caused that. Yet now, she sat opposite me at the scrubbed table, her hands clenched, her face lined and scratched with the care, that was upon her. Even the upright proud shoulders were bent down a little and still her eyes would not lift to mine. Fergus was watching me, waiting for a verdict and I put out a hand and pushed away my inheritance in its rich silk kerchief.

"I'd have liked it fine if you'd kept me on the island, Morag. I can't think of anything better than to live here and have a whole Scots island to love me and care for me. Money isn't anything. Only happiness counts. You and I would have been happy here. I wish you could have kept me, for that's my first choice — never to have to leave Corran and its people — and yourself, but you were caught by life. There was this other child in Lissarinka and no hope for it and there was a situation planked down in front of you by circumstances. It might have seemed very easy to some, but it was no easy thing you did. God knows how many people you marked out for happiness, with no thought of your own. There were so many in Lissarinka, that wouldn't have been happy any more. Mimsy would have died. You took a label and you set me out for riches and comfort and success. You turned me into a privileged child, with love on every side of me. You let your own love for me go hungry. I honour you, Morag, more than any other person I know, for what you did for my sake."

"But your real father?" she whispered and her hands were brown-clenched, her knuckles as white as the table.

I was over-young to give the judgement of Solomon but I gave it now.

"I know what Claudia was like. I've got a very real vision of her for what she was, since I came here. She was no silly child-bride to run away in a pet, because she had a falling out with my father. She chose to leave him and go away and she must have known I was already conceived, though I suppose there's no proof of that."

"She never spoke of it. She may have

known when she left him, but she may not. She had left home in the middle of the night and nothing but the clothes she stood up in — that and your bundle of strange possessions."

"If she left him, I don't want him. I stand by her decision. I don't want any part of him then or now."

I stopped up short and wondered what power had closed my lips up so suddenly then. I knew it was Claudia again, somewhere at my elbow in the darkened kitchen, the part of her that had escaped the grave to call me to come to her. There was something that troubled her, something she wanted done and she could not rest easy in her grave, till I had done it.

I told them this and my words were uneasy. I drew back the silk square and my fingers idled through the contents. I clicked the necklace round and knew I could not change anything, even at this stage. I thanked Morag again for what she had done for me. I went round the table and took her in my arms and was unhappy at the thin unprosperous state of her shoulders. God knows if she had enough to live on in the winter, but I could see to that. Vaguely I made a promise to myself to bring prosperity to Corran and I would have the means to do it one day. There was something to be done first, so that Claudia could rest on the side of the hill. Somewhere in the back of my mind, I blamed Ireland and all Bessie's upbringing for the superstition, that was a part of me. I believed with all my heart that there were people, who could not lie easy in their graves, and I believed that Claudia was such a one.

"Morag, I've got to do this. I hope Fergus will help me and I promise no blame will ever fall on you. I've got to get right to the heart of the whole story and find out why Claudia left my father and who he was, but I want no part of him and I never shall. My parents are at Lissarinka and they'll always be my parents, but this inheritance can't be spurned without some effort on my part to find out where it came from and why . . . and other things. We'll still keep it secret. Only Claudia will know and then she'll rest tranquil."

I walked over to stand with my back to the turf glow and I reached out my arms to Morag.

"Give in to me in this. I love you, Morag. I'll never put any mother above you. I owe you everything I am. Let me go and find out who Claudia was."

She smiled at me sombrely and shook her head.

"You've got wisdom past your years. They say Claudia walks the hillside on moonlit nights and that she has something on her soul. Come back and see me an odd time and don't leave for a while yet. Just stay a week or two, till you've overcome the battle up the weir like a salmon does, in the run of the year. Rest quiet and then go, but come back the odd time. I was thinking that the things in the silk kerchief were a kind of sign. They come from all the corners of the earth and it's like the gifts, that were carried to the Holy . . . gold and frankincense and myrrh. There must be a big importance to them, else she'd not have carried them all those long weary miles, not only for a bairn to play with. There must have been something very important indeed that she kept tight hold on them, till the breath was leaving her body and her soul on its way to heaven."

So we sat there and talked and our minds were in complete agreement, one with the other, and a fine future we planned for Fergus and myself, for Morag and the whole island and not a bit of what we planned that did not come true, or perhaps there was. We talked the hours away and they crept in, the Island folk for they knew there was something important in council.

I was never quite sure if they had seen the small items of my heritage or whether they had not, for they had a way of closing up like clams. We sat round the room and when there were no more chairs, was there not plenty of space on the wood form and after that on the floor? The bottles appeared and were passed round. Morag and Janet the Post, myself, half a score of other ladies passed more solid nourishment and presently an old man, who was known as the 'Prophet' began a long saga in the Gaelic and everybody listened to it, as if were the ten commandments heard for the first time. My eyes were weary with the desire for sleep, and I could not understand any part of it, except the odd word, that belonged to the Irish, I had learned at school and that was no help at all. Then suddenly, he fixed me with an eye as piercing as any the ancient mariner could have had and he spoke out clearly in the Sassenach tongue, his white beard making him prophet indeed.

"Mind yoursel' well, lassie. Maybe it's in your head that it's a fine thing to live happily ever after, but there's one that walks this earth and he'd like well to see you in your coffin and laid beside your deid mother. Watch out in the darkness. I tell you, Fergus Kennedy, keep guard on her with all the strength in your braw arm, for there's death that walks towards herself . . . and maybe no power on earth to stop it."

At that the party broke up and everybody called down shame on the Prophet that he could drink so much as to descend to speaking the Sassenach tongue and with such wicked lies in his mouth too. They begged Fergus and myself to pay no heed to him and turned back the topic to the things that still lay in the silk kerchief on the table. There were wild guesses about what they might be, but not an idea in any head, not but that there were many heads too fuddled with the product of some of 'the wee stillies in the hills' to know what they were talking about. They went home when the sun was well up the sky and it was time to let out the hens and milk the cows, so wearily we got on with the tasks of the day. Yet all the time, I held in my mind, the picture of a white kerchief still white against a scrubbed kitchen table and the things that had lain inside it for almost twenty years . . . the necklace, the barrel, the paint box, the cigarette holder, the bottle opener . . . all so small and all so delicately made and from the four corners of the world . . . and in my mind that picture stayed, till one night near the end of our stay on Corran I had it. I knew what they were. I knew where they must have come from. I could even conjure up circumstances that might fit the whole picture, but I said nothing to anybody, not even to Fergus, just kept the knowledge close to my heart. Then one day, when it was very calm and the sea was a tame animal, instead of a savage beast, Fergus and I said goodbye to Morag and to Corran. We stepped into the speed boat and went out across the Little Minch with a wake astern and our bows lifted up to face into the future, and no thought in our heads that the future was not as bright and happy as any future ever was. We had promised to come back soon and we fully intended to keep that promise, and very soon too.

The journey across the Atlantic to Obaig was one of those magic travels, that took no time at all. There are some days, when you go from one place to another and it is a long weary trip, that seem never to come to its ending. Then another time, the whole thing is done in a space of time, that passes quickly as from one moment to the next. It is all bound up with happiness and with who your companion may be, with youth and health perhaps, but they are not essentials. Perhaps your mind has interesting problems to solve, or something excessively good to find at the end of the day. Yet you can have all these things and still know that miles drag long and the day runs slow. This time, we left Corran and there were a great many difficult sea miles to be raced, but looking back, it was all done in a flash, and that was quite impossible. Bessie would certainly agree with me that there was magic about, for in no time at all, we were turning round the point at the end of Kerrera and slowing down to make the speed boat secure at her usual mooring.

Perhaps it was that night or the next night, that I told Fergus about the old man on Obaig Pier, who had mistaken me for Claudia. I know that Fergus had made his peace with the Manager about his abduction of the speed boat, but the Manager was as easy-going as the people of Corran. He used the boat mainly for his own use and he had been too busy for the last few days. It had been a good excuse not to have to take visitors out for trips up the Sound of Mull, for that was one of his chores, and a tiresome one when there was work, that would have to be finished late at night, if he couldn't get at it in the afternoon.

"Besides, you had to go out to Corran and fetch your affianced bride. It was a fine romantic way to go about it — don't know how else you'd have gone, for it's a world of its own. I think it's the most isolated place in the islands. There's nothing there but sheep and a few crofters. They keep themselves to themselves."

I cornered Fergus over dinner and said I was glad to hear that I was 'his affianced bride'.

"I know I've been in a hazy sort of state, but I can't seem to remember anything so definite as a proposal and an acceptance and a notice in *The Times*."

He grinned at me across the table and dared me to repeat the statement I had just made. He could not know the affair of honour that a 'dare' had been in the old days, nor what the consequence of Phil's last dare to me had been.

"I never refuse a dare."

"If you repeat that last remark, as I said just now, I promise you that I'll get up from this table and put my table napkin down on the carpet. I'll kneel down and propose formally to you for your hand in marriage. I'll go on to tell you my prospects and promise that I will love you and cherish you till the day I die . . . also of course, that I will keep you in the state of life to which you have been accustomed."

We were very merry about it and very much in love. Then I remembered how I had arrived in Obaig and I told him that I had had one shoe that had a sole half off . . . Then the old seaman jumped into my memory and I told Fergus all about him. Fergus was full of enthusiasm at once, fired with imagination. We must find this man and he would be somewhere about.

"We're playing Sherlock Holmes, my darling. We can use every clue we can find."

It was a warm night and we walked along the front when we had finished dinner. His arm was tucked companionably in mine and I would have been content to walk along for ever, with the sun gone down behind Kerrera and the sky a glory of red to delight any sailor's heart. We went right down to the place where the trawlers had come in and watched the unloading of a catch. The seamen were dressed in salt-crusted, rusty rose jerseys and jeans and pink knitted caps with a pink bobble on top and they looked ready to take the stage at Drury Lane in a marvellous new musical show. We watched and there was a magic there as it had been on the journey from Corran, but I knew it was Fergus, that turned everything to glory for my senses. I knew at last what it was to fall in love and inhabit this new kind of world and then I remembered that we were sleuths on the trail of something that might be less romantic. We went back along the front and found him, my old seaman, near the ticket place on the pier again, drowsing on a bench with his back up against the side of one of the buildings. I put a hand on his shoulder and felt like somebody on an identification parade. He was disorientated for a moment and then his eyes fastened on mine.

"So ye cam' back. I waur thinkin' ye micht."

We had a conversation for the next half hour and things were conducted in a slow gentlemanly way, such as is the custom in Scotland.

I could not rush in like a bull at a red flag and ask him what I wanted to know. Besides, Fergus had gone off to a shop across the road and was back presently with some 'baccy' and I loved Fergus for knowing that this had been the right thing to do, loved him and loved him and knew that this was the way life would be between him and me, gentle and understanding and kind ... never harsh cruel, or ugly.

The old man's eyes lit up at the sight of the 'baccy' and he put his hand in his pocket to find the coin to pay for it, for a Highlander is nothing, if he is not a proud man.

Fergus was quick enough to grasp the situation for he explained that he had no intention of being in a man's debt and had not Himself helped his affianced bride on her journey to Corran?

So the old man introduced himself and his name was 'Tam' and he had a Scots brogue, that you could cut with a knife, and it made communication that bit difficult.

"And how was the lobster fishing on Corran this year?" he asked after he had made many extravagant remarks about the 'affianced bride'.

It was like finding out an oat from a bag of chaff. He took out his pipe with a suspicious eagerness, ground the tobacco between his horny palms and filled the pipe, tamped it down with the same gadget, he had used before and when he had finished and had the pipe ready to light, I took the little object out of his hand, while Fergus gave him the box of matches, that went with the baccy.

The pipe cleaner was marked MADE IN SHEFFIELD and it was a good candidate to be blood brother to the little things in the white silk scarf. The people who had made these things were craftsmen, yet there was no great fortune for the making. It was what the civilised sophisticated world made of them in places that might be far away, where cash registers ring the sound of success. The makers' hands would be poor; as Tam's hands were. I loved Tam with a love born straight from pity, for I knew, though how I knew it, I do not know, that he had had no 'baccy' for a few days. Tomorrow was pension day. For all I knew, he might be hungry and pension day would still be tomorrow. Claudia had loved him, just as I loved him. She had had nothing to give him, but one of her small treasures.

"I think my mother gave you this pipe cleaner," I remarked casually. "She came through the Pier and you were having trouble with your pipe. It was blocked on you and she had just the right gadget."

I got a flood of 'braid Scots' at that and interpreted it not a quarter, except how was 'Her Leddyship', and did she still reside on Corran and were all her weans as bonnie as mysel'?

"She's dead."

He seemed to shrink into himself at that, asked in a whisper if she lay in the green grave on the black and we knew the green grave was the sea. He tried to comfort us and he mixed up one generation with the other and sometimes it was me, he spoke about and sometimes Claudia. Then would come a lucid spell and his brain as sharp as a needle.

"She was a gentle bonnie lassie and

she had a white silk scarf and all sorts of wee articles in it and she giv' me the pipe instrument, like you said."

"When?" said Fergus and again "When?"

Tam had been thinking it over the other night after seeing her come through the second time, but of course that would be myself. It had been eighteen-nineteen years before . . . it was just after Christmastide . . . St. Stephen's Day, no, it was nearer to Hogmanay. It was easy enough to remember for he lost his job a day or two after . . . got a wee bittie drunk on Hogmanay . . . lost his job at MacBraynes, but it was no matter. He got a good post on an ocean-going collier and he was out of the country for years. There would have been no chance of him hearing news of Corran. It was all adding up.

He looked at me in confusion and wandered into his old age again.

"But I saw you not two weeks ago. I'd ha' been at sea by then. The collier was a man short, when she docked here and they took me on. Och! That's na' the way o' it. It was yer mither. It perplexed me how a high-born lassie could come all the way frae Lunnon, on her feet with her shoes wore out, picking a lift where she could, runnin' as if the de'il waur at her heels. She was bowed down with sorrow and at Christmas too and her a married woman, for she wore a ring, but there're not all wed, that hae rings on their fingers . . . "

He sighed.

"Her name was Claudia. She did na' tell me what her ither name waur."

How could we say we did not know it either? We had tried to explain what we wanted to know, but always the vagueness came down like the clouds, that were gathering on the horizon.

"She died on Corran when I was born," I said. "I never knew her and she never knew me."

"Do you tell me?" he exclaimed shocked and there was talk of how the Almighty could allow such a thing to happen, but in the Islands, life was not a vale of milk and honey, like it was the other side of the Border.

"But they tell me it's a rat-race the

ither side of the Border," he went on and that "Hadrian was the canny mon, to hae pit up sich a defence, but they get past it now in charabangs and in cars and on motorbikes, even tramping the countryside in short breeks, leaving rubbitch every place they traverse."

Fergus put his arm through mine and invited me in silence to see that there was humour in any situation. It was a great property he had, of calling forth laughter from tears. Now he was inviting me to notice that Hadrian had set up his famous Wall against the English and not the Scots, to the old sailor's way of history.

"So Claudia came from beyond the Border?" he said aloud, casting a line over the trout pool.

"She cam' frae Lunnon, frae a fine hoose, but she were called away sudden and no time to bring her traps wi' her. I thought after that mebbe somebody died on her. She cam' frae Lunnon, but she were a country lassie."

He looked up at me with intent eyes and the glass of his mind clouded over again. I was Claudia again and of course,

I'd know for myself that I didn't like Lunnon.

"Just tak' a keek at ye and ye ken ye're country bred. Ye stood ower there with yer airms stretched oot tae the sea and ye tuk in great braiths of fresh air."

"Isn't it a bonnie thing to suck in clean air after the filth of a big city?"

"That's whit she said tae me."

We were collecting Sherlock Holmes facts, one by one.

I stood squarely opposite the old man and looked him in the eye, asked him if I were so like my mother, that he added us both up and made one person. He looked back at me very soberly.

"If ye waur to stand afore a glass, wid ye no see her again, even if she's in the black grave? She'd cam' walking oot tae ye. Her left hand wid be yer right and her right hand yer left, for that's hoo it is, wi' a glass on the wa'. They say a mon can never see himsel' as he truly is, but wi' right tae left and left tae right. I dinna understand a deal of it, the noo."

"But you're certain sure she came from Lunnon," I pursued him and he smiled at me.

"But you'll ken that for yoursel' lassie. She went back there or I think she went back, but she can't have gane back . . . not if she sleeps on Corran . . ."

★ ★ ★

As for the island of Corran, the Manager of the Hotel had the last word on that.

He stood on the steps of the hotel to bid us goodbye.

"And this isle, you're so interested in, it's a gey strange land. It's miles from civilisation and none the worse off for that. The folk have turned their back on the rest of us and what we're making of the Highlands. They've got no law on Corran, but their own, you ken. They don't give a damn for electricity laid on or for piped T.V. They incline to the belief that such Inventions come direct from the devil, like the Revenue men. The Revenue men are for ever putting their noses into other people's business, kegs of whisky washed up on the sands and harvest that's rightly theirs. I mean it's rightly the Islanders' or rightly the tax man's, depending whether you live on the land or the sea . . . "

He walked down to the car and opened the door to put me in my seat.

"The people of Corran do far better than the rest of us. There's peace out there. Haste ye back. We'll lay on a craft safer than 'the speedy boat' and you can sail off among the islands for your honeymoon. Goodbye now and mind how you go."

A hundred miles to the south, we stopped the car and walked up a heather hill to have our packed picnic lunch. There was chicken and Scots rolls and butter, fresh crisp salad too and plastic knives and forks, that might have surprised Morag. The butter was done up neatly in cubes of silver paper, very different from the way we had it at Lissarinka, served in a generous circle, six inches across with a cow punched out on the side of it or maybe a shamrock or a Scots thistle, There were throwaway beakers for the wine. The plates were throwaway cardboard and the plastic cutlery was throw-away. Fergus said that if we did not soon stop this throw-away cult, we would all be sitting on top a plastic throw-away mountain, that would be quite indestructible. Still, it was a wonderful lunch, with Scots tablet, as they call 'fudge' up there, and sherry trifle with enough sherry and to spare, to get the taste of it.

When we were finished, I lay back in the heather.

"The things in the white scarf, Fergus. I wanted to wait till we were on our way. I can't see the significance, but I know what they are. I think you know too."

He propped himself up on his elbow and looked down at me.

"Morag knew," he said, "I'm quite sure of it. I don't rightly understand why we all three put up such a smoke screen of ignorance. I think it's this delicacy about a man's feeling that's so strong on Corran. I imagine that nobody else there knew what your inheritance was. Morag was too kind to say out loud that all you'd got was a handful of Christmas cracker charms. A dowry is an important thing on Corran and there wasn't one that would put tongue to the words that a fine milch cow would have been worth a cartload of such stuff as Claudia had left behind her."

"Oh, Fergus. Of course, they were Christmas cracker novelties but you and I know the great value of them. They're teeming with clues. Alter what old Tam has told us, we know Claudia lived in London. She left near enough to Christmas and it all adds up."

He took up the trail for me. It was the Christmas before I had been born. Something awful must have happened to make her leave the house, the hotel, the party, whatever it was . . . in such a hurry, that she took only her handbag and the collection of charms.

"Maybe she was setting the Christmas table," he said, but I struck that off at once.

"No, that's not right. The crackers had been pulled. The dinner was over. Claudia must have been clearing up the table . . . probably made a pile of the little novelties the way one does, and they were expensive crackers, the kind that come from Harrod's or maybe Fortnum's. Why did she take them with her? It makes no sense. Oh, Fergus, do you think we'll ever find out who she was and why nobody came looking for her?"

"Morag made slightly sure that nobody came looking for her," he said drily. "She wanted you for Lissarinka and she bent a few rules and every single body on Corran aided her and abetted her. Small chance the 'polis' would have against the inhabitants, when their minds were made up. Anyhow, I'm glad it happened the way it did. I met you and you met me."

There was a lovely interlude on the side of a Scots hill, when he demonstrated just how glad he was. We talked personal intimate details, that would interest nobody but our two selves.

We went back to the car at last and decided that we would go through Edinburgh. We had been so absorbed in each other that we took a wrong turn somewhere and agreed that it was a great advantage. Neither of us had ever seen Edinburgh from the Castle and it was high time we did. Then we walked along the Royal Mile, went over and looked into the windows of the shops in Prince's Street. Then it seemed to have grown very late indeed. It was far too late to face the drive down the A1. We booked into a hotel and had a wonderful dinner, but we were so very happy in each other's company, that I can remember nothing of what we ate. I went down to breakfast the next morning and saw Fergus coming out of one of the phone booths. He had been fixing up accommodation in London, he said, and over good Scots porage and bacon and egg, he told me.

"Con McCracken has a houseboat on the Thames, shares it with some of his Dartmouth pals. It's empty at the moment for he's at base just now. They're off to sea on some exercise tomorrow. He says we're welcome to camp out there."

We set our faces towards the south later on and by now the mountains were just a beautiful memory. On we went down the main path to London, on roads where Speed is King and it's every man for himself. We were glad when we found Con's boat. All the way from the border, we had turned the question of the identity of Claudia over and over and over again. We had discussed what must be done next with the material we had garnered so far. He was well in with Fleet Street, and through crime reporting, with the police. Yet we must not involve the police too officially. There was a chap called Inspector Stafford, that could keep a thing 'off the cuff'. Then there was a man called Fleming. Fergus had been at school with Fleming and Fleming was something on the *Telegraph*, so there was the 'Old Boy Network', so out of fashion today, but still capable of miracles.

We were tired of talking about in circles. It was exciting to find the houseboat and go aboard.

"Everything will be ship-shape and Bristol fashion," laughed Fergus. "You know Con. I've been regretting not having my own flat any longer — but this is far better."

Of course, there was no provisioning and that had to be done. The basic stuff was there, the pepper, mustard and salt, as I said and tins of many useful foods, but it was fun to play house. I changed into black jeans and a sweater and rope-soled pull-on canvas shoes, that

I had bought in Prince's Street. Fergus appeared in sun-bleached slacks and a sail cloth jacket and so we set up home together. We found shops. We chose goods. We carted a big cardboard box containing everything we could think of. It was satisfying to come back to the boat, at the dying of the day. We tidied everything away into lockers, fixed up bunks, poured drinks, stretched ourselves comfortably on the long seats, that ran one each side of the main cabin. The sun was a long path across the water and there was no sound except the lapping of the Thames against the pilings, that, and the sirens of the ships on the river.

Then hunger drove us into the galley. We had Scotch broth to start with and it came from Fortnum and Mason's.

"Fortnum's," I said. "That's where those crackers came from."

Back into my mind sailed the picture of Fortnum's at Christmas and the cracker department and the one time I had been taken there by 'Father', as a big treat. There had been special crackers, in white or in red or in blue maybe. They cost a fortune, but it was a special occasion as my first visit to London. There had been an old man, who had served us, in pin-striped trousers and black jacket. He flashed on the screen of my mind and was gone again, but I filed his picture away and listened to Fergus, who was demonstrating his skill at making omelettes.

"I must get my hands on a missing persons' list," he was saying. "It shouldn't be impossible. I'll start off tomorrow and I have definite leads ... the year and the approximate time, evening presumably. Surely somebody must have reported Claudia missing? Was there an explanation?"

We were too tired to do anything but sup our Scots broth and feed Fergus's omelette to the Thames fish, for it had turned out to be a disaster, though in the besotted stage of my love, I would have eaten it, if it had killed me. He took the pan and scraped the contents over the side. Then we ate sliced ham in our fingers and opened up a can of chocolate mousse and spooned it up together, share and share alike, and I was sleepy, so sleepy that my eyelids were closing.

I woke up three hours later and found that Fergus had tucked me up in a warm tartan rug in the forward cabin, so I closed my eyes and sighed and slept again.

I had bought fresh eggs, but not as fresh as the eggs on Corran or in Lissarinka. I had bought rashers of bacon, in no way as good as home-cured bacon would be. This was civilisation and you had only to go into a shop and buy the things. You had not to feed animals all the years round, all the dark months of the winter, with the water slopping into your Wellingtons and out again. Still, Fergus must wake up to the smell of frying rashers.

It was not strange that the delightful atmosphere of playing house, two children playing house, had gone, quite gone. An uneasy, uncomfortable, eerie, sinister feeling had crept in, a doubt, a half-fearfulness . . .

It was all Con McCracken's fault, God bless him! He must have been hard put to send out the signal to us from Dartmouth. He must have found a messenger late in the day, but not too late.

We had not had occasion to use the brown tea-pot, that stood prominently on the galley shelf. I had reached for the coffee pot, the evening before. Con would have been sure that the tea-pot would have been seized upon five minutes after we came aboard. Was he not used to Bessie and her teas, her brown pot, that was a twin of this one? He had assumed that we would find the note, as soon as we reached the boat and entered the galley. God only knows why he did not tell his messenger to leave the note on the saloon table, propped up in a prominent position. As it was, I found it, curled into a roll in its envelope and addressed to Constance T. and Fergus. I found it as I made breakfast. I read it, took it along for Fergus to read, for it was marked *Urgent* and it was urgent and very important. Over and over again, we talked about it, while I fried rashers and eggs and later ate them, but the taste had gone out of them and the smell was not the old wonderful smell of rashers and eggs frying for breakfast.

It was as laconic as the note that Wemmick had left for Pip in Great Expectations, which had just said 'Don't go home' or some such terrifying thing. Con had never had words to spare and he had none now.

"Signal from Con McCracken. Phil in London and his knife is turned against you. The Brave has put on war paint and the sense is gone from his head. Had this information after your call to me. Keen watch must be mounted. This imperative, repeat imperative."

There was just enough of the old childhood games mixed up with the message to give me nostalgia for the days when Bessie and the kitchen and Lissarinka were fortresses of safety, where harm could never befall any of us, but this was no childhood game. There was no mistaking that it was genuinely from Con, or we thought there was not. Still to make sure, Fergus went ashore and tried to get him on the phone, but he was not available, would not be available for several days. He was at sea on an exercise. He had left a message in case Mr. Kennedy rang, to tell him there was a note awaiting him in London. He had thought there might have been a call last night, from Mr. Kennedy . . .

Con thought we might suspect Phil of playing a trick on us. At least, Fergus scotched that one. Con had obviously gone on some exercise at sea — but we knew that a keen watch must be mounted. Maybe we were not so well trained as Con McCracken was in the mounting of a keen watch.

7

The Cracker Man

FERGUS was a stranger in his dark suit and white silk shirt. Gone was informality. The game of playing house was over. He was bound for Fleet Street and did he not know it like the back of his hand from his apprenticeship there? It was important for newspaper men to form a brotherhood and I had no part in it. I would have been a strange figure in jeans and a sweater and not much better in good Scots tweeds and a wool jumper. Fergus was unwilling to leave me on board by myself, not after Con's message. I had no intention of staying on board anyhow. Had I not London at hand and much shopping to be done? I managed to persuade him that a woman must get her hair fixed and get some civilised gear and he was kind enough to say that he liked me as I was. I convinced him that I could not come to any harm in the West End.

"You're to take no risks," he said. "Don't go alone anywhere. Stay in the shops. Con was never an alarmist."

I had not begged to be taken along. I knew that there might be sordid details and I would be an embarrassment to Fleming and Inspector Stafford, even maybe to the Old-Boy-Network. It did not include women.

"Inspector Stafford will have access to the Missing Persons' file at Scotland Yard, Constance-Tenacity. We have the date of Claudia's arrival at Corran and the approximate date of her departure from town. We have a host of clues from old Tam. Let me take that kerchief and its contents."

"You can take it tomorrow. There's something I want to try out. Please, Fergus, let me have it for today."

He told me that I was not to be getting up to any Tom-fool tricks and then he gave in to me.

"Very well then. I'll take it tomorrow, but it's all got to be so damned hush-hush. We can't involve Corran. We can't involve Lissarinka and every person in the story. It's unofficial and it's got to stay unofficial."

We took a taxi to Harrod's and he dropped me off with a final warning not to do anything foolish. Above all, I was to take care of myself and not forget Con's signal. When I came out of Harrod's and he presumed that I would be there all day, I was to take a taxi back to the boat and lock myself in ... not answer to anybody, till he came back and he would not be late. He expected to be there 'after the shop shut in Fleet Street' and that would be sixish. I could see to having my hair done, but for heavens' sake there was nothing wrong with it ... and oh, yes, he loved me very much."

I watched his taxi slide off into the traffic. Then I went through Harrod's like a vacuum cleaner. Lissarinka had an account there and I made full use of it. In a very short space of time, I cast my skin. I became regenerated, although I had no use for the hairdressing department and no time to use it. A good brush through was all my hair wanted, that and its childhood washing in soft water from the rain butt at Lissarinka, but I would have to wait for that.

My tweeds and good wool sweater went into a cardboard carrying box, labelled with the famous name. It gave me much snob value. I bought some clothes. I even bought a small gold pin for my cracker-charm-gold-keg and pinned it to my dress for good luck. I had purchased this cream sleeveless dress and the gold keg barrel, pinned near the throat, made it something quite splendid. The keg looked genuine gold worn against that dress. The lizard strap was lizard, was lizard, was lizard. How dared it look anything else in Harrod's?

I bought a cream handbag, that had to be big enough to carry all the other novelties, but Fergus had no idea that I was not going to spend my day at Harrod's, however tempting it might have been to do so. For a moment, I thought of trying my plan in a special department there, but there was something which drew me out through the front door, to step into a taxi that waited at the kerb.

My hat would never have suited Corran. It was mink and it was not more than two inches square. It toned with the strap of the keg and it had damaged Father's account quite a bit.

"Fortnum and Mason's please."

I scanned the pavements for Phil. Arrived at Fortnum's, I paid the cab and stood looking into the window for a while, afraid to do what I had set out to do. There was the shadow of a man reflected in the glass ... a man, who stood behind me and for a second, I thought it was Phil. I spun round, but it was some strange man, the same build, the same bright hair. I would not have been afraid of Phil. I thought suddenly that I could have talked to him and made friends with him again. I had a deep guilt about him. If I met him, I would put out a hand to him and we would make it up as we had done so many dozens of times. They had said he was mad, but of course, he was no such thing. He just liked to be King of the Castle and he had a quick temper and he was given to cruel jokes. Then I turned and went into the lobby of Fortnum's and remembered uneasily the things I had told Morag in the night. Unbalanced perhaps, but never dangerous, I thought, and then I remembered the slide down the scree on the island. They said that sometimes, a person is murdered by somebody and is not afraid up to the last moment, when it is too late.

I pushed the whole thought out of my head and walked into the heavy scent of the flowers and along to the elegance of the displays. Up the half stairs, I went, slowly and more slowly and very glad of the white sleeveless dress and the gold keg-barrel. A young man in a pin-striped trousers and black coat came to know my pleasure.

"I'm looking for the cracker counter, but it's the wrong time of the year for that, isn't it?"

He took in the mink hat and the good shoes, with a sweep of long-lashed eyes and smiled at me.

"It's never the wrong time of the year for anything here, Madame. If you'll tell me what you want . . . "

Over his shoulder, I saw an old man — an old man, well past retiring age, but with dark jacket and striped trousers still, with gold-rimmed spectacles, that slipped down to the end of his nose. There was a lost doddering look about him, but I by passed the young man and made for the old chap, as if I were steel and he a magnet. I hope I made some excuse to the young man, but I rather fear that I forgot my manners and just went walking past him.

"You're the cracker man," I cried and was as pleased to see the old chap, as if he could give me the answer to all my puzzlement.

It was a very disjointed talk we had at first, but we seemed to understand each other to perfection. I had come to Fortnum's with my Lissarinka father, years and years before. 'Fitzgerald' the name was, and we lived in Lissarinka in Ireland — and we came to buy crackers. It was the first time I had been brought to London for shopping before Christmas and it had seemed a wonderland after Ballyboy. There were never such things to be seen anywhere, for it was before my days of 'being finished' at the boarding school and I had had no fraction of civilised spoiling. I had stood mouth agape at the splendor that was London and the high spot of it all was Hamley's toy shop, with Fortnum's a good second, for the sweets and the luxury of it all and the crackers . . . and the taste of a walnut stuffed with marzipan that this old man had given me to sample.

"You were on the cracker counter. It's a long time ago now."

"A long time," he agreed with a smile that was all artificial teeth and he kept them from slipping with an effort, for his job might slip with them.

Then his face lit up with a real smile and it was as different from his shop smile as it could possibly be.

"Miss Fitzgerald of Lissarinka. The family has an account. You picked out the decoration for the Christmas table and I felt so glad that there was still such a child left. Even then, we got far too many children that have everything, but you believed that the fairy for the top of the Christmas tree was a real fairy. I never forgot you — must have been ten-twelve years ago — perhaps more, the years go fast now."

He looked lost for a minute and then pulled himself together and asked me what it would be his pleasure to show me today.

I was as lost as he at that, and could not think what to say to him and he sensed that there was something troubling me, or I think he did.

"If there's anything I can do to help you?"

He was not a bit put out that I wanted somewhere quiet to talk to him. He must have been used to many strange creatures in such a world. He brought me to a small office and pulled up a chair for me, sat down behind a desk, which he apologised was not his, but 'Sir' wouldn't mind as it was the lunch hour. Then haltingly I put him in the picture and he made no great amazement of it.

"Indeed, Madame," he said now and again, just from force of habit.

Of course, I did not tell him of the white coffin, or one quarter of the whole story, just that I was trying desperately to find a missing person and I knew where she was, but not who she was, only my real mother — and still, he did not make any great expression of surprise, just sat in silence and waited while I produced the kerchief and set the articles out on the desk before him.

"You're correct of course, Madame. These are the contents of crackers . . . a box of crackers or maybe two, but I think one, otherwise there might have been duplication. There would have been paper hats of good quality too and mottoes and balloons . . . "

"No mottoes," I said and there was a silence for a while. Then he excused himself and went off, came back presently with a small pile of catalogues full of pictures of crackers of every sort one could imagine. He leafed through them and then pushed one across to me . . . the sort of thing a manufacturer's salesman might carry.

"If you could have given me an idea of the year," he muttered, and I was on to that like a terrier on a rat.

"But I know the year."

"That's simple then."

I looked down at the page he showed me and saw a box of crackers in a fine coloured plate and there was a picture of some of the contents and there was my Indian and the paint box and the bone-handled penknife. In small print too was a mention of the carnival hats, the balloons, the mottoes. It seemed that no effort had been spared to search the manufacturing empires of the world for trinkets of good quality . . .

He was fingering the little objects and he must have had a lifetime of selling boxes of magic for children, for there was love in his face for such business and for the joy he must bring in a peculiar prismatic sort of way.

"I thought I might get names from you."

My voice cracked with nervousness and I was abject in my apology, for surely such a shop could never disclose secrets about its customers?

"If my real mother or my father bought them here, and if they were customers with an account . . . I know it's an awful thing to ask, but if you had access to old accounts, you might be able to find the names of customers, who bought such crackers and charged them, that particular year."

He lifted his brows and looked at me for a long time, pushed his gold-rimmed glasses down even nearer to the end of his nose.

"I wouldn't want you to lose your job here — your position, because of it," I whispered and knew it was an impossible thing I asked him to do.

"The years lose every man his job," he said sadly, "But it's difficult, you know. There are other stores and these same crackers would have been sold elsewhere ... Harrod's and Jackson's and many others ... and London isn't the only city in the world — and besides there's a deal of stuff that the customers stump up for in cash — and — and — and — "

"Claudia was my mother," I said softly. "That's her silk kerchief there and she lies asleep on a Scots hill and I don't know — Oh, God! I don't know! She *wants* me to know and I'm trying to find out. I've tried to explain to you and I know it's a crazy plan I have, but I have the feeling she guided me ... paced my feet every inch of the way from the Outer Hebrides to you in this place."

He looked startled at that and well he might, excused himself again and went off and I had an idea that he had gone for the police and hoped that Fergus's Inspector Stafford might be able to get me out of any trouble, I might find myself in.

He was gone a long time and I wondered if I would hear the siren of a police car through the muted roar of the traffic, not that there was much sound of traffic here. There was no window, only a dusty skylight with thick pebbled glass to keep out what brightness might be found in a city sky. I got up and walked back and forth and knew myself for a stupid fool. If my real father or Claudia had bought the things for that Christmas, there was no proof that it was here they had come. Yet Fortnum's was Fortnum's was Fortnum's and there was still a feeling that I was being drawn rather than that I had reasoned it all out. I had come involuntarily rather than with intent. I could feel something deep down inside of me, as I had on the Scots hillsides, that led me along a predestined path. I could feel a whisper in my ear and it was not Con's voice, but just the essence of thought.

"Watch how you go, my darling. Look

behind you and don't walk alone at night. Phil McCracken's evil and he wills you evil. Take care of yourself ... for me, my darling."

Of course, I had Bessie's training and all the Lissarinka legends and Puck's Castle behind me. I would never have admitted that I did not believe in the Little People or in ghosts, but what Irish person would dare to deny them? The time ticked on and it was obvious that the old man might have forgotten all about me. Then after a hundred years he was back, with two ledgers in his hands.

He was full of triumph, the triumph of the old over the young, who seek to push those like himself off their thrones, and down from power, who want to take over — the usurpers — who think the aged are outdated and to be classed as 'old fools'.

"I don't know if I can be much help," he said, but he did not mean what he said.

"You were a customer here yourself from Lissarinka. Here's the entry." He banged the ledgers together and sent up some dust. Then he opened the newer-looking book.

"Here's an entry of our account with Lissarinka House in Ireland — a Mr. Fitzgerald, for a Christmas order, when you were a very small girl and we sold you some of the magic of Christmas. Mr. Fitzgerald had it charged, as if a person could ever charge magic to an account, but there it is and promptly paid too — a box of crackers, but no such fine ones as the ones you're after, the two boxes of stuffed walnuts and some of our own special chocolates, the fairy for the top of the tree. It's a funny thing that I never forgot the child that believed I sold fairy princesses. You were a charming little girl, even then, and you were so full of love for the master of Lissarinka . . . "

He looked at me for a long time and said again that he remembered me well.

"It's sad, if you weren't his daughter, but love him, child, never stop loving him."

I had thought him too old to have grasped one half of story I had told him, but he had it down to the last item. He turned to the other ledger.

"I think there ought to have been a pipe cleaner and perhaps a few other things, with these items," he said.

"There was a pipe cleaner. I saw it. Claudia gave it to a man on the pier at Obaig and there was a . . ."

His face lit up and his teeth smiled with the same smile, that must be non-skid, or one became redundant.

"That's it, then. I've no doubt that I've got the right year, for there was trouble about those particular crackers. There was a complaint from a very high-up person in Iran about that pipe cleaner. I recall that this customer claimed the metal was deficient in the pipe cleaner. He might have been buying an air liner and complaining about what they call metal fatigue nowadays. The actual round tamper-down piece snapped off short when one of his wives tried to open a bottle with it. It's strange how a complaint like that sticks like glue in your memory, when sometimes I can't hold a person's name for two seconds, but I remember that year and the bonbons and they were very fine — very fine indeed — better than the stuff, they're sending us nowadays, but you hadn't a pipe cleaner in your kerchief."

I might have assured him that the pipe cleaner had had no such thing as metal fatigue. Had it not outworn the elements of the seas for nearly a score of years, but there was no time to tell him, for he had gone on with his part of the scene.

"I know without doubt that these things were contained in the bons-bons of the year you have specified, but there's a difficulty for you compared with which the labours of Hercules might be easy. I can show you the lists of what people bought these crackers and charged them, but I can't see that it will help you. There are so many — American citizens over here for an English Christmas and half the Princes of Araby. There are all the ordinary people in Greater London, ones rich enough to come in here every year, ones that come just because Christmas is Christmas and they forget the New Year with the accounts on the door mat and the envelope from the Inland Revenue."

He was a philosopher. Of course, he was a philosopher, and how he wanted to help me.

"People come year after year, living on their pensions some of them, but they remember the food parcels we sent their boys in two world wars and want to keep faith with us too."

He sighed and I thought maybe he had such a soldier — son — grandson, who was dead now and would live for ever in this man's heart and that was the stuff life was made of, with sorrows that would fill the Atlantic with tears, if they were all out-poured.

"There are a great many names in this book and it's all most confidential. I'm sorry that it took me so long, but the secretaries were at lunch. The only bright spot was that you'd been able to give me the initial of the surname. Without that, it would have been quite hopeless."

My hand went to my forehead, for I was all confusion and no thought would follow another thought with any sense in the sequence.

"Did I tell you that Fergus is almost certain to get a missing persons' list? I want this list to check against it. It might — must give us a clue. It's a chance . . ."

I tried to thank him at last and made a poor job of it, told him that I would never forget him, never be able to repay the help he had given me. I knew him for another like Morag, like her Islanders, who had taken a stranger within their gates . . .

Then I remembered him as a perfectionist and thought there was one small thing I must really say.

"About the pipe cleaner," I smiled just before I said goodbye to him. "You might be worrying that that pipe cleaner was defective, but it was no such thing. Claudia gave it to a man on the pier at Obaig. That's God's truth. I saw it myself and he told me — saw it the other day again and twenty years gone past. It's still mint new . . . as good as the day it was 'Made in Sheffield'. Don't worry about that rich customer from Iran . . . he was way off."

I got a taxi back to the river, with the cardboard box on the seat at my side, my bag in my lap and the list of Fortnum's customers in my hand, those with the initial 'C', who had bought crackers at Fortnum's, that particular Christmas, crackers of that special sort and had them charged to an account. There were a great many names, page after page of them. There was a great doubt in my mind that Claudia's surname began with 'C'. It was just as likely that she had two first names, each starting with the same initial. Claudia Cicely ... Claudia Clare ... Claudia ... Maybe Claudia had never shopped at Fortnum's in her life. Maybe the things had been ordered by post and paid for by cheque. I was crazy to think I could solve the problem the way I had gone about this. This must be the longest shot in living memory. I would be an object of amusement in Fleet Street and maybe Scotland Yard. I zipped the list in the depths of my bag and wondered if I could even bring myself to show it to Fergus, especially as I had had instructions to stay put all day and not go wandering off. Then I wondered if Phil would be at the boat waiting for me and if he was, what I should do. There was nobody there and I was glad of it, glad to get aboard and close the hatch. I snipped the bolt home and wondered what had become of the girl, who had stood at Fortnum's and thought that she would never be afraid of Phil. Here by the river, it was lonely and eerie. As I slid the bolt, I asked myself, if Phil might have come aboard before me and if I might be locking myself in with him. Then I pulled myself together. There was nobody at home and my heart slowed down to its normal pace.

I tidied the boat and remembered too late that I had promised to provide a supper. I had had time enough, but my excitement of getting the list had shot every other detail of practical living out of my head. Fergus would be home at six and it was that now. There was no chance to find a delicatessen. I scrutinised our supplies and found them totally without glamour and it was past time for Fergus to come. He was never late and soon it was seven and well I knew that he would never come. Phil had met him. Of course, he had. Phil's hand would have been turned against him. Con had warned us. Phil would not stop short of murder and soon a police car might come to collect me to go and identify Fergus in a place of hell called a 'morgue'. No, they would not even know about me. I would hear nothing, just know that nobody came home. I might try ringing Fleet Street and asking for Mr. Fleming, but he must have gone home by now. Inspector Stafford might be able to help, tell me where Fergus's body had been taken.

I longed for the lovely silent Hebrides, where a lassie stood at the head of the pass and watched for her laddie to return, where she sat by the sea shore and scanned the Atlantic for his boat, but there was the green grave there and the black grave too. I opened the hatch and went ashore, sat myself down on a bollard and contemplated the river.

Then Fergus was behind me and his arms were about me and all my dark trouble vanished like mist before the sun. In no time at all, we were on the boat. I had the list out to show him and there was no doubt he was excited by it.

"This is something solid. I know it's a long chance, but it's a *chance*. You're quite some girl, Constance-Tenacity."

We went down the lists with our heads close together at the table in the day cabin "C . . . C . . . C . . . C . . . "

"Tomorrow, Stafford will have the List of Missing Persons, and this will cross-check with it, but it's complicated. There's a deal of persons, who disappear and are never reported missing. It's a sordid business, so sordid, that Stafford doesn't want you at the Yard till we get something far more definite than we have now."

I started to argue with him about that, but he said it was time for us to go and dine. He had a table booked in Soho. He had forgotten that I had promised to cook supper. He apologised for being so late and for worrying me, but there was a chap called Fouracre, he had had to go and see. I'd know how important this was in a day or two, but not now. Now was the time to dine.

I was glad of Harrod's silk dress with the high-jewelled collar, which had been another lightning purchase, glad of the evening bag in green enamel, that had a powder compact inside it, which played in a tinkling little voice, when the lid was opened.

We had a magic evening in Soho, yet I think that both of us watched the shadows for Phil, but there was champagne to drink and luscious sweet liquers and Turkish coffee and it was another world from the darkness where street lights did not reach dark corners and the oily ripple of the Thames water on its way to the sea ... and tomorrow was another day and now we were safely back aboard and the hatch locked and double bolted, and I had been kissed and tucked up in bed. Tomorrow I would not argue about accompanying him to Fleet Street and the Yard. I would understand that Fleet Street was a rough arena for young ladies and there were things that must be discussed. If I insisted on going, they would all have to tread carefully.

"Good God! Here's a past that may need trampling out by the black oxen of the years, and it's your father and your mother, we're dealing with."

There was a saloon cabin and another cabin aft with a bunk to port and another to starboard. The lights ran in from an electric cable on the wharf and they were shaded into dusky comfort. Here was safety indeed, the Robin Crusoe atmosphere again, where no harm could come, with strong fortifications built against the natives, that might swarm outside the stockade.

Fergus took himself off to sleep on the port settle in the day cabin, for he was a very proper young man, this 'Son of the Tribune'. I closed my eyes and was glad he was such a man, for he fitted in with Lissarinka and with Ballyboy and with the fifty-years past standards, that still made Ireland such an enchanted place. I would have Fergus fashioned in no other way. I closed my eyes and was asleep and in the morning, it was I who picked it up under the letter box slit.

It was a picture postcard ... a shot of the stretch of the Thames, where we were moored. You could see the bank on the opposite side of the river and somebody had inked in a cross, just directly opposite where we floated. It must be from Con McCracken, I thought, as I turned it over, yet Con was in Dartmouth or may be at sea and this had been pushed in the letter box slit. It bore no stamp. The blocked letters were higgledy-piggledy, in the way anonymous letters are supposed to be written and I felt the small hairs stand on the nape of my neck.

"X marks the spot. That's the spot where I stand and watch you, but don't come looking. You'll find no joy. I'll come for you, when I'm good and ready. I'll find you, just when and where I want to find you and that'll be the end of you and of me. Phil."

Now there was no possible chance of my being left unguarded, while Fergus went off about his detective work. There was no talk about the sordid business detection was, or about Fleet Street being too hurly a burly for a gentle maiden like myself. He took me into his arms and held me close. There was no word between us, only a great knowledge, that passed in silence from each to the other, that we possessed the most precious thing in the universe. There must be no chance of loss, ever, down the years of eternity, 'till death did us part' and afterwards, along a million, million years.

He loosed me at last, and changed from one moment to the next, to the ordinary world of everyday life.

"It's past time you met John Fleming. You'll like him."

There was this extra-sensory perception between us. He did not say it, but I knew his thought.

"Fleming will know somewhere safe to hide you. If it were Ballyboy and the Slieve Bloom Mountains, I'd be the expert, but not here. Fleming's a Londoner . . . "

Fleming's office was executive, not as important as his father's would be, for that was near the top of the line. John Fleming had his name in gold letters on the door and an antechamber with a secretary at a desk and she dripped glamour as honey from the comb. There was not one white blonde hair out of place and there was a welcome in her face that might pass for genuine, if I had not the imagination to know it would be stock-in-trade. It must be learnt like sums at school and it must turn on and off like an electric arc light. It must be an art, difficult to learn, to banish without offence and to admit with such welcome, that a visitor felt important. Her voice was soft and modulated and her every gesture was studied in grace. She had survived the toughness of Fleet Street without scar, for she was the heroine on the front of any woman's paper, yet with a brain behind all that loveliness. How could she hold down the position of secretary to the lord high executive's son, without great expertise?

"I wasn't expecting Miss Fitzgerald, but Mr. Fleming will be delighted to meet her."

She stood up when we came in and put admiration into her eyes, as she looked at me, said how pleased she was to meet me and we must go in at once.

I was glad of the cream dress and the mink scrap on my head, glad of the gloves that were still clean enough to pass, hoped that the big handbag was not too motherly, but it had to be that size to hold all Claudia's toys.

If I had met her in Lissarinka, perhaps I could never have felt the inferiority. I was almost certainly far better than she would ever be, on the back of a horse, but that knowledge did me no good. Horses were few and far between here.

Then I was in John Fleming's office

and he was getting to his feet, reaching for a stick. Fergus had not told me he walked with a limp, that he had such kindness to him. His hand came out to take mine and his teeth were as even as an American film stars' and there were laughter wrinkles at the corner of his eyes. He made me welcome, drew out a chair for me, talked about Ireland and looked down presently at Phil's letter, read it and read it again, did not quite believe it and then worked it out that it was the reason that Fergus had allowed me to come with him. They might have discussed it all aloud before me, for I could pick up every thought, that passed between them. They must keep me out of harm's way.

Presently, John Fleming was asking me a favour. It seemed that there was a task, that must be done and I was the obvious person, for I knew every facet of the case.

"We have a place downstairs. It's rather an uninspiring department, but it has all the old numbers of the paper. We wanted somebody to go carefully over every edition, every Southern edition of course, starting way back at the Christmas before you were born. You know what we're after . . . "

I had produced the white kerchief with all the strange little objects and he was obsessed with them. He picked them up one after the other and said that of course, they were Christmas cracker novelties.

"Harrod's, I'd say, or Fortnum's, Jackson's perhaps."

I passed the list over to him and he looked at me in surprise, managed to convey that he would never understand how such a lovely girl should possess such brilliance, but his eyes hurried back to the list of names.

"We've got a break-through here. My God! We've got a break-through. Stafford will be pleased with this."

Maybe I was carried aloft on the admiration and praise, but I had no hope of sitting in on the conference. John Fleming put his arm through mine and guided me along the corridor to the lift and we descended to the library-like gloom of the basement room, where the old numbers were held for reference.

He introduced me to the man in charge and I was provided with a pile of books, that might have been good props for the giant in Jack and the Beanstalk. He showed me how to find my way about them, just by slogging through one page after another of the bound papers. I knew what I was after. If I found anything, I was just to note the date and the page. He snapped his fingers and a new jotter appeared on the table by my side and a new felt-tipped pen beside it. Here indeed was a young prince of power, but it was Fergus, who got my parting smile, got the reproachful shake of my head, and the loving look.

Then after a while, I saw that they were taking no chances. A young man came down the stairs to basement level and through the open door to the reference section. Ten minutes later, came the second, but they had no knowledge of each other, only went across to the counter and asked for some issue of the famous Daily. Inspector Stafford had had time to arrive upstairs. He had seen Phil's picture postcard and read the higgledy-piggledy writing and he had not thought it a silly joke. I imagined that he had rung some source of young men with polished black shoes and with dark blue trousers. These were not plain clothes men. They had been summoned quickly. They had discarded uniform top and chequer-board cap, but they had that clean look about them and they matched each other too well. One of them sat at a table, that commanded the door and the staircase. The other was near me, both of them near enough to keep what they would call surveillance. In another time, in other circumstances, I might have thought it fun to lead them on a false trail, but the time for laughter and childish games was over. I bent my head and skimmed on and on and on and my fingers were soon slate-grey with printing ink, the life's blood of the whole building. I passed from the account of one accident to another and wondered why the public had to be told all these horrible things, why they should read of wars and rumours of wars, of children burnt in fires, of massacres, of disasters, that wiped out a thousand people at a time. I was on the look out for a lady, who might be missing and maybe she had been the body in the burnt car on the Great North Road, as yet unidentified and I was in some mid-February by then and she lay peacefully on a Scots hill. It was all so long ago and in the first month I had not even been born. It was interesting to think how all these things had happened and I had not been there. By the first mid-February I had been safe in my mother's womb and she had been safe on Corran and perhaps Morag had been told of my existence.

The minutes ticked into hours and after a time, one of my policemen guards, left his book of bound volumes back to the custodian and went up the stairs. Sure enough, presently a girl arrived and of course, she was a policewoman, but she did not last long. They were just changing the scenery and she would never have been heavy enough to tackle Phil in a fair fight. A burly middle-aged man with greying hair came in and made a great to-do with the man in charge, about some old number that nobody could find. I could hear the argument, which terminated when they remembered that there was no thirty-first of June, even as far back as 1960. Very well then, it must have been the thirtieth. He would have to make do with the thirtieth, and so it went on. Presently, my lunch came in on a tray and they had done me proud — a very excellent sherry and a stack of smoked salmon sandwiches. Of course, Fergus would have chosen them. There was very good coffee too and some small cakes, that might have been made by angels.

I imagined the meeting that must be going on in the office and thought the fare for lunch might not be so dainty upstairs.

Then John Fleming's secretary came to collect the empties and to tell me where the ladies' room was and presently I was looking at my reflection in the mirror there. I had produced nothing whatever to earn my keep, I thought, and then I looked with dismay at the keg-barrel, that swung from its imitation lizard strap at the neck of my dress. I had not produced it with the other things. I had forgotten all about it and it might be important, although it was probably not.

I went back to my chair at the table and worried in case they might think I was a fool to have overlooked it. It might be the best thing for me to take it off and to ask the man in charge of the reference basement to bring it to Mr. Fleming. I walked over to the counter with hesitant steps and noted how my guards alerted themselves, but so slightly that nobody would ever have noticed it, if they had not, like myself, been addicted to reading fiction about crime and the police.

"Do you think I might send something up to Mr. Fleming's office with a note?"

"Mr. Fleming isn't in the building, Madame. He left shortly after he came downstairs with you, but he's expected in his office during the afternoon."

Back at the table, I thought of the keg barrel, fingered it, as it hung at my left shoulder. Something had started to nag at my mind, something from one of the papers, hours before. I had looked at it and passed it by and now it cropped up again, like a tune, that will not be forgotten. I was sure of it. It was a sense past all understanding. I leafed backwards through the great pages. It had been before the sherry and the smoked salmon. It had been before the policewoman came in and distracted my thoughts of detection with the way her hair swept up in a golden swathe. I had wondered how she got her cap to sit right, on top of such glamour. Before she came, I had been looking at . . . looking at . . . looking at . . . I put my head in my fists and the newsprint flashed past my shut eyes like the lit pictures in a fruit machine. Then I swung the pages backwards in time and back again. It had been something to do with presents, a woman's page article. I spun from one Christmas to the Christmas before it. The concentration of thought jabbed me with a sharp needle. I was back at the edition where I had started and there was nothing . . . nothing . . . nothing. I could not come on it. My brain was worn ragged and my eyes ached. Maybe the police 'on obbo' were asking themselves what possessed me to flip from one set of woman's pages to another, like a terrier after a rat in a heap of chaff. Then I had it, really had it, in an article headed "WHAT ARE YOU GOING TO GIVE HER FOR

HER BIRTHDAY?" It was the illustration that made me gasp now, though I had passed it over. I had seen it and my sub-conscious mind had photographed it...

It all depended on how much you had to spend, but it was the thought that counted. Blah! Blah! Blah! There it was, right before my very eyes, as somebody says in some programme ... some famous comedian, and my brain started to work on that one, till I pulled it back. This present was for the rich. It was 'pricey', but it was super. She was guaranteed to love you ever after and it was guaranteed to bring you good luck.

It had not brought good luck to Claudia. He had not loved her ever after, yet I had no proof of that, had I? It was of gold, the best there was, and none of your nine carat variety. It had been fashioned in Switzerland, this magnificent locket. It was banded with lizard and there was a genuine lizard strap to hold it. Better still, the strap had a miniature gold buckle fastener, that had to be seen to be believed. It was a heart-warming thought that such craftsmanship still existed. The buckle actually undid and did up, as if it were a real buckle and not made by fairy hands . . .

I bent my head down and looked at the illustration and it was there in every last detail, my keg barrel. I had made a great error in classifying it among the cracker novelties.

I unfastened the nine carat pin that held it at my throat and saw that indeed the keg was a whiter, better gold. I examined it for a hallmark, for surely it must have one, but I could not find one. With hindsight, it was quite obvious that here was no Christmas cracker plaything.

The policemen had changed again, one, ten minutes after the other and now they were C.I.D. men, or I imagined they were. For all I knew, they might be ordinary men, who just wanted to check some reference in the newspaper reference library, yet they seemed interested in me and watched me gravely, as I pinned the keg back at the neck of my dress. One of them had slacks and a sweater over a shirt and a tie. The other had a gaberdine coat with military epaulettes and his shoes were too clean. I wondered where Fergus was, or John Fleming or Inspector Stafford. I should contact them with this new vital information. I even thought of asking one of the C.I.D. men, but then I was not quite certain about them. I imagined my embarrassment if one of them was an ordinary citizen going about his business in a normal way, so I waited and waited and waited and tea arrived. If only John Fleming's secretary had brought it down, I could have asked her what to do, but it was another girl, dressed in a white overall, and she was no executive type, just the tea girl, weary with pushing trolleys all day long and just that bit put out that she had had extra work to fetch a cup of tea down to me and a plate with two biscuits, on what Masefield had delivered up the channel — a 'cheap tin tray'. Then I felt guilty at having considered that Mr. Fleming's personal secretary might be a superior being to this poor girl. God alone knew what I was myself and who was I to judge status and rank and worthiness? I thanked the girl far too effusively to try to come to terms with my conscience and then made things worse by leaving a fifty pence tip under the tea cup. She would probably never find it and it would probably get into the machinery of the washing-up machine and short the whole building and bring the production of tomorrow's edition to a halt and that shows what frame of mind I had developed . . . and still I waited.

Then the lift doors wheezed. I could hear them well, for the lift was close to the stairs, though very few people used it. I watched the door and wondered if there was to be a change of my guards, but it was Fergus. I could scarcely believe that he had come for me. He looked a different person from the Fergus of Lissarinka, far more different from the Fergus of the Corran hills. He came over and put out his hand to take mine. His face was white and his eyes were very sad indeed under the tufted slanted brows. I had wanted so badly to find him and tell him about my discovery, but he shut my lips with his first words.

"We've broken it, or we're pretty sure

we have. Let's get out of this capital of law and the media and back to the river."

I was standing at his side at the kerb and a taxi pulled in. There was no trace of memory about the keg barrel in my mind. Then we were at the river and the water poppled in a slight breeze and the leaves twinkled.

"Do you know, Fergus? My father?"

He was unhappy. He glanced sideways at me and there was no missing the fact that the news was not good news.

"Wait till we get to the boat. We'll make a cup of tea."

That confirmed it. People always said that before breaking bad news. We were not far from the boat and I asked him to stop the taxi and let us walk along the embankment and I was losing spaces of time. We walked along the wide concrete path and his hand had taken mine.

"It doesn't matter, Fergus. It all happened so long ago. Just so long as you still want me and there isn't some awful thing to tell . . . "

"I want you all right. You'll never know how much I want you. I love you so much that I can't bear to bring you pain."

"So it's pain?" I said, and he nodded his head and stopped to lean against the wall of the river, put his arm about me as if he would shield me against the hurts, life can deal. He said nothing and we stood like that, till I prompted him.

"I've known that Claudia isn't happy in her grave. Maybe now I shall know why?"

He looked at me for a moment and away again, out towards the river at the ships, that crept up and down along the sea lane.

"You solved it, Fergus? You did say you'd solved it?"

"Your list from Fortnum's," he said. "That let us through, but without Fouracre, we'd have got nowhere. It's sleasy. There's no joy, no matter how you twist and turn it ... no joy from start to finish, only damn fool human idiocy ... and we're damn fool idiots to stand out here, where Phil could take a shot at us."

He started off along the pavement with my hand held so tightly in his that there was no chance of escape from him, even if I had wanted to escape and on the way to the boat I found that I had been right about the identity of my police guards. "Stafford took it very seriously, very seriously indeed," and he had been warned to keep a look out and a nice way he was doing it. So we came to the boat and let ourselves in. Fergus went to the galley and presently came back with the cup of tea and he had shed his formal suit and was in jeans and a sweater, and still he was having difficulty in telling me what must be told.

"Please," I whispered.

At that it came out, one fact after another and all in a flat voice, as if he felt that what he was telling me was hurting me very much indeed.

"Your father's name is Clifford, Nicholas Clifford. There's no proof of it only circumstantial evidence, but it's true ... no doubt of it. God send there's a hereafter and they'll be together again and make peace with each other, for the way they flung their happiness away."

"So he's dead now?" I whispered and his silence answered me.

He went off and found a sheet of paper torn from a typist's jotter and he spread it out on the cabin table. Then he sat down beside me and on the table the cups of tea grew cold.

"So my name is Constance-Tenacity Clifford?"

"Your name is Constance-Tenacity Fitzgerald, legally by deed poll and you know that already. It'll be Constance-Tenacity Kennedy as soon as you'll marry me. What importance is there in a name? You're you and I'm me."

He got it told at last, how there had been Nicholas and his wife Claudia, and how it had been Christmas. Claudia was expecting a baby, but she had not told anybody about it. It was to be a big surprise the night of the Christmas party. This was presumptive evidence, but that was how it seemed to have been. The party had been a good one. There had been too much to drink perhaps, but there was still no proof of that. The likely thing was that Claudia was clearing the table after dinner . . . later. It would have been later. Maybe she had felt sick and she had gone to the bedroom and the fun was progressive downstairs . . . or that was how it seemed.

"She must have gone up to the bedroom and she had the cracker novelties in her hand, wrapped up in something or other. This chap, Fouracre, Inspector Fouracre, was a good friend of the family. He wasn't at the party, but your father told him how it was. I'm sorry. It's not nice. They left me to tell you, for you've got to know. Your father was a man. There was no real harm in him, but he couldn't . . . couldn't leave women alone. He had Claudia and Fouracre said she was a lovely girl. Your father was a fool and we must remember the fact that he didn't know about the baby. That's for sure. In his eyes, the whole thing that night was a party."

There was a pause so long here that I thought it might go on for ever, but he looked at me miserably and let me have it.

"She went into the room and came on him in their own bed, with a tramp of a girl."

I shook my head in denial and he took me into his arms and kissed me, as if I were a hurt child and then he looked over my shoulder through the port, watching the little ships slide by.

"If he had known about you, he'd never have let it happen. As I said, it was a party to him and then it was all over, for Claudia was finished with him. She got out of the house, as fast as she could. She told him that she was glad he was enjoying himself. That was the last he ever saw of her. She just left the house and the party and everything else and she vanished. He never saw her again and he never knew what became of her."

"It can't have happened like that," I whispered. "It's impossible. How could anybody know?"

"He went looking for her, when he found she had gone, drove up and down half the night. In the morning, he rang Fouracre and Fouracre tried to help every way he could. If a person walks out like that, the police do not class it as a missing persons' case. They call it 'a domestic'. They hate to get involved with a quarrel between husband and wife. It all solves itself in a day or two and the police find themselves unpopular with both parties for interfering. Fouracre told your father that Claudia would be back, but he didn't know the full circumstances, not till he got your side of the story and the tale of the crackers and the Fortnum's list. There was no chance of foul play. People had seen Claudia walk out through her own front door on foot with a bundle tied up in a white head scarf — and a small case. She had obviously run off, God knows why, they thought. It was 'a domestic' and that was that, but she didn't come back and Fouracre got a feeling about the case. He was uneasy and he put down Claudia Clifford's name on a file. Stafford found the file at the Yard, checked it with your Fortnum's list and Fouracre was called in to help. He's been retired for years . . . "

Inspector Fouracre had kept a memorandum on the whole affair in case anything grim happened. He had kept it in his own personal files and he had been able to produce an account of the whole case, grim sequel and all, to Inspector Stafford and John Fleming and Fergus today. They had gone in a squad car to the house in outer London, where Fouracre lived. The retired inspector was more interested in his greenhouse nowadays, but he took time off from it to rummage around in an old desk packed with papers.

"Your father tried to forget Claudia," Fergus told me. "He tried to write her off and he began to drink in earnest. He was killed in a car accident a year or so after that Christmas party, came out of a side turn on to a main road in front of a lorry. Fouracre was involved again. It would have been a drunk in charge case, but your father was dead. Claudia had vanished and the trail was cold. There were no relatives and no real friends, enough money to pay his debts and no more, a few companions who missed him for a week or two and then forgot all about him."

Fergus still held me in his arms, but now he put me a little away from him, took my hand in his and his face was bleak.

"I saw the files on the case . . . all written on that special foolscap paper the police use for statements. Fouracre had closed the account, drawn a line and that was the end of it. I can see it now, Constance-Tenacity, the writing at the end of the last page and he had written, in cynicism maybe, or in regret for an old friend. 'And that was an end to a Christmas party.'"

Fergus picked up the sheet of paper torn from a typist's scribble pad. He had used it for notes, but the task of telling me what had happened was over. He had done with the memos and the short little notes and as far as he was concerned that was the end of it too. He rolled the paper in his hands and tossed it through the open port into the Thames. It rode lightly along the surface of the water, bobbed with the poppling and made for the estuary on the ebb of the tide.

"Let there be no moaning at the bar," he said. "Let him go. Let them both go and may they rest in peace! Forget them and set them free. You never knew them. Don't try to cling to what is lost . . . to what is lost, even before the day you were born."

I knew that this was good advice, but

in the back of my mind, I was aware that Claudia's ghost had not been laid, any more than the Thames had been turned back to run reverse direction to its source. My hand went up to finger the locket. I had told nobody about the locket, so I told Fergus now and that it was the sum total of my research in the basement of one of the most important dailys in Fleet Street.

"I've tried to open it but it doesn't open."

"It's lovely. It was obviously his last Christmas present to her, but the case is closed. The sad story is finished and now comes the happy one. Wear the locket in memory of Claudia, but marry me soon, very soon. Let the water that has run down the river go out and lose itself in the sea . . . "

We were two children again, playing at house. We made fast the hatches against the villains that might lurk outside. We even found candles and lit them, stuck them in saucers to make the dining table more romantic. We built fairy castles for the future and we pretended that life was pink champagne and magic and rose-coloured spectacles, that there was no ugliness left in the world. It had all vanished and soon we would go home to Lissarinka and began to make plans for the wedding.

I did not tell Fergus that Claudia's spirit still haunted me, not in any great dramatic way, but in an unease of mind. When I had gone to my bunk, she was there again in the darkness. I switched on the light and opened the port a little. The night was warm and nobody could come through the port for it was small, far too small for an intruder. My gear was all tidied away. Under the port on the shelf was the gold keg and its lizard buckle and its nine carat pin. All was well. I switched out the light again and she came walking back along the years, Claudia, whom I had never seen, Claudia, in a long dress, that was like a white mist, that dazzled about her. I switched on the light once more and of course, it had been a dream. Yet again and again, she was there, in all my dreams and sometimes, I was she and she was I. I walked into the room to tell Nicholas about the baby. I loved him. No woman had ever loved a man as I loved him. There he was and the details of the nightmare were shameful . . . sordid, mind-destroying. The woman was naked and so was he and there was a scene. Oh God! There was a scene in my own bedroom that branded my soul.

I woke up in the pitch blackness and stretched a hand for the light, switched it on and no light came, only a brilliance that made an orb of fire out of the port. A klaxon screamed and there was shouting.

"Ahoy there! Ahoy there! Is there anyone aboard? You're drifting beam on in mid river. For God's sake, look alive, Royal Iris. Show yourselves lively and come about. Ahoy there! Ahoy there!"

A flashlight dazzled my eyes still more and Fergus had come into the aft cabin. I was half between dream and reality. There was a crash of breaking glass from the main cabin as the boat lurched and Fergus had turned his torch to the lockers. A pair of jeans and a sweater descended on my bunk, with curt instructions to me to get dressed, and still I was half in the dream that had come from twenty years before.

Was it a shameful thing that I had been found aboard Con's boat? Fergus's voice brought me to my full awareness. I knew who I was and where I was.

"The power's off. Somebody unhitched the moorings and cast us adrift. I'm a fool not to have thought what Phil might do."

He was nothing if not cool in a crisis, but I was astonished at some of the language that came out of his mouth, as he found auxiliary lighting for me in the form of candles in saucers. Then he was on deck and dealing with the river police and I was struggling into my clothes. Very soon, I was on deck beside him, only half realising the danger we had sailed and both of us asleep. We were a little way down river and drifting, dragging the mooring ropes. Fergus had got the engine going and another police launch had arrived. They helped us back to our mooring, helped make us fast. Then they wanted explanations. It had obviously been done by some of the yobboes that hang round the embankment at night. Fergus gave them Inspector Stafford's number and voices passed back and forth across the air, tinny small voices, that jumbled one's ears. Yet presently it was sorted out.

"We'll catch this character. It's not as if we had no description of him. He won't be able to resist another try at it."

It was hours later and I had stretched out on my bunk. From this angle, I could see something white under my hair brush. I swung my legs out of the bunk and found a small piece of white paper, folded small. It was in Phil's writing, as awry as his brain must be. Again, I thought of the Alice in Wonderland Queen and how she had wanted me to breed stability into her son.

"Ladybird, ladybird, fly away home. I'll have your locket safe waiting."

The locket was gone. I knew exactly where I had left it on the shelf under the port and I should have noticed that it was gone, when the river police were there. I should never have left the port open. He had only to put in an arm and pick out the locket and my flesh crept with the idea of him, standing on the walk that ran round the hull, perhaps with a flash in his hand and how the gold of the keg would betray itself.

He was playing the old cruel childish games again.

"Ladybird, ladybird, fly away home. Your house is on fire. Your children are gone."

I knew what he was planning to do. He was on his way home. He could fly Aer Lingus to Shannon and I loved Lissarinka. It was only a matter of getting there quickly. Who would be on guard against him? Who would ever believe that he planned to burn the house? He must aim for Puck's Castle and get his plans laid. Then it was only a question of a match and a can of petrol. I thought of the haystacks in the paddock. I thought of the big thatched barn. I thought of the dry weather. It would go up like tinder. They would not come alive out of it . . . not Mimsy, nor my father, nor Bessie nor Tim-Pat . . . my children, if ever anybody had children. They were my responsibility, my loved ones.

I went along to Fergus in the day cabin and found him asleep. He was wrapped in a blanket and he looked warm and comfortable like the cat in the advertisement for electric blankets. He cannot have been properly awake, when I poured my hysteria down on him.

"I know Phil. You don't. It's 'Boys and girls, come out to play', all over again. He went to the trouble to get the others to sing that under my window at night. I know he did. He's mad, Fergus, totally and inescapably mad. His mother practically admitted it."

He looked at me with sleepy troubled eyes, with the lock of hair over his brow, wondering if I had had a nightmare and was still in it.

"He's on his way home. I know it. He's gone to burn Lissarinka and destroy it for ever. We'll have to go at once, but even then, we'll not catch him for he's had a start on us. It's like Rebecca all over again. Rebecca and Manderley. We'll fly to Shannon and then get a car and when we come near the house, we'll see the lighting of the skies. We'll be too late. The whole hill will be crowned with flames and the trees blazing. The pines will burn like torches. There's been no rain for weeks. They'll all be gone, Mimsy and Bessie and Father and Tim-Pat . . . the horses in the stables and the stock in the yard . . . "

He took me into his arms and gentled me as if I were any terrified beast.

"You've had an awful time, Princess. Could you leave this to me?"

I opened my mouth to protest and he laid his finger across my lips and then kissed me.

"We'll be gone within the hour. I promise you, but there are things to be done. You've forgotten there's law and order. I'll let Stafford know and he'll have the ports watched. He'll contact the Guards in Ireland. We'll get the whole place impregnable and no harm will come to the house on the hill. Don't you know 'it's rotten with fairies'. Phil might as well try to walk through a fairy ring, as get past Sergeant Murphy of Ballyboy."

His light mood calmed me, yet he knew my terror and we left as soon as we could.

"He's stolen Claudia's locket," I told him and as soon as the words were out of my mouth I remembered that a locket was an item of jewellery that almost always contained something. There was some important thing in the keg barrel, but Phil could not know that. He could not ever have seen it till tonight. It must open! Claudia willed it into my mind that I must find the locket and open it.

"What if he has taken it? Don't you think I'm not capable of taking it back from him?"

He smiled at me and kissed me, before he went off to telephone the police.

"I'll get it back for you, if it's the last thing I do," he smiled, and in the distance of the stars, I heard Claudia's voice, low and urgent.

"Don't let it be the last thing he does, Constance-Tenacity, for it might well be."

I was tidying the boat and shoving my gear into a case and I blamed Bessie for all the superstitions she had put into my head, but I was convinced that Lissarinka was in grave danger, even if Fergus was only going home in a hurry to put my fears to flight.

"Don't let it be the last thing he does."

Here was the greatest fear of all.

8

The Storm Of Wrath

IT was early morning and the clouds were soft white banks. I wondered if Claudia walked in such a land, till she could find peace. We were high over the patchwork of Ireland, with its little fields, so impossibly green. We were coming in to land at Shannon and we could see the roads now with cars like black beetles, running along them. We could see the houses and the runways of Shannon and now we were touching down on the tarmac with never a bump. It took a little time to circle the runway and then the door was open and the gangway was out. There were soft slow kind voices all about us. A Civic Guard picked us out as we left the plane and there was no question of delay in the customs, or anywhere else.

"Miss Fitzgerald of Lissarinka? Mr. Kennedy? We're expecting you. There is a car ready and waiting outside."

The evening was coming down and the sky was darkening. There was no chance of us getting home till midnight and I knew that for all they were doing, I would see the glow in the sky. That was how Rebecca had seen Manderley and that was how we would see Lissarinka, no matter how often Fergus told me it was out of the question.

"They'll have put a watch on the place hours ago, Princess. I promise you. We've done no good by rushing home, except to lay your ghosts. Please, don't worry. You've found me and I've found you and there's to be no more of this scrambling your brain with Celtic tales of imagination and horror."

Hours later, we passed through Ballyboy and he was kind enough not to insist on stopping off at the Newspaper offices. He understood the terror that rode me through the night. Here was the long bog road and we bumped at speed along it and still there was no glow in the sky.

"There won't be a glow in the sky, Miss Fitzgerald. I promise, cross my heart and hope to die."

"Don't say 'hope to die', Fergus."

There was a light at last, the reflection of the gates of Lissarinka, the letters picked out in gold in the headlamps. I was out of the car in a moment to let it through, shutting it again behind the car, for there was stock loose in the fields. There was no light showing, least of all a fulminating blaze.

"It's all right," he comforted me. "We did the sensible thing. I agree with every word you said. It was possible. It was probable and now I admit it."

He got out of the car and came to take my hand in his.

"Thank God I managed to find a girl like you."

He kissed me lightly on the cheek and held me in his arms.

"If you weren't you, you'd be set on buying up half London for your trousseau. You'd have had to have your hair fixed. Maybe you'd have insisted on doing the rounds at Scotland Yard for a look at the murder bag, or murder room or whatever they have there. At the very least, you'd have taken Fleet Street by storm and seen the papers roll off the presses. Then there'd have been theatres and shows, that we mustn't miss, but oh, no, a Ladybird's home, is her home, is her home. It's here we'll live, you and I, and here our children will be born. It's here your heart is and will always be. I love you more than I thought it possible to love any woman. Your house is safe.. As for the locket, I'll get that back for you. Don't fret."

In my mind, I heard her voice again.

"Don't let it be the last thing he does, my darling, for it very well might be."

The spice of the pine trees was all about us and soon the old familiar stable smell. The horses were whinny-snickering at visitors so late. The moon was coming out through the racing clouds. The stable clock was five minutes past midnight and all was well with the world.

Lissarinka House came awake gradually. There was a light flashed on in Bessie's bedroom and the window opened. Bessie's head, caught fast in a hair net appeared. Her hands rested on the sill and she stared down at us.

"It's all right, Bessie. It's only me and I've got Fergus with me. Don't wake anybody. We'll just come in quietly and not disturb the house."

If I had hoped to achieve that, I had hoped in vain.

Bessie clutched the neck of her sensible Viyella nightgown close to her throat at the mention of Fergus and she relayed the news to Tim-Pat, who was obviously in the bed behind her.

"It's Constance-Tenacity, all the way from London and she has company with her, the Son of the Tribune."

"Glory be to God!" came Tim-Pat's voice from the dark interior of the room. "And how does she look, Herself? Is all well with her?"

There was a family altercation about that, sotto voice, demanding how Bessie could possibly see how I was by the light of the moon. Then all conversation was cut short.

"Don't fret now, Honey. I'll come down and open the door to you. Leave the luggage lay where it is. Tim-Pat will see to it later."

I was in a kind of exhilaration that Lissarinka House still stood fast on its foundations and was not a blazing torch from end to end. My home was not ashes and it seemed quite obvious that my children were not all gone. So Lissarinka House came gradually to life.

The light flashed on in my father's room, for why should I call him 'foster father' when my own father was dead and gone and had never known me? Father would move quietly, knowing that Mimsy must not be disturbed. Then one light after another flicked on in the façade of the house . . . the light in the library . . . Bessie would be setting a match to the pine cones that filled the grate. Then the light over the front door illuminated the whole drive and the flowers tidy in their ornamental urns, but their colours grey, because the sun had gone. The lamps in the hall were already burning and almost at once the door swung wide to the full and they were all there, Bessie in her flannel dressing gown, but with hair net removed and with hair fresh combed, Tim-Pat in a nightshirt, covered decently with a top coat, my father in his red silk dressing gown, his hair ruffled from sleep and a kind of apprehension all about him, that I could feel, but it was no obvious thing. He knew very little of what I had discovered. For all he knew, I might have found a real father, who must claim me now and leave him daughterless in Lissarinka. There was a fear that sat upon him and a great sadness ... almost as if I had died again. I had been young enough not to realise that he might have experienced such fears and I blamed myself now that I had not telephoned him fuller news from London, but Ballyboy telephones had eavesdroppers. Still I might have calmed his misery, when I had not even remembered ... realised that he might have had misery. I could have given him a cryptic message by wire, but I had only thought of my panic at Phil's message. "Ladybird, ladybird! Fly away home." The mere thought of the little verse could put me on the roller coaster again and send me down the slide. Now there was the light of Lissarinka streaming out to Fergus and myself and faces, and every one of them anxious enough.

I hurled myself up the steps and into Father's arms, almost strangled him with the fierceness of my grip on his neck, till

Bessie unlocked my hold on him.

"It's bad news?" she asked miserably and suddenly I thought of these three faithful people, who put such value on my presence in the house. I looked from one face to the next, knew myself totally unworthy of such loyalty, such love, when I had done nothing to deserve it.

"I found out all about myself. I have it down to the last line, or maybe to the second last."

I was shamed by the look in their eyes, yet moved to tears myself, that they should care so much.

"It's a long story, but it's finished, or I hope it is. You're stuck with me, as daughter of Lissarinka House. There isn't anybody left, who wants me, only yourselves — nobody else to take me in as once you took me in and gave me so much . . . so very, very much."

Seo arrived silently from somewhere and threaded herself round and about my legs, till at last she jumped to my shoulder and draped herself to decorate my neck like a fox fur.

Everything always seemed to happen automatically in Lissarinka in moments of crisis. We found ourselves gathered in the library, where all important things are discussed. The cones had caught fire in the grate and there was a welcome and a warmth and a comfort in the room. From somewhere had appeared a silver tray with whiskey and ginger ale, with ice too, in case there were people present, who might not think ice an insult to good whiskey. The water was in a cut glass Waterford jug. There was coffee bubbling in a percolator and the coffee cups were set out, even the special coffee sugar in its silver bowl. There was cream from our own cows.

Bessie and Tim-Pat stood and waited to hear all that had happened, but Bessie had had time to make sandwiches of Limerick ham, well daubed with fresh mustard. Yet to my eyes, she had not even left the room, just stood behind my chair with her hand on my shoulder to steady me and Tim-Pat had been ramrod stiff, behind the 'Master's' chair, on guard duty and ready to serve Lissarinka to the death. That about summed it all up, God bless them both!

We sat there presently with a dram in

our hands and they waited to hear the news. Slowly I told them, with many stops and starts and with Fergus filling in a deal of detail for me, when the story thickened my voice past speaking. Between us, we omitted none of the principal happenings.

"It's a happy ending as regards us, but Phil, there's no doubt that he cut the cables and set us adrift, after he took the locket. I don't say he wanted to kill us, but he wanted to get a start on us. I got it into my head that he intended to burn this house, but I think that the locket was the important thing. It was a locket, though I never thought to try to open it. At least I did and then, came to the conclusion that there was no way to unscrew it or unclip it. Still, they wouldn't have called it a locket, if it hadn't contained something. I think Phil has guessed it's important and knows we must have it . . . "

"That's only a 'come-on'," put in Tim-Pat. "He's thrown down something he imagines is precious to you. He knows you'll come after it. It's like the old days when you played 'knights and dares'. He knows well that you never refused a dare in your life. It's only his trickery, Constance-Tenacity. You'd best turn your back on it."

My father agreed with him. Besides, there was nobody at Puck's Castle. They were not in residence and the place was all closed. The McCrackens were on holiday somewhere abroad. It was like a dead house. Even the maids had been sent off home on holiday.

"I went over there and looked in the windows the other day," Bessie told us. "There was dust over everything, except for where they'd spread white sheets over the furniture. The people hereabouts always make up a tale about that Castle. They have it now that the ghosts have driven them out at last, but they're gone on holiday, on a cruise to some foreign place. As usual, there's always a sensible explanation."

She squeezed my shoulder.

"I wonder did Herself leave somebody behind her to put down the chickens' blood on the flagstones. If she didn't, I'll lay that there'll be nothing, but dust on the hall floor this minute."

We were far past ready for bed, when we heard footsteps on the stairs and the whisper of the carpet against the bottom of the door, and Mimsy came into the room.

"I heard it again, the singing. The children are outside and they want to come in. They shouldn't be out so late."

Father had her in his arm to bring her to the fire and we all stood there listening. There was nothing except the ticking of the clock and then I heard it and so did Fergus. He was across the room in an instant and was throwing the window wide.

"Boys and girls, come out to play.

"The moon doth shine as bright as day. Leave your supper and leave your sleep . . . and join your play-fellows in the street."

It was still black night, though the dawn must soon be here. We both heard it plainly, the hoarse whisper.

"Hide and seek. I'm hiding out from you, Constance-Tenacity. Come and find me. I've got your locket."

Tim-Pat was beside us and he might

have been talking about fat stock prices, for there was no excitement in his voice, only a sorrow that a person should go out of his mind and behave in such a way.

"That's Master Phil playing at ghosts like his Ma does," he said. "They're on the watch for him and they'll catch him. 'Tis best to be shutting the window and getting off to our beds. We'll think it over tomorrow."

We went to our beds. At least, we pretended to go to our beds, but I knew Fergus by this. He had no such intention in his head. He kissed me goodnight at the door of my bedroom and whispered in my ear.

"I'll get your locket for you, Princess."

I watched him go along the corridor and into his room and I went after him. His window was open and he was gone. God knows how he got out into the garden so quickly and silently. After a bit, a car started up and drove off and Bessie was spying out the 'carryings on'. She had had suspicions that what had happened was going to happen and now she transferred her suspicions to me.

"Follow him you will not, Honey! It's

men's work and Tim-Pat's after him and the Guards will be on the watch out. Come on away to your bed now, like a good girl."

She hung about till I almost screamed at her to go.

"We forgot to tell you about your oak-tree," she said. "It's the queerest thing you ever heard in all your born days."

"But Fergus will be almost at Puck's Castle by now," I said and she took no more notice, than if I had said nothing at all.

"You know the way you planted the sapling and said if we all had faith, it would turn into an oak tree. We had to have courage, you said, and hope. Master Phil was mighty put out with you, but it was only because he was jealous. They say you were careless enough about the whole thing, just took a torn off a weeshy bit of the oak and shoved it into the ground and trod it down gentle and firm."

I pretended an interest, but I had no interest. My mind was three miles across the valley, walking at Fergus's side.

"It's taken. The sprig of oak is taken. It was all about it in the paper this week, for it has a wee pair of new leaves and people coming for miles to have a look at it. They say you've worked a miracle. I've cut out the bit from the *Leinster Tribune* . . . "

It might be a sign that God fought on my side, but He was not helping me now. She went away at last and in the hall as I crept out, I met Tim-Pat.

"If you were thinking of following Mr. Kennedy to Puck's Castle, I'd put it out of your head," he told me complacently. "I waited a bit for I knew you'd get past Bessie, but you'll not go. I'm away after him myself in the car and there's no other car in the garage, that'll start. Can't you leave the affair to men to deal with? There'll be plenty to take him. Go back to your bed."

I waited till I heard the second car leave the stable yard and then I was downstairs as fast as light. There were horses in the loose boxes. Had I not heard them?

I was wearing jeans and a sweater. I crept along the half doors to the horse stalls and heard a whicker of welcome from Sultan. It took me half a minute to get his bridle and slip it over his ears. Then Seo found me again and twined herself round my legs, as if she wished me to fetter me to safety. I put her in the manger and gave up all idea of saddling the horse. I led him out on the cobbles. There was no time to find a saddle and fiddle in the darkness with the straps of the girth. What need had I of a saddle? Sultan came with me as if I led him on a thread and we were at the edge of the front lawn and I was up on his back, turning him off towards the stone wall, thanking God for the high full moon and for the swathe avenue through the fallen elms. I gathered the reins in my hands and put my heels into his sides and he was off like an arrow. The grass was quiet velvet to muffle his hooves. The front lawn was a silver landscape and I leaned forward to whisper in his ear that we must hurry. The dry stone wall was coming up in front of us and I prayed that it was not a crazy thing I was trying to do and knew full well that it was.

Here was the place where Phil had

picked out two stones and challenged me to a contest the day after the storm had scattered the elm trees like matches and murdered the great oak ... and the sapling was going to grow. I stroked the ebony neck as we came to the wall and then lifted Sultan for the leap and he flew through the silver light like a bird. Claudia's whisper had driven me to attempt this race through the night. I could hear her as clearly as if she had been at my ear.

"What if it's the last thing he does, my darling?"

I had been wrong about the burning of Lissarinka and I was probably wrong about the great danger, that walked abroad tonight.

Now we were racing down the hill and the cemetery appeared on my left, with the slabs of tombstones white in the moon. We cleared the stream with feet to spare and went away up the hill and I knew every inch of the way. The creaking of a church door had no importance to me tonight. We gathered speed uphill, though it seemed impossible to move faster. The battlements of the castle were solid against the sky and we were getting near and nearer. It was time to rein in and move with silence and stealth. I had no way of knowing where Fergus was or Tim-Pat, nor if there were guards about, in an ambush to trap Phil. The castle was in total darkness. There was no light at any of the many windows, only the reflected moon against the glass panes. I pulled Sultan to a walk and he went along the grass verge of the back avenue. The gate stood wide. I had used it a thousand times when I went there as a child to play, or as a young lady to visit. I knew it like the back of my hand. There was a rail where a horse might be tethered and I tethered Sultan, only stopping to pat his neck and put my cheek down against the satin of his face. Then I was stepping quiet as a mouse to the back door, foolishly expecting to find it open, for it was always open. Of course, the whole castle would be closed up. Had I not been told so? I whimpered a little. There was another way in. As children we had had many secret entrances, the door to the tower, the door to the dungeons. It was dark in the shadow of the great building and Phil would be waiting. I had no doubt of it.

"Come and find me. I've got your locket."

The door to the tower, that was the one to try. I edged myself round the walls and came on the squareness of the stone bastion. My fingers groped for and found the door, searched for the wrought iron circle that was the handle. Then suddenly and silently the door swung open and my wrist was caught and held. A torch flashed on and off again but in the split moment of time, I saw Phil, in the tower hallway, dressed in black slacks and sweater, a dark scarf half across his face like any murderer. He drew me inside and his fingers punished my wrist, as they had often done when we were children. I had had one good look at him, as his right hand trapped me. The gold locket was dangling in his left, dangling from the strap, that I had thought was mock lizard, the small barrel shining out its true gold and the buckle of the strap too, that might have been made by fairy hands in Lissarinka Hill.

The torch went out as quickly as he

had snapped it on.

"I thought you'd come after it. It's important, isn't it, the locket? No, don't expect lights. I've put paid to the electricity, same as I did on Con's boat."

The door closed at my back and I was alone with him in the square stone tower that stood in the oldest part of the Castle. He drew me by the wrist across the flagged hall to the place of the ruby blood stain.

There was no laughter in me now that it might be Mrs. McCracken, that kept the stain fresh with chickens' blood. Here was the blood of two young lovers, who had leaped from the top floor of the tower, so many eons past. High up, was a circular ceiling of glass like an oriel window, that kept out the wind and the rain. From where we now stood, there was a circular staircase of stone, that led upwards and upwards to the place they called 'the Leap'.

The moon shone through the 'oriel' roof and it was beginning to overcome my sudden blindness. I could see Phil in outline, see the glint of the locket, that swung to and fro in front of my face. Ah, God! There was still the glint of the moonlight on that hair of his, that might have been ripe Jack wheat in the fall of the harvest. There was great sadness in my heart for what might have been, if life had not turned agley and changed its predestined path, to find out the cruelty of fate and what time can do to the young, who set so hopefully out on the journey.

"You had to come and get it. You know it holds the secret of your birthright. You'd be damned if you'd acknowledge to be a bastard, if you were no such thing. Is that the way it is . . . and has the going got tough with the Son of the Tribune, if you've failed to find out if there's a bar sinister or if there ain't? A bastard is a bastard is a bastard . . ."

I could only think how bright the moon was in his hair, as he stood there with his head thrown back and himself laughing. Then I whispered to him that he would not get away, that the police were after him.

"And why should the law be after me? I've done nothing. Well, maybe I have, but I'm too clever for them. I knew what I mean to do here tonight and it's worked out so far. You came, didn't you? That's the first part done. Then I sewed it up tight. I left some clothes on the bank of the river earlier on ... shoes, pants, jacket, even my wallet and a farewell note. By now, the Guards will be dragging the Drowning Hole, unless they've left off for the day and mean to start again come morning. They think I'm mad. By now, they're quite sure I've taken my own life, but they don't know the plan. That's the important thing."

He had moved slowly to the bottom of the first step and I had no choice but to go with him. I did not notice till we stepped up on the first step, where the suit of armour stood to guard the stairs, grey against the stone of the steps and the stone of the castle walls, the flags of the hall ... grey.

"I'm going to pack it in and I'm not going alone. I got it in my head that we'd climb to the top of the tower and save Ma the trouble of sluicing the chickens' blood round the place ... not that she does. It's spite, that says that and the jealousy of jumped up people with no tradition behind them, who'd give their right arm to have a history behind them like Puck's Castle has."

There were round landings every now and again and we reached the first of them and I thought how like the second suit of armour was to a guard watching the safety of the tower of the keep. I wondered where Fergus was and Phil read my thought, almost before I thought it.

"You're wondering where the Son of the Tribune is, the shy young man, who came stepping into the kitchen at Lissarinka that day, like 'a parfait gentyl knight' and yourself and himself looking at each other 'across a crowded room' like the song says and that was the end of me, not that you ever cared a tinker's cuss for me, only because your father and my father wanted the match and you were a dutiful daughter or thought you were. God help you! You may have been dutiful, but you weren't his daughter. It's a laugh, when you come to think of the whole affair. For all you know, you might have been got by an Irish tinker out of a barmaid in a ditch in any lane, and that would make fine breeding to match up with Lissarinka and Puck's Castle."

He stopped and looked at the suit of armour.

"I'll tell you where Fergus is. He's down by the Drowning Pool this minute. He's looking at my car, upside down in the water. He's in the company of a few gaping Civic Guards. If he came after you tonight, the Guards will have turned him off the Castle road. 'Mr. Phil's after driving his car into the river,' they'll say. 'You can see the wheels of it through the water, so he'll be drowned surely, God rest his poor troubled soul!'"

There was no happiness in his laugh, just the wash of a mind adrift in a sea of madness. He read my thoughts just as I read his and he answered the question before I asked it of myself.

"Tim-Pat will have tagged along too and maybe your father . . . your foster father, but Fergus Kennedy will be in charge of operations. He's so bloody gallant. He'll dive down after the car to try to find my dead body, in an upside down car, ten-twelve feet under a swift flowing river. Tim-Pat will be running up and down the bank trying to get him to stop it, telling him he's off his head to risk his life after a dead body, but the Son of the Tribune is a person like yourself, Constance-T. He's not one to give up and he'll not give up tonight. He'll just choose the wrong moves in a game of chess."

It was all so possible. I could see it happening, yet Fergus might spot the clue.

"It was a God-awful trick getting my car into the river upside down. I as near as damn it went in with it."

Fergus must have been told about the clothes on the bank. That would get past Tim-Pat, who only cared that his people of Lissarinka were safe. Tim-Pat would be past logical reasoning, but Fergus must ask himself why the clothes on the bank, but perhaps he would be so involved in the horror of it all that his thinking might go wrong.

"We're going to jump off the top floor, you and I," Phil told me now, but I had known it anyway. and it was no shock to me, only confirmation of a great terror.

"Fergus . . . " I said and I intended to say that Fergus would come for me, but I shut my mouth up tight and remembered the story of Scherezade, but I must play the part in reverse. If Fergus was coming, I must make time. The thought of him was a small candle that burned in the darkness of my terror. The nightmare switched off, yet it was no nightmare. It was actually happening to me, more slowly than it actually was, as if somebody turned over frame after frame of an old movie picture. I left the role of Scherezade to Phil, just managed to find the questions to keep slowing him down on his climb to the top landing of all.

"Nobody opened the locket," I said and knew it was a strange gambit.

"I opened it," he said in the voice of arrogance, that I knew so well. "It has a fool trick, that's supposed to make it unopenable, but I opened it. I told you that, didn't I? It opens clockwise. Every other locket opens counter-clockwise. It was stuck fast from the times, when people tried to undo it and only made it tighter and tighter. I tried everything to get it open, but in the finish, it didn't beat me. Nothing ever beats me."

"It must open counter-clockwise," I said.

"Wrong! You're like everybody else. It opens clockwise. Clockwise, counter-clockwise, tick-tock, tick-tock. Times running out for you. What the hell does it matter? I'm going to have the honour of your hand tonight, in death, if never in life. If I can't have you, no other man will and what's the importance of a locket, when you'll be dead in the next five minutes?"

Here was another small round landing and I reached out my hand to touch the gauntlet of the knight in armour.

"If I can't have you, nobody else will. Do you hear me?"

I went on up the next circle of stairs and asked him carelessly if the locket had held any great secret, tried to make my voice casual and did not succeed in the least.

"You're frightened of me tonight, aren't you? You've good cause to be. Christ! The times I've tried to put fear into you and you'd never admit it. Cub-sized, with the tears wet on your face, you'd scowl up at me and as near as damn it, spit in my eye, you little vixen."

He sighed and loosened his grip on my wrist, but as soon as I moved, he had it again in a vice.

"There's no hope of your getting away. Don't try it. You'll not survive the Leap and neither shall I, no more than the lovers, Ma is always on about. We'll jump from the spot on the Leap floor and that's the highest landing in the Castle and I don't care, for you'll belong to me and I'll belong to you, right down the years, like the first lovers, that tried the same escape route."

I pulled him back to the locket, praised him for opening it, asked him what he had found inside.

"It was a thin sheet of paper, the sort you'd use for Air Mail or making cigarettes — had to be, there was no space. The hallmark was inside and that was a damn fool thing too . . . a person would never be sure it was gold. I suppose it was some sort of puzzle, but it didn't beat me. I told you. One day I'll be King of the Castle. I'll be the King that will reign for ever in a great new legend, that will match your new oak tree. That piddling little sapling will die in the first hard winter, but your blood will be down there on the stones, running free with mine, and you will be walking the plains of heaven with me, queen to my king for the rest of time."

I pulled my wrist free from his grasp and there was a click and a streak of silver and a knife opened in his hand.

"It takes a tenth of a second to spring . . . a second maybe to kill. You haven't been more than a second from death, since you came sneaking soft shoe to the tower door."

I managed to laugh at that, but it was the strangest sound I ever made. I teased him that he was no different than when we had played at cowboys and Indians together.

"It's no game," he said, "But you were like an Indian Princess that day in your Paris suit and the Pocahontas band about your hair. It was the day after the second storm and Kennedy had come into the kitchen. If I had had a knife that day ... but that's fool talk ..."

"This whole thing is fool business, Phil. Tell me about the note in the locket. I won't try to get away."

His mind could grass-hopper like Mimsy's and I knew how to turn Mimsy's mind from one subject to the next. I had had plenty of practice at it.

"Please, Phil, I promise, I won't try to escape."

That was a childhood statement too and I crossed my fingers as I said it and knew that I would give up my life with a hard struggle, even if I gave my word that I would not.

"The note?" I prompted.

"There was small writing on it, neat. I've seen her grave on Corran, the place where I flung you down the cliff. I don't know what was going on ... don't care much. The note was signed Claudia. That was the name on the tombstone. You're no bastard. Did I tell you that? I can't remember sometimes. Your pa married your mother."

He grabbed my wrist again and swung me round to face him.

"My mother kicked you out, just

because she thought you were a common little tinker. I have the proof in this locket that you're nothing of the sort, but I don't care any more. They all say I love myself best. Well, maybe I do. Con says I'm mad but I ain't mad. My mind's scrambled and there's one thing I know is true. It's a fine wild thing to hold a girl's hand in yours and jump down from six floors up. Marriage can last no time at all. You get old and the girl's a crone and the soft look gone . . . and maybe a few brats to grow into manhood and grandchildren round your feet . . . take all the power over from you and sit you in the chimney corner. I've done it here. I know. Mine is the power and the glory and my old man takes second to me. What I say goes and the men in the fields are afraid of me, but in time, it'll be me in the chimney corner and you'll be old and grey and the Indian black gone from your hair and the soft look and the litheness of body, the way you can sit a horse like a queen. I'm offering you eternal youth and eternal happiness . . . and never a sad thought in your head any more. There's a glory for any bride, that's been jilted by a man's mother, who'd chop off your head as soon as look at you."

He looked up towards the glass roof and the moon was caught in the clouds, but it still made an areola about his head.

"This place is full of ghosts. We'll have good company."

I tried to back away from him and came up against the armoured knight on one of the landings, but I had lost all count of them by now, only knew that the ceiling oriel was very close. Phil clicked the knife in and out like a silver tongue and then shoved it into the band of his slacks.

"I love Fergus," I whispered and he laughed at that, said it was a pity that in that case he had no intention of marrying me.

"It would be fun to be married to an unwilling bride."

"What was written in the locket, Phil?" I asked and knew that indeed cruelty was his god and he would find ecstacy in unwillingness, far more so than with a joyful loving girl, coming to him in gentleness.

Fergus might have gone down to the river to look at the car. The Guards would have turned his car off the Castle road, and Tim-Pat's too. He might not even have been told about the clothes on the bank. God above! They might not even have found the clothes and the note and the wallet. Fergus might be diving out at the Drowning Hole and it was a place of horror, where the river ran fast, where bodies had been taken out with grass still clasped in dead hands. There was a chance, a tiny chance that Fergus had heard about the clothes and the car and known that two and two sometimes did not make four . . . and here was a false sum if ever there was one. Suppose he had come to the tower, had found Sultan, had come on the scene being enacted on the stair that spiralled to heaven, I looked down from the height of the staircase and saw the great dining hall below me, almost invisible in the moonlight, but still I could make out the long table and the chairs shrouded in ghost dust cloths and the tracing of the coat of arms over the fireplace, as far away from where I now stood as if it were in another world. I knew it so well, with its grandeur, tattered now, as war banners are tattered, when war is over and are hung on church walls in honour. One day, I knew with a great certainty that Con would be master here and Con was the right one to restore the fortunes, the broken fortunes, not by marriage, but by steady hard work and with loyalty in his heart. Con would be the one and the paint would be fresh again and the whole place restored to its rightful state. Con would stand Puck's Castle back in its rightful place, when Phil and I were just an addition to the ghostly company. With the clarity of the eyes of those about to die, I knew that would be the future and was glad of it, yet still I kept on with my Arabian nights ploy, whispered to Phil that he had not told me all that was in the locket, and so spun his mind about again.

He and I were alone now. I had very little hope that Fergus was anywhere near. Yet he might know of the knife. He might be somewhere waiting his moment, but I knew that all hope of this must be past, for the last floor was upon us.

The words tumbled out of Phil's mouth.

"There was the name and address of a man, your father. Nicholas Clifford. You're Miss Clifford, after all. There's an address. It's traceable. He'll come over to the funeral. Claudia was married to him. That'll please her, I daresay, him coming to your funeral."

"What else?" I asked, and the words tumbled out again and went round in circles and repeated themselves, mixing up and turning back and forth, veering off to talk about something else. His face twisted with emotion sometimes and sometimes, he was so sane and sensible, so reasonable that you might have been fooled and not realise that you could not trust him from one step to the next. He might have killed Fergus — killed Tim-Pat too. I got an awful sureness that Phil and I were really alone together, one with the other, and there was no escape for either of us from what was going to happen.

"There was a storm on Corran, she said, Claudia said in the note. They couldn't get medical help. She had only

Morag and a few handy-women. I knew Morag. She used to be housekeeper yonder before Bessie. They say she was a great old character, but she wasn't a nurse."

"Claudia was afraid she'd die in childbirth," I murmured. "She thought she'd die, when I was born."

My whisper went curling down the staircase and up again and we were close to the top landing now and the sand running down the glass.

"If she died, and she did, didn't she? Well then, Morag was to take you . . . if she wanted to take you . . ."

He went off onto a jumbling of words about life in the Islands and how the people there were tough as tigers, I drew him back to the letter, but it was he who spun the story.

"Claudia was a silly damn girl . . . no thought in her mind from one moment to the next. She ran off and left her husband after some kind of a muck-up. He was to have a second chance. Morag was to let him see his child and give him the first pick. That's a rich way of carrying on. If he gave you the thumb's down,

Morag was to have you for keeps but she could have you anyway . . . It was all codology, but Claudia wasn't fooling. She never stopped loving your father and she was fool enough to think he still loved her. Still, you were born in legal wedlock and that'll please Ma. Maybe she'll still dabble the chickens' blood on the stones, after we are dead and gone, God rest our souls, if she ever did it in the first place."

I spoke aloud now and my voice echoed back and forth in the round tower, as if there were goblins and ghosts and spirits who spoke the words back to me.

"Claudia still loved him. He still loved her. He couldn't help being the way he was. 'It was a party'. That's what he said."

"And what's that all about?" demanded Phil, who could know nothing of Fleming, or Stafford or Fouracre . . .

I shook my head and noticed that dawn was on its way. The black darkness was turning to gunmetal and the shadows were lighting, but imperceptibly.

Here was the circle of the top floor

of all and we stood side by side on the spot, where the lovers had made the leap so many years ago.

"This chap was to see his baby or not, as Morag chose. If Claudia came through, she intended to go back to him. 'Love's not Time's fool,' that's what she wrote in the locket. That's the last bit of it and that's a good requiem for us. Let's go."

"I love Fergus and I'll love him for eternity. If you force me to jump down there, I'll not be with you, not my spirit. You'll go by yourself into eternity and it's lonely and dark, and you know in your heart, that's how it will be. 'Love's not Time's fool.' There will be no glory and no legend, just the story of poor sick man, who threw away his life for something, that never was."

He caught my hair in his hand and I felt the locket tangle with it and the next moment, my face was over the bannister and I was looking down on the flagstones, still only coming lighter grey with the day. I shut my eyes against the depth of the fall and was conscious of the buckle of the locket pulling my hair, as it tangled. There had been a queen on a scaffold, who had said 'Lord Jesus, receive my soul', and I wondered if I should be thinking the same words now, and my courage had run out, as time had run out. This was the end of the golden life, the end of the joy of Lissarinka, the end of happiness, the end of everything.

"I'll wait down there for Fergus. I may jump with you, but I'll wait down there, till the time comes for Fergus to fetch me. I'll be just another ghost that haunts Puck's Castle."

"Fergus doesn't care a damn for you. If he did, he'd be here now. Let that be the thought you die with, before you decide to wait for him down eternity."

He let me go at that, the locket still tangled in my hair. I put up a hand to free it and over Phil's shoulder, I saw the suit of armour, that guarded this last landing. There was a shadow that separated from it and slid with no sound, closer and closer. Then there was a scuffling and the knife gone from Phil's belt.

"But I am here, Phil. I've been waiting for you."

I knew it was Fergus, who spoke, quietly and calmly as if he still could pull some fragments of safety from disaster. He threw the knife over the balustrade and after a long time, we heard it clatter on the flagstones. I had no emotion left any more than a marionette. I just stood there and watched the scene enacted before me. Phil's mind snapped like a bow string. His face contorted as if he were a child about to break into tears. He might have been insanity itself in the spirit of man. He loosed me and turned to face Fergus and I thought that Fergus had thrown the knife away. He would face him in equal combat, Knight to Knight. Then Phil had spun away to put a foot on the balustrade, to give a spring out and away. He gave a raucous cry as he fell, that I will remember till the day I die, that and the dull thudding crash, so different to the clinking of the knife.

The cry had roused the rooks that lived in the trees about the Castle. They rose to circle the tower like so many great black bats, their cries begotten from his cry. I wondered if his soul would go spiralling up through the wheeling of them, as they bade their farewell to the man, that should one day have been the Master of Puck's Castle. I looked through the oriel at the coming of the first shaft of dawn and I spoke in my heart.

"Goodbye, Phil."

We went down the staircase, Fergus and I, and here was the hall and the flagstones and no need for chickens' blood now. Phil lay with no life left to him, one arm outstretched as if he slept untroubled and perhaps he did.

That was the way we left him, to be another legend and nobody would ever know the full truth of it.

On the way home, we looked back at the tower and saw the rooks wheeling still, but after a time, one by one, they settled down and came to rest, after the storm of wrath.

***Other titles in the
Ulverscroft Large Print Series:***

TO FIGHT THE WILD
Rod Ansell and Rachel Percy

Lost in uncharted Australian bush, Rod Ansell survived by hunting and trapping wild animals, improvising shelter and using all the bushman's skills he knew.

COROMANDEL
Pat Barr

India in the 1830s is a hot, uncomfortable place, where the East India Company still rules. Amelia and her new husband find themselves caught up in the animosities which seethe between the old order and the new.

THE SMALL PARTY
Lillian Beckwith

A frightening journey to safety begins for Ruth and her small party as their island is caught up in the dangers of armed insurrection.

THE WILDERNESS WALK
Sheila Bishop

Stifling unpleasant memories of a misbegotten romance in Cleave with Lord Francis Aubrey, Lavinia goes on holiday there with her sister. The two women are thrust into a romantic intrigue involving none other than Lord Francis.

THE RELUCTANT GUEST
Rosalind Brett

Ann Calvert went to spend a month on a South African farm with Theo Borland and his sister. They both proved to be different from her first idea of them, and there was Storr Peterson — the most disturbing man she had ever met.

ONE ENCHANTED SUMMER
Anne Tedlock Brooks

A tale of mystery and romance and a girl who found both during one enchanted summer.

CLOUD OVER MALVERTON
Nancy Buckingham

Dulcie soon realises that something is seriously wrong at Malverton, and when violence strikes she is horrified to find herself under suspicion of murder.

AFTER THOUGHTS
Max Bygraves

The Cockney entertainer tells stories of his East End childhood, of his RAF days, and his post-war showbusiness successes and friendships with fellow comedians.

MOONLIGHT AND MARCH ROSES
D. Y. Cameron

Lynn's search to trace a missing girl takes her to Spain, where she meets Clive Hendon. While untangling the situation, she untangles her emotions and decides on her own future.